Helen and Iago are a mother and son team. Helen loves to write and Iago likes to think up plots and ideas.

Helen was born in Liverpool in 1953 and has spent most of her life working in science and research.

Iago was born in Bern in 1982 and runs a village pub and microbrewery of which he is part owner.

For Ellen, Nine, Harold and Taid.

Helen Roberts

Iago Roberts

Deadly Imprint

AUSTIN MACAULEY PUBLISHERS™

LONDON * CAMBRIDGE * NEW YORK * SHARJAH

A CIP catalogue record for this title is available from the British Library.

ISBN 9781035801213 (Paperback)
ISBN 9781035801220 (Hardback)
ISBN 9781035801244 (ePub e-book)
ISBN 9781035801237 (Audiobook)

www.austinmacauley.com

First Published 2023
Austin Macauley Publishers Ltd®
1 Canada Square
Canary Wharf
London
E14 5AA

Vaughan who knows why.
Elfed for Lakeside.

Table of Contents

Chapter One

You could say that books were her life, and until that day, she would have happily agreed with you. Elaine made her living through books and she lived in a town famous for its second-hand bookshops.

Today, she had a day's annual leave to catch up on housework and gardening, so once the chores were finished, Elaine decided to walk to the town centre to browse around. She often used to make the same shortcut through the park to reach the shops. The alternative was to skirt around the museum, but this meant following the narrow footpath close to the main road. On this day, she found the park barred by police tape. The September sun slanted through trees which were just beginning to turn various shades of gold and russet. It was going to be an early autumn after the long dry spells of summer. Normally, Elaine would have turned back immediately, not one to intrude on another's misfortune, but something made her want to know what was going on, an unaccustomed curiosity drove her. The green paramedic uniform drew Elaine's attention to an elderly gentleman sleeping on a park bench, a book lay askew on the seat next to him. It may have been a recent acquisition because it rested on tissue and brown wrapping paper which were still partially folded across it. Elaine thought the book looked old and valuable, a solid leather-bound tome. The paramedic turned and spoke to a police woman standing nearby. The seriousness of the old man's situation hit Elaine and she felt a dart of shame as she realised that she had been staring. Elaine turned to leave but as she turned, she saw that the space beside the man on the bench was empty where seconds before she had clearly seen the book. Could she have imagined it? She was sure she had definitely seen it and yet it was impossible for something to just disappear like that.

The paramedic caught Elaine's eye and her sense of shame returned; retracing her steps, she headed towards the centre the other way.

As she picked her way around the alternative path, the morning commuter traffic was moving fast. It seemed more sensible to turn back home, she felt a few spots of rain and she was no longer in the mood for book hunting. Unwilling to give up, she carried on until a wing mirror came just too close and sent her heart thumping, why didn't they widen this path? It's only a matter of time before someone gets hurt. Taking the next left turn into a narrow side road, she found herself in front of a shop she'd never entered before. The Victorian shop front had a single large window pane on each side of the entrance. There were a variety of dog-eared second-hand books in the window, car maintenance manuals for models which hadn't been seen around for thirty years or so, faded recipe books and old medical text books. *There must be a limited market for this stuff,* she thought but nevertheless something drew her inside.

The interior of the shop leaped out in stark contrast to the outside. A young man was sitting reading behind a solid oak counter, his blond curls cascading down to the book he was studying. Apart from a huge roll of brown paper in a dispenser, a credit card machine, a till and the book there was nothing else on the counter.

Shelf after shelf of leather-bound books stretched far back into a cavernous space. The smell was intoxicating, a pleasant hint of mustiness combined with overtones of furniture polish. The bookshelves themselves were solid wood and highly polished. The man had not looked up when she came in.

"Hello, I've just popped into browse." Elaine offered.

He met her gaze but said nothing; his expression neutral, he returned to the book, a paperback novel as far as she could tell. Half tempted to walk straight back out Elaine hesitated but found herself drawn between the rows of shelves despite herself. How had she missed this treasure trove before? If the glory of books itself wasn't enough of an attraction, the space in which they were contained would have been. The floor was solid parquet and it was clear that someone lovingly polished it, there was no delineation at the edges of the bookshelves, and the floor has the same hue and shine right up to the edge. *How on Earth do they manage that?* She wondered.

There was a little artificial lighting, the rows of shelves stood perpendicular to windows at the far side of the shop. *Has this previously been a church?* The hardwood frames were gothic arches and had clear panes. The daylight radiated in with an Arctic clarity.

Lorna Doone Blackmore, the title and author stamped in gold drew Elaine's attention; her aunt had had a similar copy and it was one of the books she used to admire as a child. She shot a furtive glance to the shopkeeper as she took the book from the shelf, half expecting him to boom at her in fury. There was no reaction.

Published by Nelson. There was slight mildew on the title page. Turning to the flyleaf, she found an inscription: *To my dear Emily with love Sonia. March 1935.* Elaine always found inscriptions fascinating. *Was Sonia a friend or a relation? Was Emily a child or perhaps a young woman?* Carefully replacing the book, she continued browsing, she was now out of sight of the shopkeeper, feeling more comfortable, she ran her fingers over the spines and breathed in the heady atmosphere. The sunlight showed tiny specks of golden dust in the air, as she carried on the specks became denser. Deeper into the interior of the shop where it was slightly dimmer, she found another section. Windowless, this area was dark and surprisingly dusty but the books and shelves were similar to the rest of the shop. One book looked as if it had recently been placed there because there was a line in the dust in front of it and yet there was no dust on the shining gold leaf of the top edge. The title *Feral Justice* seemed anachronistic to the type of binding. It looked expensive, and not the sort of thing that would normally interest her but she was curious, so she gently eased it off the shelf. Carefully opening it up, she was very surprised at what she found. The pages of good quality paper were white and clean, they had an almost silken sheen. Obviously, a reproduction as although it had all the physical features of a new book, it had the style and typeface of a Victorian novel. Elaine was intrigued, this was unusual in the book world. In artistic circles, work is frequently copied from an older style but this doesn't often happen with books. In fact, in all the time Elaine had worked for the publishing house, she had never heard of such a thing. She would have to have the book; it would probably stretch her budget but that was the last thing on her mind right now.

Even as she walked towards the counter, she wondered why she was being so uncharacteristically impetuous. Normally, she wouldn't buy so much as a tin of tuna without due thought and examination, and yet here she was with an expensive item she had only just lit upon and she was rushing to secure it. Laying the prize gently on the spotless surface of the counter, she took her purse from her rucksack. The shopkeeper continued reading, Elaine contemplated the top of his tawny head for a moment.

"Could I take this one, please?"

He looked up and without looking at the book he shook his head.

"It's not for sale."

Taken aback, Elaine frowned.

"But it was on the shelf on display."

Then realising, this was a weak argument she added, "Do you have anything similar that isn't already sold?"

"It isn't 'already sold' because it was never for sale in the first place." His voice had an edge like steel on glass.

Elaine was never one for an argument and she would normally have apologised and just left the shop at that point. She could feel that her face was on fire but she persisted.

"Could you tell me which books ARE for sale then, please?"

"Do you actually want to buy a book?"

"I ACTUALLY want to buy this one but you say it's not for sale. This is a bookshop, isn't it?"

"No, it's a car showroom." His face showed no hint of a smile.

That was enough for Elaine, she slammed her purse back into her rucksack and turned to the door.

"I wonder that you stay in business at all with customer service like that!" She was close to tears.

"What sort of thing were you looking for?"

It's amazing what a show of temper can achieve sometimes, Elaine thought. *Let's try again.*

"To be honest, I didn't have anything in mind." She realised this made her sound like the timewaster he obviously considered her to be.

"I love old books though and I find your shop fascinating." *Maybe a little flattery would appeal to his amenable side?*

"Well, there are plenty of old books here as you can see but I was hoping for something more specific?" The edge in the voice had returned.

"It's this book I want. Look, I know, you said it isn't for sale but do you have anything similar I could look at?" She pushed the book towards him.

"No, there's nothing else like this one, nothing at all." He lay a reverential hand on it and drew it towards the back of the counter. "I'm sorry, it's unfortunate you picked this one but…"

She looked up and met his eye, she saw hesitation. "If it were for sale, how much would you be asking for it?"

"Seven hundred and fifty pounds, but to you three hundred."

"What?" She wondered if she had been the victim of an elaborate scam. "Do you mean you will sell it to me?"

There was a look in his unblinking eyes which suggested a silent affirmative.

"Thank you, I'll take it!" Even as the words left her lips, she thought she must be going mad. This was so much against her better judgment.

Without a word, the shopkeeper produced a piece of tissue paper from under the counter and laid the book diagonally in the centre, then gathering the pointed edges together he secured them with a sticker which resembled a gold seal. He then tore a neat rectangle of brown paper from the roll and made a tight parcel which he tied with fine twine. *Is this all part of the con?* she wondered. He took seconds to produce a pristine parcel! Despite her doubts, she was eager to produce her card for the payment. The bookseller took the card but paused and regarded her for a moment, he had a curious expression in his dark blue eyes, a gentle compassion which belied his previous rudeness.

The transaction went through smoothly and Elaine headed out of the shop feeling as if she had just purchased the bargain of a lifetime.

Not wanting to risk the narrow footpath on the way home, Elaine decided to go back via the town centre. As she passed the clock tower, she saw a familiar face at the other side of the car park. "Tessa!" she waved and smiled.

The elderly lady waved back and came trotting towards her.

"It's a nice surprise to see you out this way!" Elaine didn't often see people from work in the town; it was one of the down sides of having a long commute.

Tessa regained her breath for a moment before replying. "I thought I'd do a bit of early Christmas shopping. I love coming out this way, sure, there are so many lovely little shops out here. Its lovely to see you too dear. Have you time to stop? Maybe we could go for a coffee?"

Elaine shook her head. "No, I must get back, maybe another time?" She spun around and left Tessa standing there. It wasn't until she had walked some distance that she realised how rude she had been. Elaine turned around and looked back down the road but it was too late; Tessa had gone.

Chapter Two

Laura followed Lilly into the hall and closed the front door with a hard shove. She secured the chain, closed the curtains and leant her forehead on the soft velvet for a moment.

Lilly protested, "Don't shut the light out, Mum, it's only half way through the afternoon."

The sun streamed in as Laura swept the curtain open again, she turned and smiled a bright smile which didn't quite reach her eyes.

Lilly was rummaging in the bread crock. "I'm going to make a sandwich do you want one?" She took the Marmite, peanut butter and raspberry jam out of the cupboard and lined them up on the work surface.

"No thanks, love." Laura wasn't hungry; besides, she didn't share Lilly's taste in sandwich fillings.

"I can do you a ham one?"

"No, pet, I'm fine for now, I'm going up to read my e-mails in a minute, do you want to talk first?"

Lilly's reply was indistinct through a mouthful of bread but it was something about watching "Love Island." She dashed into the lounge oblivious of her mother's weary tread on the stairs.

Laura picked at her thumbnail as she waited for the computer to boot up. She briefly looked through a bunch of leaflets the hospital had given her before stuffing them in the top drawer of her desk. She opened the drawer again and started to take the leaflets out then changed her mind and slammed the drawer shut. Looking over her shoulder, she saw that the study door was open. She moved to close it, and looked out to see where Lilly was. The skinny teenager was engrossed in the TV, still munching on a huge sandwich, long legs draped over the arm of the sofa. Laura felt a pain as real as if someone had stabbed her in the heart.

The internet finally connected as Laura sat back down, she was careful to leave the study door open just a tiny crack. She needed to talk to somebody. It was only at times like this that Laura felt the lack of a partner to share the parenting with.

Miss Maitlin had been very patient and thorough and she had given Laura so much information. At the end of the consultation, the soft-spoken surgeon had asked Laura if there were any questions. Laura's mind had gone into a kind of shutdown the moment amputation had been mentioned as one of the worst-case scenarios. Luckily, Lilly had been out of the room at the time. Laura had not been able to think of a single question but Miss Maitlin had emphasised that her secretary was always available through the day and that he would ensure any messages got through.

If only there had been someone with Laura to help take in all that had been said. Laura's sister had offered to go with them. Laura should have taken her up on the offer, it was just that she felt that she would have been made to feel it was all her fault somehow, her sister had a knack for making Laura feel inadequate. A small voice in her head told Laura that she shouldn't let her pride affect her actions at this time but she supressed the thought.

In the absence of anyone else to ask, Laura turned to the internet for advice. Searching on Google brought up a plethora of information, most of it very well set out, but Laura couldn't be objective, a terror had gripped her, she just wanted to read somewhere that all this wasn't really happening, that life could go on as normal. What she read was more or less what Miss Maitlin had explained to her that after treatment, life would probably soon go back to what it had been before. Gymnastics, ballet and all Lilly's sporting activities could be resumed. All that would be left to remind them would be a small neat scar. That was what Laura had been told, that was what was written on the internet. Through a black tinted fog of fear, all Laura heard, all she saw, was the fact that a very small percentage of cases required more heroic treatment. With her hurt and swollen mind, Laura perversely identified Lilly's situation with this tiny minority, and the bottom had fallen out of her world.

Laura got up to check on Lilly, she had a glass of smoothie now but was still engrossed in the TV.

Returning to the keyboard. She typed, *Alternative treatments for childhood Sarcoma.*

Most of the options which came up were sites which Laura had seen on previous searches. It took more searching to find a site that actually said something different, and in her eyes more optimistic.

As she followed link after link, Laura began to form a picture of a community outside the medical profession who had a different way of looking at disease. She frequently saw phrases such as 'treating the symptoms and not the cause' and 'treatment needs to be tailored for the whole individual'. A lot of this made sense to Laura, but as before she was overwhelmed with information. She longed for a simple instruction telling her, 'This is what she needed to do', and then she found it.

The website was a British one. The man who smiled out of the page 'Dr Alan Sharmer' had the look of an expert. He was sitting side on, his suit spoke of quality, his benevolent smile was confident. The treatment offered claimed to be one hundred per cent effective with no side effects, and according to the website, it could be run concurrently with conventional treatment without interference. Laura took this to mean that the conventional medicine would not interfere with Dr Sharmer's treatment. Laura delved deeper. The website talked of treating the whole person and the power of positive thinking. Laura became particularly interested, where she read that boosting the body's immune system would allow it to attack the cancer from inside, she had read this elsewhere; it seemed that a person's immune cells were constantly on the lookout for rogue material to purge.

Dr Sharmer's treatment, according to the website, used a unique mixture of natural ingredients which tackled the problem from two sides at once. 'Natural ionising radicals' which would strengthen the immune system and 'apoptosis chain stabilisers' which would target tumour cells specifically. The medicine could be used on its own, but Dr Sharmer recommended that his dietary and exercise plan be followed to gain maximum benefit.

For the first time in weeks, Laura felt as if an enormous weight had been lifted from her shoulders. She hastily took the number down and stowed the note in her purse.

Skipping out of the room she called out to Lilly. "Hey, you got any room left for lasagne?"

"Have I?" Lilly rolled her eyes but the grin was wide. "What do you think, Mother?"

Chapter Three

The way was still barred through the park, there were police patrolling the area which was still taped off. Elaine had to double back and brave the narrow path again; she held the parcel close to her chest to protect it from the threatening cars. Once she reached the subway under the main road, she knew that she would be back to quiet residential streets, from there it was only a short walk to home, a Victorian two up two down terrace. Her car was still parked safely outside, there was seldom any problem with vandalism in Cotswold Street or any of the adjoining roads, the most disorder the residents ever got were a few good natured but noisy revellers turning out of The Carter's Arms on a Saturday night. The key reflected in the highly polished brass lock as she opened the door. Walking into the cosy hallway, it appeared that the central heating had clicked in on cue.

Elaine picked the post up from the mat before going into the kitchen to switch the kettle on.

Iris was immediately rubbing around Elaine's ankles in greeting and purring like a tiny chainsaw.

"Ok, puss I'll feed you in a minute." Elaine bent to stroke the silky black head; she was just about to unload the rucksack onto the work surface as normal but stopped herself. Although it was her habit to wipe the benchtops completely clean and to thoroughly dry them with a clean linen tea towel afterwards, Elaine found herself worried about the possibility of damp or greasy spots.

In the centre of the lounge, there was a low walnut coffee table. Apart from a couple of books, Elaine always kept it free of clutter. Grabbing a new soft yellow duster from the cupboard under the stairs, she polished the whole surface and then laid the brown paper parcel down.

There was an urgent plaintive meow from the kitchen. *Should she make the coffee or open the parcel first?* Elaine was tired and in need of a drink but she hesitated, the thought of her prize sharing the same table space as a coffee cup just didn't work. On the other hand, she didn't want to spoil the pleasure of opening the package by having anything distract her.

Taking up with the duster, she cleaned a perfectly dust free piece of bookshelf and slotted the parcel in there. *Let's delay the pleasure,* she thought.

As the kettle was heating up, Elaine fed Iris and pondered the events of the afternoon. *That poor old chap, he didn't look homeless; he was quite smartly dressed. Perhaps, he was suddenly taken ill in the park and he was unable to call for help. He may have had a family at home waiting for him, how sad.*

The coffee tasted good; she stood in the kitchen to drink it. Normally, she would have switched the TV on and watched a quiz show or similar, savouring her drink with a couple of chocolate digestives. All she wanted to do today was to get the coffee out of the way, make herself comfortable, and unwrap her treasure. She had to wash and dry the coffee cup first, and store it back in the cupboard. "I must be getting OCD." She said to herself.

The water was hot for a shower, so Elaine went upstairs, switched the bathroom heater on and dug out the track suit she used for lounging around the house. The hot water and aromatic shower gel was soothing, she felt the tension of the day slipping away and her muscles relaxing.

She hadn't been aware of the tension within her. The steam in the bathroom clouded the mirror, as she looked at her reflection it occurred to her that it could be anyone looking back at her. *Someone in a mirror universe trying to communicate with me.* Elaine startled herself with such a strange thought.

There was a stew defrosted in the fridge, batch cooking was one of her things, she'd make large amounts at the weekend which could be kept or frozen for the week ahead. It saved time in the long run. She set the herby stew over a very low heat on the hob. There were two dumplings wrapped in cling film in the fridge ready prepared, she would put them into the pan once it had been simmering for about half an hour. The kitchen clock showed half past five. *I'll put them in about six,* she thought. Taking the parcel from the shelf, Elaine called Iris in to sit with her. Iris curled up in a furry black ball at her side.

Half an hour, she would unwrap the book and just read the first page. Untying the twine, she wound it into a neat ball. Playfully, she turned to Iris to let her play with it. Iris wasn't there, she was out in the hallway, her tail like a bottle brush and her green eyes dark with suspicion.

"Oh, puss! You are silly!"

There was no tape on the package, so the brown paper fell neatly open; Elaine took the paper from under the book, smoothed it out and folded it three times matching the edges precisely. The seal peeled easily off the underlying layer without ripping it, the tissue paper was then subject to the same meticulous folding.

The goatskin binding was soft to the touch, Elaine's fingers slid deliciously over it as she placed her right index finger under the top corner of the cover, as she opened it the blank flyleaf shone out at her, there was no inscription. The title page was puzzling, *Feral Justice* by Aurelian Wright, Requite books. No place name. Elaine had never heard of the publisher or the author.

The light was just beginning to fade outside, so Elaine turned on her reading light. A long-stemmed aluminium daylight imitating floor lamp. It stood like an inquisitive friend peering over her left shoulder. The pages of the books shone out brilliantly under the light's honest rays.

Most books take a little while to catch you, but from the first page, Elaine was hooked. The story drew her in, she could completely identify with the main character; in fact, it could have been her the author was writing about, and it was uncanny.

An acrid smell slowly entered her consciousness, she looked up, "The stew!" running to the kitchen she noticed it was pitch dark outside. The stew was completely ruined, it was burned on the bottom and totally inedible. Glancing at the clock, she was amazed to see that it was gone nine o'clock. The pan hissed as she filled it with cold water, it felt like a reprimand. She went back into the lounge to find the book face down on the floor, its splayed-out leaves crumpled and folded under the weight of the heavy binding. Distraught, she picked it up and tended to the creased pages.

"How could I have been so stupid?"

She had left the book on the arm of the chair in her panic to get to the kitchen. It must have slipped off.

There was even a little rip in one of the pages. Elaine was furious with herself. For the second time today, she was close to tears. Tired and hungry, she decided to call it a night. She straightened out the book as best she could and enclosed it in the tissue paper. Taking volume eighteen to twenty of the Oxford English Dictionary from the shelf, she laid them on top of the book in the hope that the weight would flatten out some of the creases if left overnight.

Suddenly exhausted, she switched everything off downstairs and dragged up to bed where Iris was already waiting curled up on the duvet.

The next morning dawned bright and sunny, the *Today* program played on the radio. Elaine felt a dark cloud fall on her as she remembered her damaged book. Grabbing her dressing gown, she went down and briefly surveyed the messy kitchen, she would clean that later. The first thing on her mind after feeding a very hungry cat, was to see if the heavy book treatment had worked, and was amazed to see that it had worked better than she possibly could have imagined. There was no sign of any damage at all. She wondered what special paper could have been used for it to behave in this way.

The post box rattled and something hit the doormat with a heavy thud. *That's unusual,* thought Elaine, the post doesn't usually come until after nine, well after I've left for work.

She stretched around to look at the kitchen clock. It was ten-thirty! Elaine ran up the stairs two at a time to inspect her radio alarm, it displayed ten thirty. What time was it set to alarm? She checked and found the setting was at the usual time of six forty-five. "I should have been in two hours ago, what's wrong with me?" She asked herself.

Elaine's mobile phone lay on the bedside table, snatching it up she selected 'work' from the menu and tapped to dial.

There was an answer on the second ring.

"Hello is that, Trish?"

Bad luck, she knew that Trish wouldn't let her forget this in a hurry.

"Hi, Trish, I'm sorry but I've only just woken up, I'm not feeling very well." She didn't know how else to explain.

"No, no it's nothing like that, I've just got an awful headache." She was a bad liar, she knew.

"No, I stayed in last night reading but I just couldn't wake up this morning." She started to feel irritated by Trish's interrogation, she laughed weakly.

"No, not a single glass, I forgot to eat though maybe that was it."

"No, I'm not trying to diet, I just got absorbed in the book, listen I will be in tomorrow I'm sure it's just a passing bug."

She realised too late that this was a mistake.

"Don't worry, I won't bring in anything infectious, see you tomorrow. Yes, yes, see you in the morning then, bye, ok, bye."

Elaine never took time off sick, even when she felt quite poorly, she would generally battle it out.

Pondering on events as she cleared the mess from the kitchen, Elaine tried to analyse the situation, she had never slept in before by even a few minutes, besides she was sure that it had been the alarm which had woken her but where had the time gone in that case? The *Today* program finished at nine and it was definitely this that she had heard as she woke. All sorts of thoughts crossed her mind. At thirty-eight surely, she was too young to have had a mini stroke.

Thinking back, she realised that she had been reading just a page or two after surveying the damage to the book. It was quite normal for her to get so wrapped up in reading that she lost track of time, but never to this extent.

Elaine had some bacon in the fridge and some fresh eggs given to her by Mrs Williams down the road. Mrs Williams kept chickens in her long neat back garden. All the houses in the road had long gardens, but Mrs Williams lived on the end of the terrace and her garden was especially wide. The nut-brown eggs from her hens always had deep golden yolks and because they were always day old fresh, the whites had a different quality to shop bought. When fried, the albumin stood proud and didn't spread out, when boiled, the whites were milky and light as Greek yoghurt.

Deciding to cook a Full English, Elaine looked in the freezer for hash browns, she was in luck. The grilling bacon smelt wonderful, she suddenly realised how famished she was. Not surprising, she thought after yesterday's stew disaster. Cooking extra bacon, she planned to make a packed lunch for tomorrow, she didn't want anything to delay her in the morning, she certainly didn't want to turn up late for work. There was plenty of hot water, so she washed up as she went which meant that after she finished eating there was only one plate, the cutlery and a mug to wash up. This done, Elaine adjusted the heating to warm the lounge, and treated herself to another session with her book. It wasn't even noon, so however absorbed, she got she had plenty of time.

About four o'clock, there was a faint knock on the door. Elaine went to the door; it was Mrs Williams. Fond as she was of her neighbour, she wished not to have been disturbed, Elaine had been at an especially interesting bit and she desperately wanted to carry on reading.

"Come in, come in, what a nice surprise!" Elaine opened the door wide.

Mrs Williams tottered in. "Hello, dear, I saw your car outside and wondered if everything was alright. Are you not in work today?"

"No, I wasn't too well, so I stayed at home." Elaine felt bad lying, but she couldn't think of anything else to explain her presence on the spur of the moment.

Mrs Williams looked at the cosy throw on the sofa and the open book on the coffee table.

"You get back in there, my dear, I'll make us a nice cuppa tea, go and sit yourself back down."

Elaine protested. "No, I'm not too bad really I'll make it, it was just a headache and it's almost gone."

"Nonsense, nonsense." Mrs Williams physically bustled Elaine back into the lounge. "I'll be two ticks."

Elaine closed the book memorising the page, and pushed it to the far side of the coffee table.

As good as her word, Mrs Williams was soon back with the tea. Elaine's in a thick straight sided mug, her own in the floral China teacup that she knew was kept especially for her. Elaine stood up and took the mug. As Mrs Williams sat down and put the cup and saucer down, she didn't line the saucer up with the coaster properly and this caused the teacup to tip and splash tea in the saucer. In an effort to retrieve the situation, Mrs Williams made a lunge at the cup which only made things worse by splashing tea all over the coffee table. To her horror, Elaine noticed spots of it on the top edge of the book.

"Oh, dear, oh, dear I'm so sorry." Mrs Williams started to mop up the spill with tissues.

Elaine grabbed the book and ran to the kitchen for a clean tea towel. She rubbed at the stains but they wouldn't come off.

"I'm so so sorry, dear." Mrs Williams sounded distressed.

Elaine fetched the tissue paper from the shelf in the lounge and wrapped the book in it, securing the edges with the gold sticker. She then wrapped the parcel tightly in another tea towel and put the bundle straight into her rucksack.

Mrs Williams voice was teary, "I'm such a clumsy fool; can I pay for a new book, Elaine?"

Elaine had been ignoring her neighbour but now seeing Mrs Williams's quivering mouth the book seemed less important. Hugging the kind old friend, she did her best to assure her that everything was fine.

They sat chatting for the rest of the afternoon, the upset forgotten. Once Mrs Williams had gone, Elaine opted for an early night; she wanted to make sure she was fresh next morning.

Half watching the local news in bed, Elaine's attention was drawn to a mention of her town in a report. It seemed that a renowned professor of English Literature had been found dead in the park. Paramedics had rushed to the scene but they were unable to revive him. No foul play was suspected. Elaine switched off the TV and settled down but thoughts flew around in her mind about the poor man dying alone.

The next morning, Elaine did wake punctually. There was plenty of time to get into work. She packed her lunch in the lower compartment of the rucksack, locked up and started the car. The traffic was light at this time of the morning and it was easy for her to join the flow of cars on the main road. Elaine had gone for less than a mile before she started to daydream. If I get in early, I will be able to read another chapter before I start work, she mused.

Elaine heard the bang before she felt the car jolt heavily, her head whipped back and slammed into the headrest. The rucksack fell into the foot well on the passenger side, Elaine's first thought was of the book inside it, *I hope there's no damage,* she thought.

Chapter Four

Elaine felt her blood run cold, she pulled the car to the side of the road and stopped. A white Renault Kangoo pulled in behind her and a man got out. Elaine was shaking, she had no idea what had happened, she cautiously climbed out. *Don't say sorry* she thought to herself, that will get things off to a bad start.

"Don't you look before pulling out?" The man strode towards her, his short arms swinging from hunched shoulders, he had a mobile phone clutched in a cement-stained hand.

"I'm sorry." *Damn!* She thought. "I didn't intend to pull out, the wind must have blown me."

The man snorted, "Well, you want to learn to watch out for that sort of thing love, it's not even that windy, you haven't been drinking, have you?"

"It's early morning, no I haven't." Elaine was indignant.

He really did take the moral high ground now. "Well, the effects can hang on from the night before you know." He put the phone to his ear. "I'll ring you back, mate, just got pranged by some woman." He paused. "No, the van's fine, she caught the bull bars." He paused again. "Yep, yes, see you later, this won't take long." He hung up.

Elaine looked at the damage to her rear offside wing, there was a nasty dent and the pearly pink paintwork was badly scraped. She ran her hand over it, now there were sharp burrs where there had been a highly polished smoothness.

The man was at the front nearside of the van. "You're lucky, there's no damage to my bumper, no harm done." He wiped the back of his hand across his mouth leaving a chalky trail. "You're ok to drive, aren't you?" This was a statement of fact rather than a question.

Elaine failed to notice his genuine lack of interest, *for the first time, he showed a little concern for her,* she thought. Her knees must have been visibly knocking by now, she felt wobbly but didn't want to admit it.

"I'm fine but shouldn't we exchange insurance details?" Elaine wasn't sure how these things worked; she had never been in an accident in all her twenty years of driving.

"No point." He seemed knowledgeable. "I'm not going to claim, there's no damage to the van." He whacked a heavily booted foot against her tyre. "Only superficial damage to this." He poked a finger at the dent. "Wouldn't take much to knock out."

He turned back to the van. "Sure, you feel ok then?" Without really waiting for an answer, he swung up into the cab and drove away.

Elaine sat back in the car, she was still trembling slightly as she turned the key, she sat for a while watching the cars and lorries zoom past. Eventually, there was enough of a gap in the traffic to enable her to accelerate back into the flow. The remaining journey to work went without incident and by the time she turned into the car park she felt calm again. It was still quite early despite the interruption to her journey. *I'll have half an hour for another chapter of my book,* she thought.

Clearing a space on her desk, she took the book out of her rucksack, and unpacked it carefully. The gold letters shone out at her; she was used to handling old books but this one was by far the most beautiful she had ever seen. She savoured the sheer look of it for a while. *Shame about the tea stains,* she thought as she turned the top edge towards herself to examine the extent of the damage once more. Frowning, she turned her desk light on even though there was bright daylight streaming through the window. She took a magnifying glass out of the drawer and looked again. There was no sign of any stain at all.

The computer wasn't booted up but Elaine resolved to Google, 'stain repellent paper' later, she wasn't quite sure how she would word it: 'stain proof', 'stain repellent', 'stain absorbing'; she felt uneasy wondering if she had imagined the whole thing.

There was time for a chapter still. Elaine had marked the place with a special bookmark, an oak leaf wrought in thin gold. Only a very special marker was good enough for this book.

Elaine started as she became aware of a figure to her left-hand side.

"Feeling better today?" Sylvia beamed at her. Sylvia almost always had a sunny expression.

Elaine looked at the clock, it was twenty-five to nine. She closed the book quickly.

"Yes, much better, thanks, it's strange I don't normally get headaches but this one was a stinker." *Lying is coming too easily* she thought to herself.

"What's the book?" Sylvia craned her head round to look. "Wow! It's beautifully finished, isn't it! Is it old?"

"It's hard to tell how old it is, there's no date of publication. I've never heard of the publishers before either. I think it's a recent print made in an old style, but they have made no attempt to artificially age it to make it look antique." Elaine wrapped the tissue paper around it again and secured the edges with the sticker of the original wrapping. It was curious she thought that the sticker had retained its stickiness over multiple uses. "Sylv, have you ever come across a stain proof paper in books?"

Sylvia frowned. "Well, there are various papers that are waterproof for use in menu printing, for example, and there are stain resistant papers that are used in the food industry. None of these would be suitable in book binding though, they'd be too thick, it would give you too few pages per inch for a start, apart from that the feel would be all wrong. Are you thinking of branching out into book binding now? Haven't you got enough on your plate?"

Elaine smiled. "No, it's just a thought I had, it was nothing, thanks!" She looked across at the piles of manuscripts on her desk. "I better get started on these, I suppose." Sylvia grimaced in sympathy and headed towards her own desk.

By now, the others were in and were starting work, the trilling of the PCs starting up was like a strange dawn chorus in the background.

There were twenty work stations in the office. Some people, like Elaine, had their own permanent desks but the part-timers shared so they didn't tend to personalise their work space very much. Sylvia on the other hand made her desk a home from home, even to the point of having a brightly coloured striped rag rug at her feet. Trish had very few personal items on view, but she did tend to label everything. Even the waste paper basket next to her desk was carefully labelled 'Trish's bin'. She would unfailingly retrieve it if the cleaner left it by someone else's desk.

The desk next to Trish's and in front of Sylvia's was shared. James, who worked from nine till one three days a week, had just breezed in to take his seat, the rest of the time he worked as a reporter for *THE CRONICLE*. He took a few items from his shoulder bag: A glasses case, his personal mouse mat (white with a pencil and pad graphic) and a soft leather-bound notebook with elastic closure. He arranged these neatly on his desk as he started to boot up his PC.

Sylvia smiled at him. "Hi, James."

"Good morrow, Sylvia, Patricia," and to Elaine, "feeling better today, Lainey?"

"Yes, much better, thank you." She smiled and returned to the document.

"Any interesting stories lately, James?" Sylvia's amber eyes were wide with anticipation.

Trish looked up from her work and scowled, her short dark bob wobbled as she shifted in the chair and repositioned the manuscript she had been reading. With a loud sigh, she hunched back over the document.

James spoke in a hushed voice. "I was investigating on quite a sad story yesterday actually. A professor of English Literature found dead. He didn't have any close relatives it seems but he was friendly with his neighbours who seem to think that he had been in good health."

"It must have been a shock to them then?" Sylvia's mouth pulled down at the edges.

"Yes, his next-door neighbour was very tearful." James looked across at Elaine who had not been responding up to this point. "He lived in your neck of the woods actually, Lainey, he was found in Westcott Park."

Elaine looked up startled. "I saw him! I was going to town on Wednesday afternoon and saw an elderly gent in the park on a bench with paramedics around. The police had the whole area taped off."

"Haven't you three got any work?" Trish's face was flushed and she had spun her chair around to face them.

Elaine reddened. "Sorry, Trish."

"I'll catch up later," she mouthed to James.

Sylvia had put her head down as soon as she saw Trish sitting up. She feigned absorption in the papers on her desk. Once Trish returned to her work, Sylvia nodded to the other two and indicated the tea room with her eyes, she made a circling motion on her watch. The other two nodded in comprehension and each flicked a look at the office clock.

Chapter Five

Laura only had half an hour for lunch, so she went outside before eating her sandwich to make the phone call, she wanted to be sure that there was plenty of time for it. Normally, Laura made any calls in the canteen but it could be a noisy place and she wanted to get all the details down properly. Something else made her want to be private, she couldn't quite put her finger on it, not embarrassment but something close to it.

The number for 'The Dellamare Practice' was written on a note in her purse, she held the note with one hand and keyed in the number using her thumb. There was an answer straight away, the woman on the other end sounded crisp and efficient. Laura found herself stuttering in reply.

"Erm, hello. I'd like to book an appointment with the Doctor please."

"Yes, a consultation for my daughter please."

"Yes, I know it's private, could you give me a rough idea of how much?" Laura felt cheap counting the cost of her daughter's wellbeing. She crouched down to rest the scrap of paper on her knee and made notes of the sums given. She bit her lip; *I could try and get extra shifts,* she thought.

"Could we make it Wednesday?"

"Three o'clock would be fine."

"Yes, I'll pay by card, thank you, thank you."

Laura kept her voice low as she answered questions about Lilly's condition and the hospital appointments she had had so far, she didn't want all and sundry hearing Lilly's personal information, by the end of the conversation she felt quite drained.

Despite her exhaustion, Laura was pleased with the speed the appointment had been made, no waiting really, just a couple of days. She could even have had an earlier appointment if she had wanted, but Wednesday was the first time she had 'off shift'.

The school was very understanding when Laura asked to take Lilly out before lunch on Wednesday. Lilly herself was quite excited. The practice was about three quarters of an hour's drive away, Lilly had been to the small town last year on a school trip, they had gone to the poetry festival but had been allowed to look around the numerous second-hand bookshops as long as they went in pairs. Laura had promised her that they would have time to browse around after the appointment.

The car park was in the centre of town and Laura found it easily. She had printed a map off the internet to get them to where they were going. Her phone wasn't quite up to Google maps.

Lilly was delighted with the little twisty lanes and the old-fashioned shops, she said it was just like a magic town, and she skipped along despite the condition of her leg.

The Dellamare Practice was housed in a low flat roofed concrete building the shop window frontage had been blanked off with dark green window-film. The name was written in large gold letters on the outside of the glass.

"Is that it?" Lilly's pale eyebrows disappeared under her glossy blonde fringe.

"I reckon." Laura always put on a mock American accent when she was trying to lighten the atmosphere.

She pushed the door open; it too had been blanked out by green plastic. They found themselves in a small room that had once clearly been part of a bigger space. There were plasterboard walls enclosing the space, and three oak veneer doors, two on the left-hand side of the room and one facing them on the rear wall. The left-hand wall bisected the shop window they had seen from the outside. Two beech wood counters, separated by a small gap, split the room in half. There was a lady, presumably the receptionist, sitting behind the computer screen, she immediately stopped typing as they came in and gave them a warm smile her bright red lipstick accentuated the whiteness of her teeth.

"Mrs Palmer?"

"Ms actually." Laura said smiling, she didn't want to get off on to the wrong foot by sounding snappy.

"And you must be, Lilly." The receptionist stood up and stepped through the gap in the counter.

Lilly shuffled from foot to foot but smiled and nodded as her hand was shaken just as if she was a grown up.

31

"Please sit down a moment, I'll let doctor know you are here." She disappeared through the first door on the left, leaving an almost visible cloud of Gucci Bamboo in her wake.

There were three chairs positioned against the window, they sat down and Laura put her handbag on the low windowsill. As soon as they sat down, the door opened again and a short round man in a dark blue suit came out. His brown eyes seemed friendly, Laura noticed that he must have been on holiday recently, the top of his head was red shading to brown. He ushered them into the room. The receptionist asked them if they would like a drink, Lilly opted for orange juice and Laura chose green tea, coffee was not on offer it seemed.

"Please." The doctor indicated two soft low chairs in front of a large oak desk. The window extended into this room so Laura used the window ledge again to put her bag on. There was the noise of a tap being run in the next room and then what sounded like a kettle switch.

The room was about twice the size of the reception area. At the far end of the room opposite the door was an examination couch. At the bottom of the couch was a roll of tissue about a metre wide in a dispenser which had a sharp looking serrated edge. A length of the tissue had been pulled up over the couch. On the wall was an impressive looking framed certificate with an embossed gold seal at the bottom. The text Laura could make out stated 'Greenton Institute' in a Germanic type of font and the name 'Alan M Sharmer' below some smaller print. Under that she could see the words 'Doctor of Philosophy'.

Lilly wriggled herself into the chair and swung her long legs. Dr Sharmer smiled warmly and rolled into the leather chair behind the desk. He looked at his notes for a moment. "So, you've already been seen at the University Hospital and they have diagnosed soft tissue sarcoma?" He looked at Laura and then to Lilly but his gaze rested on Laura. Laura nodded, she felt uncomfortable, expecting the doctor to say something negative about this but before she could speak, he continued. "Well, you'll be very pleased to know that any treatment she receives here will be entirely compatible with the hospital treatment and can be run concurrently without any adverse effects."

Laura felt reassured.

Dr Sharmer turned his attention to Lilly. "Now, young lady, if you can just pop up on the couch, you'll need to take the woollen tights off first, I'll have a little look."

Lilly was well used to having her leg examined and she quickly rolled down the tights and almost vaulted on to the bench with an athleticism which belied her condition.

The doctor pulled some thin vinyl gloves from a box and slid them on, flexing his fingers he addressed Lilly. "I'm just going to have a little look at your leg, is that ok?"

Lilly nodded; her pale blue eyes had a trusting expression. Laura stood up and moved over to the couch, she caught hold of her daughter's hand and squeezed it.

"It's ok, Mum, honest." The bright little voice gave Laura the feeling of tiny shards piercing her heart but she made herself let go of Lilly's hand.

The doctor circled his left hand around Lilly's right shin, his other hand on her knee. He then methodically palpated the muscle of her thigh until he found the small lump. With the fingers of both hands, he probed all around the area. His copious dark eyebrows were drawn together in concentration.

The receptionist came back with the drinks on a small round plastic tray, she left it on the corner of the desk and then quietly slipped out.

Dr Sharmer glanced at the tray and then to Laura. "Please." He nodded back at the tray. Laura sat down with her tea, it was surprisingly refreshing, she had never had this sort before, she normally drunk what her work colleagues called builder's tea in the morning and coffee the rest of the day.

A curtain rail ran right across the room on the side of the couch closest to Laura, the curtain was pulled back to the left, but it was obvious that it could be drawn across to afford some privacy for the patient. Dr Sharmer disappeared behind the curtain and then reappeared with a trolley on which there was a large piece of equipment. "I'm just going to take a picture of your leg, Lilly." He addressed her directly. There was a flat screen attached to the equipment but it was angled in such a way that Laura could only see the back of it. When the doctor started rolling a hand-held device over Lilly's leg, Laura remembered the ultrasound when she was carrying Lilly. *It must be something like that,* she thought. The pregnancy had been an easy one for her physically, it would have been the best time of her life if not for the attitude of her family at the time.

After a while the doctor straightened up. "Right then," he said to Lilly. "You can hop down again and have your juice now." He rolled the machine back behind the curtain, walked around the desk and sat down to type something on his laptop.

Lilly and Laura both waited in silence sipping their drinks. A ghost of a frown passed over Lilly's face at the first sip.

Laura found herself staring at the doctor's chubby fingers as they typed as if she could glean some information in this way, the back of his hands was covered in thick black hair, his typing was laborious, the two-finger type. As he frowned down at the keyboard, Laura focused on the shiny top of Dr Sharmer's head which was surrounded by a circlet of jet-black hair, Laura wondered if he dyed the hair.

At last, Dr Sharmer looked up. "Well now, Mrs Palmer."

Laura coloured slightly. The doctor appeared to realise his mistake, flicking a glance at his notes, he didn't correct himself but continued, his voice resonant and steady. "I am confident about taking on this case, I feel sure we can help and the treatment I am going to suggest should benefit Lilly greatly. As I said before, there is no reason why you can't keep on with the hospital treatment at the same time, there should be no ill effects from this."

"The capsules I am going to prescribe will act on the tumour in two ways, as I'm sure you know, the problem is that the tumour cells are growing out of control. He paused for a moment."

Something we call the 'cell cycle' is doing the job it should do, but in an uncontrolled way. If you can imagine an agent which will take 'molecular scissors'. He made quote marks in the air with his fingers. "And cut that cell cycle, you can see that this uncontrolled growth can be stopped."

He paused. "Are you following me so far?"

"Yes, that makes sense." Laura nodded.

"Added to this, it is known that the immune system is constantly cleaning up possible harmful material, as individuals we are unaware of this of course. If for some reason, the immune system isn't up to the task then sometimes this can cause a problem such as Lilly's. The idea is to boost the body's own immune system to give it a better chance whilst attacking the tumour with the 'molecular scissors'." He made the quote sign in the air again. "This then gives a two-pronged attack."

Laura was trying to take this all in but from what she understood it sounded hopeful to her, and Dr Sharmer clearly knew what he was talking about. "Will the medicine make Lilly feel sick?" The doctor's very white even teeth appeared below his black bushy moustache. "My goodness, no! All our products are sourced from entirely natural wholesome ingredients. In fact, the immune boosting component is available as a dietary supplement for everyday use, in fact, I would recommend you consider a course yourself, Ms Palmer, you must have been under considerable strain in recent months."

Laura certainly couldn't disagree with him.

He continued. "In this practice, we take a holistic view of the patient. We consider the environment and diet of the patient themselves, and also the family as a whole. We believe that to give the best chance, the support and cooperation of other family members is essential."

Laura agreed, it wouldn't be hard though as there was just the two of them.

"What I'm going to propose, and can I stress now that you can choose to include or omit any of these suggestions as you think fit? I propose that in addition to the core therapy, Lilly is put on our controlled diet. This is not a calorie reducing diet, it is a mix of high-quality foodstuffs which will naturally boost the immune system. This shouldn't make any extra work for you, Ms Palmer." He addressed Laura. "The packages will be delivered to your door and will contain all the ingredients you need plus simple recipe cards." He turned to Lilly. "I'm afraid this will mean cutting out fizzy drinks, but we can provide herbal teas as part of the diet plan and in our experience, it doesn't take long for subjects to retrain their palates."

Lilly twisted her mouth to one side and looked at her mum. Laura smiled at her then turned to Dr Sharmer and asked, "She likes milk; would that be alright?"

He nodded, "Organic milk is fine as long as it is limited to five hundred millilitres a day."

The consultation continued for another half hour by which time Lilly was getting fidgety. Laura was satisfied that all her questions had been answered fully, and she has a sheaf of pamphlets to take home with her to study. She was to leave her bank details with reception on the way out, and had an enrolment form to complete. It was stressed that she must think carefully about the treatment plan over the next day or two, and only when she was completely satisfied with how much or how little of it, she chose to adopt. Once she was absolutely sure, and only then, should she fill in the form committing them to the program. She could e-mail the form or bring it in person.

The consultation had taken longer than expected and as they were ushered to the door, Laura wondered if she had put enough time on the car parking ticket. Once they were on their way back to the car park Lilly grimaced at her mum. "OMG, Mum, that orange juice was rank!"

Laura giggled. "What are you on about your pudding? It was just ordinary juice."

Lilly screwed up her nose. "It tasted like the stuff they used to give us in Brownies 'cheepo bargain basics'."

Laura rolled her eyes. "Oh, lordy! What a little snob I'm raising!" She squeezed Lilly close to her with one arm and tousled the top of her head with the other hand.

Chapter Six

At ten thirty, after working in companionable silence for a while, Elaine, Sylvia and James headed for the tearoom in unspoken conspiracy. The tearoom was on the west of the building and looked out on to the Japanese garden two stories below. Kessler and Drake Publishing believed in investing in their employee's comfort and wellbeing. Each of the seven floors had its own toilet block and large well equipped rest facilities. Tessa, also fondly known as Tessa the tea lady, was responsible for keeping the kitchens of all seven floors neat and tidy. Tessa was noticeably proud of the fact that this was her sole role, she was not expected to be involved in general office cleaning, that task was contracted out. As far as everybody knew, Tessa lived on her own, she got by supplementing the wages she received from Kessler and Drake by earnings from other smaller cleaning jobs. Tessa was of the old school in that she quietly got on with her tasks without getting involved with the other staff. Despite keeping herself to herself, everyone recognised Tessa as a reliable confidant and shoulder to cry on when needed, she was also a good source of advice and homely wisdom.

Just as the three of them were going into the tearoom, Tessa came out wielding her mops and sponges.

Elaine held her hand to her mouth. "Oh, Tessa! I'm sorry, I was so rude the other day, I should have made the time for us to go to coffee together I don't know what I was thinking."

Tessa gently grasped Elaine's arm. "Not at all, love, sure I know how busy ya are."

Elaine had the grace to look shamefaced, she knew that she hadn't been all that busy but she was glad to see that Tessa bore her no ill will because of the incident.

The kettle had been boiled so the water was already hot. Sylvia extracted three mugs out of the cupboard above the sink. She didn't have to ask what the other two wanted, it was always coffee, James with semi skimmed and Elaine with full fat, Sylvia herself always took soya milk.

Elaine and James had already taken a seat by the window.

Elaine quizzed James. "Do they know how the professor died then?"

James shook his head. "No, there will need to be a post mortem but I don't think they suspect foul play. He probably had a heart attack or something."

"But I thought you said he was in good health." Sylvia stirred her coffee in a figure of eight motion.

"Even fit people succumb sometimes." Elaine said sadly, her father had been a triathlon enthusiast until his sudden collapse in his mid-sixties.

Sylvia clamped a hand to her mouth. "Oh gosh, yes! I know sorry, Elaine."

James cut in quickly, "The neighbours did say that he had been keeping himself to himself lately. One of them suggested that he may have been depressed, although I think that opinion is based on the fact that he hadn't been to his Canasta evenings lately."

Sylvia smiled. "Are you allowed to tell us his name?"

"It'll be in the *Chronicle* this week." James nodded. "His name was Professor Cambwell. He was much respected in his field and quite active in his community it seems."

"I've heard of him!" Elaine put her coffee down with a splash, she grabbed a napkin to mop up the puddle. "He was quite well known in my area, he did a lot to help raise funds for our local scout hut, and he arranged talks at the library. I think he was very involved with the University of the Third Age too."

Sylvia had gone to get a paper towel and she polished up the rest of the spill with it. "I think I know of him through his books, published by the University Press. I haven't actually read any of his work though, it's far too high brow for me."

"There will have to be an inquest of course." James lowered his eyes.

Elaine remembered the long delay before her father's funeral, it had added to their distress at the time. "It has to be done, I suppose." All of a sudden, she wished it was five o'clock and she could just go home, curl up on the sofa and read her book.

The three of them carried on speculating on the personal circumstances of Professor Cambwell as they finished their coffee. When Trish came striding in, Sylvia grabbed the mugs and put them into the sink. They scurried back to work.

The rest of the morning went quickly. When it was time for lunch, Elaine put her book in the rucksack and got up from the chair. "I'm going out for a walk for a change, Sylvia."

Sylvia looked surprised. "Oo, do you want us to come with you?"

"No!" Elaine realised immediately that this sounded abrupt, she made a conscious effort to soften her tone. "Sorry, I just want to clear my head a little, it's still fuzzy from yesterday."

"Of course, do you need any painkillers? I've got some in my desk." Sylvia bought a small gingham bag out of her drawer and started unzipping it.

"No!" Elaine heard the harshness in her own voice once again and corrected herself, she smiled, "I'm sure the fresh air will do the trick. I try to stay away from pills, if possible, but thanks though."

Once outside, Elaine headed for the car park. She felt ashamed of her white lie, she had no intention of going for a walk. Opening up the car she slid inside, she felt a sinking feeling as she remembered the damaged wing, *I must ring the garage,* she thought.

Setting the timer on her phone to ring at one twenty, Elaine retreated into her book, the troubles of the day were forgotten even before she had finished the first paragraph.

A gentle rapping on the car window made Elaine look up startled, Tessa was peering in at her.

Winding down the window she felt herself glaring at the kindly tea lady.

"Sure, you'll catch your death out here, queen, why don't you come inside?"

Elaine was irritated by Tessa's interference but she didn't want to let it show. "I just wanted a change of scene and a bit of peace and quiet." The words come out sharply despite her best intentions.

Tessa stared down at the book. "You must be careful, my dear."

Elaine felt herself flush. "I won't be out here long, don't worry."

"That's not what I mean." Tessa shook her head and moved to say more but Elaine had already wound the window up again.

Elaine felt a pang of guilt as she saw Tessa crossing back over the car park with a downhearted slant to her shoulders but the tea lady was soon forgotten when reading resumed.

In what seemed to Elaine to have been about ten minutes, the phone alarmed. Reluctantly gathering her things, she opened the car door. Her arms and legs were stiff with the cold and as she climbed out, she almost fell over, she bent over and gave her legs a stretch to get the blood circulating again and then limped towards the main entrance.

Sylvia and James were already hard at work by the time she got back to the second floor.

Trish's expression said it all. Elaine was only five minutes late, but as her habit was to be back working a couple of minutes early, she supposed her lateness was emphasised by the fact that it was so unaccustomed.

"Nice walk?" Sylvia's open guileless expression stuck a dart into Elaine's conscience. James's understanding smile didn't make her feel any better either.

"It's getting cold out there!" Elaine couldn't compound her guilt with another direct lie so she side stepped the issue. "Once the clouds come across the temperature soon drops." She proffered. *How lame!* She mentally reprimanded herself.

Bundling some documents together, she made to go over to the photocopy area. In fact, she went to the other side of the room to phone her local garage, she didn't want to do this from her desk.

The garage answered the phone almost immediately. Elaine kept her voice low. "Hello? This is Elaine Harper, I'm phoning about my car, a Citroen Picasso I had it serviced recently…"

"No, there's no problem, well not with the servicing, the thing is, I've had a bit of a prang…"

"No, the insurance company haven't been notified, I didn't want to lose my no claims…"

"No, I'm not sure who was to blame but the other driver didn't leave his details."

"Yes, I suppose I should have, I was confused."

"Yes, you're right that's all the more reason to do things properly."

"Yes, look can I bring it in for you to have a look at tonight?"

"Yes, I'll pay what's needed."

"Yes, I know it won't be cheap but I'd like it fixed."

"Tonight? Yes, I'll be there well before seven, thank you."

At five, Elaine shot straight out of the door, calling a hasty goodbye to everyone she trotted downstairs nearly bumping into Tessa on the way down. Tessa raised her hand and started to say something but Elaine pretended not to hear, even though she normally stopped for a chat when she met the kindly tea lady. Elaine imagined Tessa's hurt expression as she carried on out of the building and headed for the car.

Surveying the car's damage once more, it dawned on Elaine that the garage man had been correct, it wasn't going to be a cheap job to put right. She should have been more assertive about establishing exactly what had happened. *I expect it was my fault,* she decided, *no point in worrying now I'll just have to cough up when the time comes.*

The traffic was light on the way home and there were no incidents this time. Elaine reached the garage in good time; she parked in front of the big green wooden doors. The green paint was flaking off in places and there was a general air of dilapidation, but Elaine's father had always used LM Bryce and she trusted them.

"We won't be able to do it here of course, we'll have to send it away to the body shop." The mechanic rubbed a grease-stained hand across his bald head, his name badge glinted red in the evening sun, "Jeff Boxall."

"The paint is cracked but not the metal underneath, so it should be possible to get behind and bang it out. The wing will need respraying of course, but they should be able to get a close match. Once it's polished up, it'll be as good as new, don't worry."

"Do you have any idea how long it will take?" Elaine was worried about how she was going to get to work. There was a bus service but this could be erratic.

Jeff looked at her over the top of the glasses which he didn't actually have on. "It shouldn't be more than ten days; the chap we send them to is very good."

"You don't do courtesy cars, do you?" Elaine knew that they were too small a firm for that but she asked anyway.

Jeff chuckled. "I'm afraid not, love," then seeing her worried face, "leave it with me, I may be able to sort something out with one of our second-hand sales. The body shop is usually pretty booked up so it'll probably be a couple of weeks before we can get you in anyway."

"You've got my phone number?"

"Yes, we'll give you a ring when we know what's what."

Elaine was glad that she didn't have to leave the car there and then. It was one less thing to worry about. All she wanted to do was to get home and close the front door on the world and read the next chapter of her book.

As she drove out of Bryce's yard, she intended to turn right to divert via the supermarket. There was very little food in the house and she hadn't eaten since the chocolate hob nob with her coffee at morning break.

The traffic was not heavy but she couldn't immediately find a big enough gap to swing out and turn right into the flow, so she took the first break in the traffic which allowed her to turn left. *I'll pop out to the corner shop for something,* she thought. Once she parked up in front of the house, instead of going straight to the Spar, she went inside to unpack her bag, putting the chain on the front door as she came in. Knowing that she wouldn't be cooking that night, Elaine boiled the kettle and took a packet of instant soup from the cupboard. Shaking the contents into a big stripy pint mug, she covered it with water and stirred vigorously. The sandwiches were still in her bag, so she took them out and cut them into strips which she then dunked into the soup. Elaine was still standing at the kitchen work surface but she didn't sit down, instead she hungrily ate the soaked sandwich with a spoon. It tasted surprisingly good. Thirsty, she took a pint glass, one she'd picked up at the beer festival, filled it with cool water from the tap which she downed in one. It was only now that she realised, she hadn't had a drink since morning coffee either.

Ignoring the television completely, she sat down in the lounge with her book. Elaine hesitated, somehow the environment seemed wrong, too casual somehow.

At the top of the house was a small attic. The previous owners had converted it into a comfortable if tiny extra bedroom. Elaine had never used it as a proper bedroom, but she had a camp bed in there. Occasionally, Joanna, her cousin would come to stay with her daughter Amy, the attic made a cosy private space for Amy. They hadn't visited for over a year now though and Elaine was toying with the idea of making the room into a little study.

The attic had a proper wooden staircase leading up to it, but it was steep. There was already a walnut desk up there which had taken most of a day to install, Elaine had had to dismantle it first and it hadn't been easy to put together again. It had been worth it though, it looked perfect nestled under the skylight. There was a dining chair accompanying the desk but what it really needed was a proper ergonomic office seat. Elaine did have just such a thing, a plush Jefferson chair in chestnut faux leather. After the experience moving the desk, she had hesitated to attempt to move the chair up there. It had remained unused in a corner of the lounge since she had bought it as a treat for herself six months ago.

Now is the time, thought Elaine, she felt motivated. It was an easy job to dismantle the camp bed and stow it under her bed in the floor below. As predicted, it was a hard job getting the chair up even the first set of stairs but the attic stairs were nearly her undoing. Sweaty and shaking after the effort of tackling the first flight, she went downstairs for another glass of water. The outer packaging from the book was still on the coffee table where she had left it. Seeing the strong twine gave her an idea. In the cupboard under the stairs, there was a length of thin blue rope; the sort that lorry drivers use to secure their loads. She ran up to the attic with it and secured one end to a hook in the beam at the apex of the attic. Elaine trailed the other end down the attic stairs and looped it around the chair. Then she went back up and passed the free end of the rope around the hook again, drew it taught and holding the free end she returned downstairs. Using the rope, she was able to inch her way up the stairs with her burden, resting at each step and tautening the rope as she went. When she got to the top of the stairs, she gave a final heave and she was in, she was able to roll the chair over to the desk, it was perfect.

It didn't take long to stow the rope away and bring the book up to what was to be her 'reading attic' from now on. Settling herself down, she felt a great sense of coming home. This was where she belonged. Elaine leaned back in the chair and gazed out of the attic window. The sky was just beginning to turn dusky pink with streaks of gold and blue. The gold edge of the book shone in the evening light. Elaine felt at one with the universe.

Elaine's normal reading style was close to skimming, she was an excellent speed reader and could take in the content of a page very quickly. She had built up this skill out of necessity over the years since her job involved so much reading. Now, in this room, with this book she found herself slowing right down, absorbing every word. She rolled each sentence around in her mind until she had extracted every nuance of meaning, only then did she pass on to the next one.

The stars twinkled down on her through the sky light like interested companions, she had long since turned on the reading light. Nowhere near a third of the way through, a sudden chilling thought came to her like an iceberg looming out of the mist. What was she going to do when she finished the book? She put the thought to the back of her mind. The idea filled her with dread.

Absorbed in reading, Elaine didn't hear the last revellers coming out of The Carter's Arms at half-past eleven. A fox barked from the other side of Mrs William's garden, Elaine was oblivious to the possible danger for the chickens.

The milkman trundled up the road his bottles clattering unheard by either the sleeping residents, or the intent reader in her newly appointed garret. It was not until Elaine looked up and saw a marshmallow sky that she realised how late it was, in fact it was beyond late. Reluctantly, she headed for bed.

The following weeks followed a similar pattern. Elaine spent all the time she could up in her cosy reading nest. Holly, her good friend and landlady of The Carter's Arms wondered why Elaine wasn't coming in for either their pie nights or the curry nights any more. Mrs Williams asked why her young friend hadn't popped in for a cuppa for weeks. Sylvia questioned why the Friday night shopping trips had been curtailed.

Elaine found herself becoming increasingly irritated by anything that delayed her getting to her reading time. It was such an occasion when the phone rang just as she was about to go upstairs.

She tried to keep the irritation from her voice. It was the garage telling her that she could bring her car in for repair at last. They had also managed to arrange a car for her to use whilst she was without her own. It was one they had been asked to sell for a third party, it had belonged to a recently deceased relative of a customer who had no use for it.

Chapter Seven

The courtesy car, a Vauxhall Corsa, handled well and Elaine soon got used to driving it. It had been superficially valeted at LM Bryce's, but Elaine thought it needed a good clean and polish, if she was going to be driving it for a couple of weeks then she wanted to feel comfortable with it. To this end, she dropped into The Carter's Arms on Friday night.

Holly, the landlady greeted her with a smile. "Hello, stranger! We were getting worried about you, have you come for the Friday special?"

Elaine shook her head. "No, just a half of blonde tonight please, I've been a bit tied up."

Holly served the beer. "You're looking pale, love, have you been, ok?"

Elaine took a large swig nodding at the same time, "Mmm, I've just been rushing around a lot at work. Is Barry in?"

Before Holly could answer Barry swung through the door leading to the toilets. He beamed when he saw Elaine. "The wanderer returns! How are you, pet? We were worried that we hadn't seen you lately, I was almost on the point of knocking on your door." He turned to Holly. "We were just saying this afternoon, weren't we?"

Holly nodded in agreement; her soft brown eyes full of concern peering behind a thick dark fringe. As she continued polishing glasses, she surveyed Elaine with surreptitious glances.

Elaine turned to Barry. "Barry, I wondered if you could do a job for me. I've borrowed a car while mine is getting fixed and it could do with a good clean inside and out."

Barry's pale blue eyes were just visible over his pint of dark stout. He raised his eyebrows in assent and made a gurgling sound. Wiping a froth moustache away with the back of his wax jacket sleeve, he smiled, "Sure thing, pet, I'll pick the keys up in the morning, shall I?"

"That's fine, shall I pay you now?" She rummaged in her bag for a purse.

"Just leave a tenner behind the bar for me and we call it quits, love."

The lasagne cooking in the kitchen smelt good. Elaine was persuaded to stay for another pint of blonde and a Friday special. It was the first properly cooked food she had had for a couple of weeks now and it tasted divine.

Despite the delay, Elaine was at home by half-past seven. As usual, she went straight upstairs to read. The television had not been switched on for weeks now and the washing basket was high with ironing. Elaine had been subsisting on non-iron clothing for work.

Reading until the ghostly light of dawn, Elaine reluctantly made a move towards bed. The heating had long since clicked off and her legs were stiff with cold. For some reason, she always kept the book by her bedside, she would not have contemplated actually reading it in bed, she was far too afraid the pages could get crumpled if she did that. Tucking the book securely under her arm, she held the rail with her other hand to steady herself as she went down the steep attic stairs. Whether with stiffness or tiredness, somehow Elaine misplaced her foot on the second step down, she felt her instep slide forward on the edge and in an instant she had completely lost balance. Grappling for a hand hold, she dropped the book, a second later, she landed on top of it, she felt the binding crack as her full weight went onto it. She slid forward as if on a sledge, pages flew out with a ripping sound as they caught on the wooden struts. Iris shot out of the bedroom with a yowl of terror.

Bracing herself for a big crunch at the bottom of the stairs, Elaine continued falling. It was suddenly dark; she could hear water dripping and children screaming. There was no impact but she found herself at the bottom of a pit staring up at a bright sky, she could see clouds scudding across in the breeze. A man at the top was staring down at her, he was unshaven and greasy long hair poked out from beneath a strange looking leather hat. She looked down at the wailing children clinging to her waist and knew by some unnatural sense and with an absolute certainty who they were. Thomas and Matilda, her children, the product of her union with Benedict, a man of wisdom and alchemy. They lived on the edge of the forest away from the village. Their cow and pigs grazed on the common. Elaine made cheese from the cow's milk, and trading this produce, as well as the part grown weaners, furnished Benedict with the means to obtain the materials he needed for his art. The family lived mainly on rye bread, vegetable pottage and ale but they never went hungry. Benedict practiced his craft in secret, he worked both night and day in his endeavours.

The secrecy with which her husband worked meant that Elaine had no friends she could turn to and but just one neighbour, Tess. Tess was like them; she went about her business without reference to the people in the village. Tess was regarded with suspicion too but unlike Benedict, she inspired contempt rather than fear. Tess had not been born in the village; she was part of a travelling family who had camped in the woods long ago when she was but a girl. Tess's parents had succumbed to a fever which left her alone, she had fended for herself ever since.

Although Elaine did not fear Tess, she had a deep respect for her and recognised the same profound natural wisdom in her that she saw in her husband Benedict.

A dark shadow had entered Elaine and Benedict's home life of late. Men from the village had found out about Benedict's work. They had long suspected him of practicing the black arts, but far from reporting him to the church, they sought ways to benefit themselves by using the knowledge.

Benedict could not or would not give them the secrets they wanted so they had captured and held Elaine and the children to force him to tell. They had not been gentle in the capturing either, Elaine could hardly see out of her right eye, it was badly swollen.

Elaine heard one of the men shouting. "Get away from here, you filthy tinker, this is none of your concern." There was the sound of a hard blow being struck.

Tess's voice rang out. "Let them go! They have caused you no harm. Why in Jesus's name do you persecute them?"

Elaine heard the other man curse. "You dare to use the name of the Lord?" There were more blows, harder this time. The men laughed.

Tess's voice came in rasps as she called out. "Fear not, Elaine! These beasts cannot touch the purity of your souls."

Thomas and Matilda slept. They had stopped crying, stopped shivering, and stopped moving. A second man appeared at the top of the pit, he wore dazzling white robes and the light was bright above him.

"A blow to the parietal lobe."

Elaine didn't understand what he was saying, what devilish business where they planning. "For mercy's sake," she pleaded, "take me, but let the mites go free."

The men did not reply, all Elaine could hear was the sound of something being dragged through the undergrowth. Elaine continued calling but her strength was failing her.

"We must go, mother." Thomas was upright at her side his face radiant. Matilda raised her fair head. "Wait for me, Thomas!"

Elaine felt light as a goose feather, she rose effortlessly clutching the two children to her sides. They ascended out of the pit and rose to a level with the clouds, the breeze took them towards home.

"Father!" Thomas called out but Benedict did not answer.

Elaine made no attempt to speak, she knew it would be futile.

Her husband's eyes were full of rage; he spoke through tight drawn lips. "I will avenge this act I swear. I will visit my wrath unto the fourth and fifth generation of those that have done this to my little lambs and their dam." He threw a vial into the cauldron, there was a blinding light.

Elaine saw their home grow further and further away. The children still clung to her and to each other but were peaceful.

Looking upwards, she saw an array of what looked like small faces. The little black eyes and tiny black mouths. There were red and orange eyes winking at her too. Closing her eyes, she became aware of a voice again.

"Nurse! I think she's awake."

Elaine recognised the voice. She looked again; she saw the pale face of an angel surrounded by a golden halo.

"Elaine?" The angel gently stroked her cheek. "You're back with us, thank goodness, you're awake, you had a nasty tumble."

Elaine's eyes focused. "Sylvia." The word came out as a croak.

A nurse appeared and took over, shooing Sylvia to the waiting area, the doctor was called and it was some time before Sylvia reappeared and was able to talk to her friend again. Elaine had supposed that Sylvia would not wait around as the doctors and nurses were fussing around for such an age but at long last, she was back at Elaine's bedside explaining to her what had happened.

It seemed that Barry had come to pick up the car keys on Saturday morning. He had got no reply so had gone away then tried half an hour later. Still getting no reply, he'd peered in the letter box only to see Elaine lying unconscious half way down the stairs. She must have fallen all the way down the attic stairs and then continued down the next flight.

Mrs Williams had a key, so by the time, the ambulance came, the door was open and they didn't have to break in. Mrs Williams had let the human resources department of Kessler and Drake know and Sylvia, James, Tessa and Barry had taken it in turns to sit by Elaine's bedside. It was now Sunday afternoon, so she must have been unconscious for nearly two days.

Sylvia leant across the bed and stroked Elaine's cheek. "It's good to have you back, we were all so worried about you. You were saying some strange stuff whilst you were out. Tessa said you were crying for your children."

Elaine frowned. "Children?"

Sylvia laughed. "Yes, I know you said you don't have any, mind you, James reckons you could have a secret other life that you don't tell us about."

Elaine smiled. "I'm not that mysterious. I was having some strange dreams though." She had a sudden thought. "How's my book?"

Sylvia almost laughed out loud. "That is so typical of you, Elaine! You half kill yourself and all you're worried about is the book. I'm afraid it did get a little damaged. Barry put it together as best he could and left it safely on the coffee table but I fear it may have to be rebound after this."

Elaine felt her chest heaving and let out a great wail, she surprised even herself with the ferocity of the reaction. Sylvia was alarmed and called for a nurse who reassured her that it was a natural reaction to the trauma and nothing to worry about. Sylvia held on to her friend with a firm hug until the tide of sobbing subsided.

Handing Elaine a paper tissue, Sylvia tried to think of something to say. "Don't worry, Elaine, we'll take the book to the best place and it will be almost good as new."

Elaine shook her head. "I'm not crying about the book."

Sylvia spoke quietly. "Then what?"

Elaine began to sob again. "I don't know, Sylvia, I just don't know." She buried her face in the tissue until the sobbing stopped.

The nurse agreed that it might be good for Elaine to have some rest so Sylvia reluctantly left, promising to return the next day.

As good as her word, Sylvia did return, as did James, Barry and Tessa so that Elaine was seldom without a visitor for the remainder of her stay.

Monday morning dawned sunny although all that Elaine could see of the daylight was a small patch of window at the very end of the ward. The tiny patch of blue sky was commanding all her attention so she was surprised when she heard the chink of bottles. Startled, she looked round to see Tessa placing two clear glass bottles with swing top ceramic stoppers on the on the bedside table.

"A couple of me herbal teas, lovely, one Camomile and one lemon balm. I've checked with the nurse and she says it's ok. The bottles are new, sure I got them from Lakeland, so I did. I thought they'd be handy for you to keep for other stuff later."

Elaine sat up in bed and thanked her visitor who was drawing up a chair by the bedside.

"It's good to see you on the mend, sure you were in quite a state."

Elaine nodded. "I'm starting to feel stronger again thanks, Tessa, it's good to see you. How are things at Kessler and Drake?"

Tessa chuckled. "Well apart from them worrying about you, it all seems the same m' dear, but I try not to get too involved or interfere." Tessa caught hold of Elaine's hand. "Except in your case."

Tessa looked down at Elaine's pale hand nestled in her own leathery sun-tanned palm. "I'm worried that you are getting involved with things that will do you harm."

Elaine frowned. "What do you mean?"

Tessa was silent for a few seconds and then she looked up her pale blue eyes full of concern.

"The book, I don't think 'twas supposed to pass into your hands."

Elaine snatched her hand away. "Tessa, what on earth do you mean?"

Tessa smoothed the bed clothes. "Nay, then I don't want to upset you, queen, I just think it isn't good for you."

Elaine's reaction caused Tessa to change the subject entirely and the rest of the visit was spent with awkward small talk. There was no further mention of any book.

Elaine was out of hospital by Thursday but not expected back at work till the following week. Barry came to pick her up from the hospital using the courtesy car which he had cleaned until it looked almost as good as new.

When she arrived home, Elaine discovered that Mrs Williams had tidied up the mess, given the kitchen a good clean, done the ironing and arranged the get-well cards along the window ledge, there were lots of cards, there was even one from Trish.

The book had been left on the coffee table and Barry had done a very good job of putting it back together. There were no rips or tears in the pages after all.

She must have imagined the pages coming out, the book was as good as new with not a sign of harm. Elaine wondered what Sylvia had been talking about when she spoke of the damage which needed to be repaired.

Elaine didn't get much chance to read in peace for the next few days because of the well-wishers and visitors. She suspected they had a rota for visiting her as they never seemed to come together.

Barry was the latest visitor, he sat nervously on the edge of the sofa sipping a cup of tea.

"That Corsa is running sweet as a nut, I took it round the garage to check the tyre pressures. Did you see the notebook I found under the seat with the manual?" Elaine shook her head.

Barry stood up and went to the hall table, there was a notebook under the car keys. He brought it through to the lounge and passed it over. "You may want to give it to the garage so they can give it back to the previous owner." She looked inside, it seemed to be a journal written in very neat cursive writing. The final entry was dated over a month ago. She read a line, "I have been following this course to the neglect of all other pursuits, there must be an end to it." It suddenly struck her that this journal must have belonged to the deceased. She was probably invading the privacy of a grieving family.

"I'll take it into the garage tomorrow, the walk will do me good."

Barry nodded, "So long as you don't overdo it, you had a nasty tumble there, lass."

Elaine smiled; she was suddenly struck by the incongruity of the tattooed Barry daintily sipping tea from a China cup that was normally reserved for Mrs Williams.

Chapter Eight

Laura had a special meal planned for Lilly when they got home. Pizza, her favourite, with cookie dough ice-cream for dessert. As she put the pizza in the oven, she thought to herself that this might be the last time for a while.

After dinner, they sat down together and chatted about the events of the day. Laura wanted to find out if Lilly had any worries about the visit to Dr Sharmer but she didn't want to ask directly, she knew enough about teenagers to know that you had to teasel information out of them by degrees and with subtlety. Lilly however was more than usually inscrutable this evening. The only strong opinion she seemed to have was the gross colour of the receptionist's nail varnish. She seemed relaxed about the whole thing but then again, she had been quite calm throughout, since the very first time they suspected that something was seriously wrong, even during the hospital visits, something Laura couldn't say about herself. Laura's world had been shattered; she had never felt so alone, even when she had been excluded from the family home at the time, she was found to be expecting Lilly. Lilly's father had been a member of the church but he had been young too like Laura, his family sent him off to study in America and she had never seen or heard of him again. There had been no support from either her or the boy's parents. Laura had had to learn to grow up quickly.

As it was school next day, Lilly was packed off to bed by nine. Laura switched the television off and took out the sheaf of leaflets she had been given by the receptionist at the clinic. Before even leaving the consultation, she had made up her mind that they would go for the whole package. There was discount on the meals if you went for the exercise plan, and a further discount the more individuals who enrolled for the meals. The only thing that she would have to work out was the weekly cost and how she was going to find the money. There was a limit to the number of extra shifts she could do, she didn't want to leave Lilly on her own at night.

There was little enough left at the end of the month to put by for a rainy day but what there was, Laura carefully saved. These savings would cover a three-month course of treatment. The doctor had predicted that it would be necessary to keep the treatment up for initially, a full twelve-month period. If she paid six months in advance, there would be a twenty per cent discount. *It would be worth getting a loan to pay in advance*, she thought. Luckily, the clinic had recommended a reliable loan company which the receptionist had told her that many of their patients had used.

The cost of the meals could be offset to a certain extent by the savings she would make in normal food shopping. The receptionist had made a point that Laura would make savings in petrol since the food would be delivered to the door. Since Laura normally did all the grocery shopping at work where she got a colleague discount that wouldn't actually be the case, there had been no point in contradicting that would have an unwanted negativity to the whole experience.

Laura toyed with the idea of phoning her sister, the only family member who Laura was in contact with but it was difficult to ask for help from her. There was always an element of judgement in Trish's tone. *If I approached the whole thing from a health angle though*. Laura thought, *perhaps it would be, ok?* At any rate, she had to find a way to bring the cost of Lilly's treatment plan down somehow. *I will just have to swallow my pride.*

The ring tone carried on for several moments, Laura was almost relieved at not having to speak to her sister, but eventually the call was answered. Laura tried to sound as bright and friendly as she could. "Hi, it's me, you sound breathless; sorry are you busy?"

"Oh, sorry, shall I call back later?"

"No, it was just I wanted to tell you about a great new meal plan I've discovered, I'm thinking of starting it for Lilly and me."

"Gosh, no! I don't think you need to diet, quite the opposite but I know you are interested in healthy eating." Laura bit her lip, that had come out a bit wrong. "I thought it would help for Lilly to have a really healthy diet and," she lowered her voice, "I think it might be hard for her to give up some of her favourite stuff, so I'm going to join in with it."

"It was recommended by the holistic practitioner I told you about, we went to see him today."

"No, he's fully qualified." Laura had expected this interrogation. "No, the therapy is complimentary to other treatment, it's all about giving Lilly's body the best chance to fight the…"

Laura's voice cracked, "The cancer."

Laura listened to a long lecture about the dangers of pinning too much hope on 'dubious treatments', she interjected with only the occasional grunt of agreement. When she finally got chance to speak, she carefully modulated her voice to eliminate any hint of irritation. "The thing is, Trish; I just feel it can't harm to follow a healthy diet and exercise plan and I thought if you and Rob signed up for the plan too then…"

Laura laughed, "No, I suppose it would be a bit optimistic to expect Rob to join in."

"I can show you the leaflets and you can see what you think." Laura dared to hope. "It would be great if you would think about it."

"Yes, sorry, I know you're busy, I'll let you go, I'll drop the information off and you can let me know?"

"That's great, thanks, I really appreciate it." Laura felt a surge of love for her sister, she could be a self-opinionated prig at times but she was more than capable of giving support when it was needed.

After the phone call, Laura felt exhausted but elated. A plan was forming, she felt surer than ever that she was doing the right thing, she just needed to find ways to make a few more savings and it would be doable.

A cup of coffee to celebrate. As Laura put the kettle on, it occurred to her that she would have to eliminate coffee if she was going to take the food regime seriously. It wasn't going to be easy, still, looking on the bright side, that would be one more saving to the family budget.

Lilly's leotard was hanging out of the washing machine. The ballet classes that Lilly attended weren't cheap. An idea flitted across Laura's mind to substitute the ballet with the exercise plan.

"No!" Laura bent down and touched the leotard to her cheek. The thought of even suggesting to Lilly that she should give up her ballet was horrifying to her. Even changing to cheaper classes was out of the question, she was doing so well with this teacher and had been going there since she was tiny.

Somewhere at the back of Laura's mind, there lurked the dreadful possibility that Lilly may not be doing ballet next year, she shoved the thought to a deep and inaccessible place, she didn't want to contemplate it; more than that, she *couldn't* think about it.

Laura booted up the ancient desktop, she remembered seeing something about working from home on the community notice board, she looked again and couldn't find anything about it.

She tried Google and before she had finished typing 'working from' a whole list of websites came up. The first one she looked up looked very professional, the testimonials of people, mainly women, who had tried it were very impressive. As she followed up more links, Laura found that there were many different ways of working from home. Sewing was out, she had never been very good at that, her mother had told her she had ten thumbs. Typing was no good either, she could get by but she couldn't claim to be speedy. Packing envelopes was something that she was sure she could do though, and there was something which just required a computer and access to the internet, both of which she had. She would have to think carefully about this, she didn't want to get caught up in a scam nor did she want to take anything on that would require absolute commitment. It was encouraging though.

Laura heard a faint tapping on the front door; when she went to answer it, she saw it was Tessa her neighbour. Tessa had been a good friend to her over the past fifteen years; she used to childmind Lilly when she was smaller. Tessa helped out at Polly's Pantry, a café over the road but her main job was keeping the staff rooms clean and tidy in Kessler and Drake, a nearby publishing house.

Laura smiled and threw the door wide hiding her slight irritation at being interrupted.

Tessa held up her hand and didn't move to cross the threshold. "I'm not staying, love, I just wanted to see how it went today." Laura had told her about the visit to the clinic.

"It was very impressive and the doctor thought he could really help us." Laura still had the leaflets in her hand, she held them up for Tessa to see.

Tessa looked in horror at the top one. "Oh, sure you're never going to take a loan out to pay for it!"

Laura snatched the leaflet away. "Sorry, I meant to show you these." She proffered the ones describing the treatment as she shoved the finance information in her pocket.

Tessa thumbed through the pamphlets. "Sure, would you not be better sticking to the NHS darlin'?"

Laura found it hard to hide her irritation now. "This is in addition; I want to give Lilly the best chance." Her voice cracked a little.

Tessa gave back the leaflets and held both of Laura's hands in hers. "Of course, of course, queen, now don't you be listenin' to me." She gazed at Laura whilst keeping a firm grip on her hands. "Just be careful, darlin, that's all I ask."

Tessa turned to go but she hadn't gone far before she turned back. "It will all turn out well in the end you know. 'Twill be a rocky road but it's going to be fine."

Laura couldn't bring herself to speak but she closed the door quietly keeping all thoughts about nosy parkers to herself. She had hoped that she might be able to persuade Tessa to join the food plan but in retrospect, she realised that it would be too costly for her since her cleaning jobs and state pension only just covered the bills as it was.

Next day, Laura made a phone call from the supermarket car park in her lunch hour.

"Hello, this is Laura Palmer, I brought my daughter to see you yesterday, I'd like to go ahead with the whole treatment package, I may be able to get another recruit for the food plan but could I delay that for a couple of weeks and go ahead with the supplements and medicine straight away?" Laura wanted to use up the food stocks she had already and she needed to confirm with Trish that she would definitely enrol. "I see, you prefer to start them together? I don't want to delay the actual treatment though and won't the food plan take a while to set up?

I could come and pick the capsules myself if that would help."

Laura felt the panic rise in her chest, she persevered and eventually managed to persuade the receptionist to ask the doctor. After a while, she heard Dr Sharmer's voice, he told her that he would make a special case for them but there was no need to come to the practice, a courier would bring the first two weeks' worth of medicine later that day at a time to suit her, she could tell them in her own good time when she was ready to start the rest of the plan. Laura felt a tide of relief wash over her, combined with an enormous feeling of gratitude.

When Laura got home, Lilly was watching 'Hollyoaks'.

"Hi, Mum, a man on a scooter brought that package about half an hour ago." Lilly pointed to a Jiffy bag on the hall table. It had a red and white tape across it with the words 'URGENT MEDICAL SUPPLIES'. Laura tore it open, there were two brown see-through plastic pots inside, one containing dark green capsules and the other purple ones. Laura sifted through the rest of the post, there was a pile of junk mail, an electric bill and a long white envelope with the University Hospital logo across the top. Laura opened the hospital envelope, it was an appointment for Lilly, she quickly returned the letter to the envelope and stuffed it in the back of the letter rack.

The two pots of capsules had the instructions written on the side, there were no patient information leaflets with them. Two green capsules were to be taken three times a day, they were the vitamin supplements. The purple capsules were the medicine, the dose for that was one capsule four times a day.

"It's your medicine, Lilly." Laura took the pots over to show her.

Lilly stared at them for a moment. "Oh, yuck, Mum those ones are the same colour as that woman's nail varnish!"

Chapter Nine

Elaine had fully intended to take the journal back to the garage but after days of visitors interrupting her reading time, she felt a compulsion to hole up in the attic and indulge herself in binge reading. Mrs Williams had strictly instructed her not to go up into the attic on her own but somehow that was the only space where she felt really comfortable at the moment. It had taken much wheedling and bribery to get Barry to agree to take the book up to the attic for her. Elaine had enough self-preservation to know that it would be foolish to try to hook the book up there herself in her present weakened state.

Holding the banister on each side, Elaine took the attic stairs one at a time. "Puss, puss, come on now, keep me company."

Iris had been like a shadow since Elaine had returned from hospital. Mrs Williams had looked after the little black fur ball well, there were numerous sachets of gourmet cat food and treats in the cupboard which Elaine definitely hadn't bought herself. "I love you, puss, but not that much!" Elaine had said when she found the stash of feline delicacies.

Iris purred, went into the bedroom and jumped onto the bed.

"No, puss, up here, come on!" Elaine called from half way up the stairs. Iris came out of the bedroom and weaved around at the bottom of the attic stairs but refused to be enticed up. "Iddy Puss Iddy Biddy Puss." Elaine used her special high-pitched cat-calling voice to no avail.

After several attempts to persuade the stubborn kitty and finally giving up, Elaine settled herself in the attic chair. Barry had left the book square in the middle of the desk. Sunlight from the skylight window above illuminated the gilding magnificently. Elaine ran her fingers over the calf skin, it was soft and silky, incredibly there was not a single sign of damage on it. The bookmark was not in place, no matter, Elaine knew exactly where she had left off. Turning the pages, Elaine was perplexed at how little harm had been done to the book in the fall, in fact, there was no perceptible injury at all. Mrs Williams had found the book at the bottom of the attic stairs when tidying up, so it must at the very least have fallen from Elaine's grasp at some point when she fell, how had it escaped unscathed? Elaine could think of no rational explanation. She didn't ponder for long, the words seemed to dance off the page as if eager for attention, and Elaine was soon drawn in. It was good to get back to the story, she had the strangest feeling that the main character had had to wait for her to return before carrying on his journey. *It's ok, I'm back.* She felt herself thinking. It was like returning home after a long and difficult journey. It reminded Elaine of the time once, when as she had left work, the skies had opened. Snow fell as if a days' worth had been dumped in the space of ten minutes. There was zero visibility, the traffic had ground to a halt and she had been stuck in the blizzard for four hours. Later, when the traffic had started to move, the fallen snow had frozen. Cars were slewing all over the road which was so deeply rutted that Elaine could hear the ice grinding along the bottom of the car the whole way. In the end, a forty-minute journey had taken five and a half hours. When she had finally reached home that night, the euphoria she felt stepping into her hallway was incredible. That was exactly how she felt now as she let herself be absorbed completely by the narrative.

"Hello?" A voice called from below. Elaine dragged herself from the story with a start. The pages of the book had a rosy glow, she looked up at the skylight and saw a brilliant sunset.

"Barry?" Elaine had recognised the voice, she tried to get up but her legs were stiff and cold. "I'll be right down, Baz."

Gently easing herself off the chair, she hobbled down the attic stairs. Iris shot out of the bedroom with a trill as soon as Elaine reached the landing.

Barry looked up from the hall below having obviously let himself in, he still had the key Elaine had given him. Mrs Williams already had a key due to her role as an occasional cat sitter but Elaine had thought it a good idea if Barry had one too for now. There was a bag of shopping at Barry's feet and he was shifting about from foot to foot on the doormat. "Watch that cat around your feet! Is that what happened last time?"

Elaine knew the gruffness in his voice meant nothing. "No! Don't be blaming little Iris now, that fluff ball couldn't trip up a gnat." She replied with a grin.

Iris regarded Barry for a moment, her eyes amber slits, then she turned her rear towards him, strolled over to the bedroom doorway, and began licking the base of her tail. Barry roared laughing. "That's what she thinks of me then!"

Picking her way down the stairs to the hall, Elaine wondered where the time had gone, it seemed minutes since she had decided to skip breakfast but she hadn't had lunch either, she hadn't even paused for coffee and now it was six o'clock!

"I'll make a cup of tea." Elaine turned to the kitchen.

"You will do no such thing! You look all done in. I'm here to take you to The Carter's for some nosh and a pint." Barry picked up the shopping. "Let me just put this away for you first, I'll be able to work out where it goes and if I get stuck, I'll ask you."

At the thought of Holly's food, Elaine suddenly felt ravenous, she realised her throat was very dry too. "I'd better have some water first."

Barry trotted to get a glass for her. "So, there'll be no argument then?" He arched his eyebrows.

Elaine held up her hands. "Baz, I know I don't stand a chance, so I might as well give in now." Once Barry had stowed all the shopping and put a large bowl of cat food down, which Iris tore into as if she hadn't been fed for a week, they made their way outside. Barry tested the front door first to make sure it was firmly closed and then proffered his arm to Elaine. They crossed the road slowly as Elaine's legs were still stiff with pins and needles.

The pub was quite busy already but Holly had set aside a table for them near the bar.

The food was delicious and after the first few gulps of 'Brewer's Gold', Elaine started to relax and she stopped thinking about wasted reading time. Holly joined them when the bar was less busy and she could snatch a moment. Elaine found out from Holly that there had been dozens of well-wishers who had been asking after her.

With one eye on the bar, Holly turned to Elaine. "Is your mother going to come back and stay with you for a while?"

Elaine glanced away. "I haven't actually told her; I didn't want to worry her."

Elaine's mother had been living in Hong Kong with her boyfriend for the last ten years.

Holly frowned. "Surely, she would want to know about your accident?"

Elaine focused on her glass of beer. "There's no point her coming, there would be nothing she could do and it would only inconvenience her needlessly."

Just then a customer started to rattle his change at the bar and Holly stood up. It was a false alarm, the customer laid the money on the bar and headed in the direction of the toilets.

Barry tried to talk through a mouthful of pie. "Your work mates have been keeping in touch, Sylvia rang you but there was no answer, she thought that maybe you couldn't get to the phone."

Elaine screwed up her mouth. "I didn't hear anything, maybe it's not working?"

Holly and Barry glanced at each other.

Elaine took out her iPhone, it was low on charge but it was set to ring and vibrate, Barry keyed Elaine's number into his phone. Elaine's rang out loud and clear, an old-fashioned telephone ring. Elaine squeaked; the vibration had startled her. They all laughed.

"Damn!" Barry was frowning at his phone screen.

"What's up?" Elaine and Holly spoke simultaneously.

"It's just that 'Octavius Sine' has killed and captured one of my portals." Barry was a keen augmented reality gaming fan.

"Oh, dear." Holly looked at Elaine with mock gravity, Elaine held her head in her hands.

"Ok, you two no need to take the p…" he stopped, "the proverbial!"

Just then a couple of customers came in, a balding man in a suit, his moustache implausibly black, followed an elderly kind faced gent who wore a flat cap. They didn't seem to be together. Holly hopped back behind the bar.

The man with the moustache strode in front of the older man and leant his bulk on the bar. His face was florid as if he had already been drinking, splaying his arms either side of him he commanded the space as he perused the blackboard frowning. 'I'll have a…' The elderly gent stood back, Holly gave him a quick nod and a smile but waited for the first man to make up his mind. The man at the bar spotted Barry. "Ah, Barry, I need the Merc Valeting before the weekend, you'll be able to do it tomorrow, right?" He didn't wait for a reply. "Come over at three o'clock to pick it up, I'll need it back before four."

Holly took a tankard from above the bar and addressed the elderly gent mainly by mouthing at him. "Your usual, Arthur?"

"A Brewer's Gold." The florid man cut across her.

"Certainly." Holly put the tankard down and started pulling the Gold into a straight glass.

"It's on song." Elaine smiled and raised her glass to indicate that she was drinking the Gold, she had assumed he was a friend of Barry's, so she wanted to be welcoming.

The man disregarded her comment. "No, I'll have the lager I think." He pointed at the tap nearest to him.

Holly set aside the half full glass of beer and reached for a lager glass.

Barry watched with interest. "I should be able to do it, Alan, but an hour is tight if you want it waxing."

"Well can you, or can't you? I need to know." Alan took a swig of the glass that Holly had placed before him. A white foam moustache on top of his own looked vaguely ridiculous.

Holly told him the price whilst flicking an apologetic smile at Arthur. Arthur smiled and nodded in return, looked down towards the floor, and clasping his hands behind his back rocked on his heels.

Alan slowly took out a wallet. He emptied the coin section onto a bar mat and counted out the change, he made piles of twenty pence pieces and another of the odd change. Only when he had replaced the other change in the wallet did he push the piles toward Holly.

"Thank you!" Holly smiled brightly, gathered up the change and put it beside the till whilst she served Arthur.

"I'm just going to water the 'taters'." Barry got up and disappeared through the door leading to the back.

Alan looked around the room for an audience. "Needs a kick up the rear, that one." He nodded to the door which Barry had just gone through. Elaine didn't look up; she speared a tomato with her fork. Holly feigned rapt interest in the glass she was polishing. Arthur had opened the paper to the crossword section and was running his finger down the clues. The other customers were all involved in their own conversations or too far away to hear. Alan snorted and reached into his inside pocket, he withdrew a vaporiser and put it to his mouth.

Holly was on to him straight away. "Sorry, we don't allow vaping in here." The strident tones caught the attention of all in the vicinity.

"Bloody ridiculous!" Alan looked around, but seeing no murmur of support he grudgingly put the device away. Remaining at the bar, he continued to occupy a disproportionate amount of space as he muttered into his lager. "Pigswill would taste better than this muck."

Barry had returned from the loo by this time and was pulling out the chair next to Elaine. "Well, I suppose he would know about that, wouldn't he?" He spoke quietly for Elaine's ears only, but somehow Holly seemed to know what he had implied as she looked up from her glass-polishing with a smile.

Chapter Ten

Elaine returned from The Carter's relaxed and mellow. Barry stood in the pub entrance and watched in the distance until he saw that she had had no trouble getting into the house. Elaine knew that she should go straight to bed, she fully intended to, Iris was at her feet demanding food as usual with a plaintive meow as she wove around Elaine's ankles.

"You've been fed already, greedy puss!" Elaine took out a few cat treats, gave a couple to Iris, popped the rest in her pocket and headed upstairs. Iris followed her closely behind fully aware that there were more of her favourite nibbles to be had.

As soon as Elaine reached the landing, her resolve dissolved, she hovered around the attic stairs.

Just one chapter? She asked herself, surely it wouldn't harm. She was halfway up the stairs to the attic before she consciously made the decision.

Iris skulked off into the bedroom.

"No, puss, come up with me!" Elaine rattled the treats in her pocket. Iris ignored her. Elaine wondered why the cat suddenly had taken a dislike to the attic. Elaine could hardly get Iris out of there when Sylvia had stayed on the camp bed on the night of the book fair. Sylvia was a great lover of cats and Iris had instantly taken to her.

Exasperated, Elaine limped back down and into the bedroom. Picking Iris up, she held her close with one hand and held firm to the banister with the other as she moved to return to the attic. Elaine felt the cat stiffen as she got to the top of the stairs. Putting some treats on the wooden floor, she put the cat down in front of them. There was an instant reaction. Iris immediately arched her back, the fur along her spine stood upright, her tail bushed out like a Christmas tree and she let out a low growl followed by hissing and spitting. Elaine has never seen her like this.

As soon as Elaine let go, Iris shot down the stairs so fast that it seemed that her paws didn't even make contact with the treads, she sat at the bottom of the stairs making a sound like a violin bow being dragged across the strings very loosely.

"What on earth is the matter, puss?" Elaine was perplexed. The cat was making figure of eight shapes below and peering up with hooded eyes, she didn't look as if she was in pain but she did look very angry. This was very out of character for the mild-mannered puss.

Elaine shrugged her shoulders and sat down at the desk. In the melee, Elaine had bumped against it, disturbing the pile of papers which Mrs Williams had left after tidying. A crumpled ball was wedged behind the papers just against the pen holder. Elaine examined it and realised it was the missing gold bookmark; she tried to straighten it out but it was so badly crushed that as she gently unfolded it, it broke. Elaine decided that although it was no longer any good as a bookmark, it was still a thing of beauty. It resembled an autumn leaf that was still just holding together despite being at an advanced stage of decomposition, she would put it on a windowsill somewhere as an ornament. Holding it in her palm, she stared at it. *Surely, Mrs Williams would not have screwed it up like that but how did it get so damaged?* Not pondering for long, Elaine placed the leaf behind the reading light and pulled the book towards her on the desk. The reading light illuminated the page as Elaine opened the book, it was almost as if daylight shone from within. Looking ahead to see how long the chapter was, Elaine saw that she was nearly half way through the whole book. A sudden irrational feeling of despair gripped her as she wondered what would happen when she came to the end, she equated the end of the book with the end of her own existence. Putting the morbid thought to the back of her mind, she started to read, but she was aware that she was slowing her reading speed down, savouring every idea, every phrase.

Before Elaine knew it, the day had started in the world outside, the noise of the milk float alerted her. Once again, she had got carried away with the story. Elaine was angry with herself, normally she was very self-restrained; it was always her that was the sensible one during work nights out, she never went over the top. Always a careful shopper, Elaine had never got into debt, she had paid off her student loan way before all her friends; in fact, with careful budgeting and sensible investment she had accrued a nice little nest egg for the future. Burning the midnight oil was so out of character, during exams she had always drawn up a detailed revision plan and stuck to it. The revision plan had even factored-in exercise, bedtimes and meal times, it was a bit of a joke with her friends who laughingly accused her of being 'an anorak'. *Why then could she not exercise a little restraint now with her present reading*? She wondered.

Elaine's knees had all but seized up as she hobbled down to the bedroom, pains shooting through her legs. The house had gone cold, so she quickly prepared for bed. There was a warm patch on the duvet where Iris had been curled up, the cat obligingly moved to let Elaine in and then flopped back down against Elaine's back purring like a helicopter blade, all bad humour apparently forgotten.

Elaine woke with the warm sun pouring in on her, she hadn't closed the curtains the night before, the brightness dazzled her, so she buried her head in the pillow. A vivid dream was still with her, it was one of those dreams which feel like reality and yet there is the knowledge that you are not part of that reality but merely observing.

In the dream, Elaine had been in a vault like room which had arched windows but she somehow knew it wasn't a church. There had been a large wooden bench in the centre of the room and she'd recognised her book laying open on it in front of a man who was wearing a long green robe. The man's face was familiar but Elaine couldn't place where she had seen it before. His expression was kind but very sad as he pleaded with her holding his palms out to her in supplication.

"I swear unto the Almighty that this was never my intention. The folly must finish here. I have let my anger rule without mercy. Let there be an end to this evil. You alone have the power to reverse the invocation. Let the power of my fury be disbursed, may it no more do any harm to the guiltless."

Elaine couldn't get this image out of her mind, it felt so real. It hadn't been frightening, she wished she could remember where she had seen the man before, he sounded so remorseful, so sad. She supposed she had spent so much time obsessing about the book it was only natural that she should dream about it, but the man in her dream bore no resemblance to any character in the story.

Elaine determined to take herself in hand, she wouldn't spend so much time up in her reading haven, she would take more exercise, start cooking again, fully prepare for her imminent return to work.

Just then, there was a ring on the bell. Elaine's first thought was the amount of time a visitor would take her from her reading. Throwing her dressing gown on, she picked her way downstairs and answered the door.

"Holly! Hello!" Elaine was genuinely pleased to see her.

Holly beamed back at her. "I just thought I'd pop by to see if there was anything you needed doing or if you fancied a trip to the shops if you're up to it?"

"Barry dropped off a load of shopping yesterday thanks, but let's have a cup of tea and a chat, shall we?" Elaine went to put the kettle on. "I'm feeling much better today actually, I'm hoping to be back at work next week."

"That's good to hear." Holly kicked off her boots and left them on the doormat. "My goodness! Have you been starving that cat?" Iris was giving her 'feed me now' yowl.

Elaine laughed. "She's always like that, she's a bottomless pit, and she'd do anything for food." She put the mugs of tea on a tray and carried them through to the lounge. "No, I tell a lie, she wouldn't be enticed into the attic last night for anything."

"I thought she loved sitting up there on your desk and basking in the sun?" Holly asked.

Elaine shook her head. "Not just lately, not since I took down the camp bed and made it into my reading room." Elaine had a sudden pang of longing to be up there in her sanctuary now but she was fond of Holly and didn't want her to feel unwelcome. "That meal last night was just what I needed, the beer slipped down a treat too, I slept well after that." She didn't mention to Holly how long it had taken for her to actually get to bed.

"I'm glad Barry coaxed you across, we've missed you, you've been a bit of a recluse of late I hear." Holly's warm smile softened her words.

"I've been reading a book, you know what it's like when you get into a good one!" said Elaine lowering her gaze, she changed the subject quickly. "I didn't like the way that man Alan treated Barry last night."

Holly rolled her eyes. "He is such a prat! You should have heard him after the two of you left, giving it large about his business and how he's made a fortune selling 'anti-wrinkle cream' to what he called 'vain housewives'. He finds it funny that what he's really selling them is udder cream mixed with a bit of lavender and baby oil. I can't stand the man."

Elaine shook her head in disbelief. "I thought he was a friend of Barry's at first."

Holly laughed. "No, Barry does odd jobs for him but that's as far as it goes. Let's have a look at this book then."

Elaine was caught unawares, her mind raced forward to what she would do if Holly asked to borrow it. "I don't think it's your sort of book." She snapped the words out without thinking but then instantly regretted it because it sounded like a put down. "I mean it's just a stuffy old thing." Elaine felt she was making the situation worse so she invited Holly up to see it.

Holly didn't seem to have been offended in the slightest, she eagerly followed Elaine upstairs. "It looks brand new." Holly gazed at the book in admiration. Elaine noticed how the gilding reflected in Holly's deep brown eyes.

Holly reached out and stroked the cover and then leapt backwards. "It's vibrating!"

"What?" Elaine frowned in puzzlement.

Holly was insistent. "It is, feel it!"

Elaine laid her hand on the book. "I can't feel anything." She wondered if Holly was having a joke.

"It must be that lamp; look it's plugged in at the mains, it must be faulty." Holly immediately unplugged the lamp and felt the desk. Nothing, she felt the book and leapt back once again.

"There must be something else on." Holly scrabbled on the floor around the desk looking for wires. "No wonder the cat freaked out."

"There's nothing else electrical up here." Elaine joined in the search under the desk.

"Maybe the wiring is faulty." Holly tested all around the floor by laying her hands flat and inching around. "You need to get someone to come and check the electrics, let's pull the desk out."

Elaine moved the book to the chair and helped Holly pull the desk forward, they both looked behind it but could see nothing wrong.

"It seems fine now," said Holly as she ran her hands all over the desk. "Do you believe in ley lines?"

Elaine shook her head. "Not really, why?"

Holly sucked her bottom lip. "It's just that a bloke that comes into our place is always on about them, maybe you're at an intersection or something?" Holly looked at Elaine's sceptical expression and burst out laughing. "Yes, I know it's a bit far-fetched, isn't it?"

Elaine agreed. "Come on, let's get this desk pushed back before we freak ourselves out as well as the cat!"

Chapter Eleven

Laura soon started looking forward to the food packages arriving. Each came in its own little box complete with recipe cards. They never knew what would be in the boxes and this added to the interest. Sometimes there were fresh herbs that Laura had never used before, but there was very little waste. Lilly sometimes complained to her mum that she wished she could go back to the occasional pizza but in the main, she was happy to go along with new regime.

The exercise classes were a different matter, although Lilly joined in with them, she made no secret of her dislike of attending. "It's full of old ladies, Mum," she said when Laura was driving them home from a class.

Laura had to admit that apart from Lilly, she was the youngest participant; most of the other ladies were middle aged at least. "We're not there to socialise, it's doing you good that's the main thing."

"Is it though, Mum? I get a better workout from ballet."

"The exercises are specially designed though; they probably use muscles you don't use in other activities."

Lilly shook her head. "But I don't even get tired during the sessions."

Laura tried not to sound impatient. "That's the point, love, it's supposed to make you stronger, not exhaust you."

"What are all those other ladies doing there? I know you come because you're my mum, but surely all of them can't have the same thing as me?"

"Dr Sharmer knows what he's doing, Lilly, I expect the others are recovering from different conditions or maybe they're just doing it for the healthy lifestyle; remember, the doctor said that the healthy eating plan was beneficial to anybody, so I suppose the exercise plan goes along with that."

Lilly wouldn't let the subject drop. "Well, wouldn't it be better for them to go to the sport centre? The classes are much cheaper there and there are healthy cooking classes too."

The traffic started to get busier at that point, so Laura didn't answer, she had to concentrate on the road. The class was held in a further education college on the other side of town; it usually only took them about twenty minutes to get home from there. The traffic slowed down to a crawl as the road took them past the University Hospital; there were traffic lights at the junction of the main entrance and the dual carriageway. The lights were changing frequently to allow the cars out of the site but this slowed down the traffic on the main road.

Lilly gazed at the hundreds of lit up windows in the main block. "When am I due back in there, Mum?"

Laura didn't answer, she was stopping to let a car come across from the right, the driver had got herself stuck in the hatched area, she waved her appreciation in Laura's direction.

"Mum?"

Laura flicked a glance at Lilly. "Mmm?"

"When's my next appointment?"

"Oh! Not for ages, you let me worry about all that." Laura patted her daughter's good leg.

"I'm not actually worried, Mum, in fact, I like going to see Miss Maitlin."

Laura smiled, "That's good, yes, she's a nice lady, isn't she? But who knows, maybe we won't need too many more visits there, your body might be able to fight this off by itself."

Lilly snorted. "Get real, Mum, this isn't a cold we're talking about!"

Laura frowned. "You heard what Dr Sharmer said about the body's ability to repair itself if it is given the chance."

"Oh, yes him." Lilly went quiet.

The traffic started to clear, so they were on their way again and before long, they were back home. They were both ready for the evening meal, the exercise had given them both an appetite.

Laura started preparing the food straight away and Lilly helped her as usual.

Lilly picked up a head of broccoli and examined it. "Isn't this the stuff you sell in the shop?"

Laura nodded, "Yes but it's so much more convenient when delivered like this."

Lilly raised her eyebrows. "But, Mum! You go in there every day; you could pick the stuff up yourself."

Laura was busy 'spiralising' a courgette. "But it's all thought out and balanced nutritionally and it's good to have the inspiration of the recipes."

"Mum, you have never had any trouble thinking up great recipes and I'm sure your normal stuff is just as healthy as this."

Laura hugged her daughter with her left arm. "Thank you, love, it's nice to have a vote of confidence."

"Mum!" Lilly groaned. "Courgette juice on my new top!" She started rubbing the front of her jumper with a tea towel.

After dinner, Lilly offered to wash up, Laura was grateful for the time, this saved her as she wanted to follow up on a home working site she had seen. She needed to get another source of income soon, as her small savings had already gone. The one thing she didn't want to do was to get into debt. It wasn't that she hadn't been tempted, getting a loan seemed very easy but she didn't know how long these extra expenses would be needed, she had a feeling that it was going to be a long slog.

There was a pile of post on the hall table. Laura sifted through it, mostly junk mail but a familiar white envelope with the University Hospital franking across the top, she turned it over in her hand and glanced toward the kitchen. Lilly was up to her elbows in bubbles, she was always overenthusiastic with the washing up liquid, Laura had told her before, it was wasteful and it meant the dishes took more rinsing but Lilly was humming happily to herself. Laura turned her back to the kitchen and opened the letter. As she thought, it was informing her about a missed appointment, the tone was austere pointing out the waste of resources and the effect on other patient's waiting times. Laura tried to supress a wave of defensiveness, wasn't she going through enough already without having a desk bound tyrant reprimanding her? There was a phone number to ring to rearrange the appointment for a 'time convenient to you'. Laura stuffed the letter back into the envelope and slotted it into the back of the letter rack. "Just going to work on the computer, love." She called in the direction of the kitchen.

As usual, the computer took a while to crank itself up, Laura watched the screen and bit her bottom lip as she waited. Images of Lilly's last hospital appointment intruded her thoughts. The waiting room had been full of happy healthy-looking children, some quite tiny but there had been the others. A teenage girl in a beany hat, she had no eyebrows, and there was the little boy of about eight with an artificial leg.

Eventually, the internet opened, there was something Laura wanted to look up before she did anything else. Laura knew that an adult had the right to refuse hospital treatment and she also knew that consent was needed from someone with parental responsibility before any treatment was given to a child. What she wasn't sure about was if the parent did refuse, might there be any repercussions? Could social services get involved? Laura had to find out where she stood on that issue.

Chapter Twelve

Elaine nearly missed the GP appointment that was to check whether she was fit to go back to work. Mrs Williams had let herself in because Elaine hadn't answered the door and she had been worried. Elaine was upstairs reading and had totally forgotten the time. Mrs William's appearance brought Elaine back to the present; she gathered her things together and had a wash ready to dash off to the surgery thanking her kindly neighbour for her timely intervention on the way. In the end, the doctor had decided that she wasn't happy with Elaine's progress and she advised her not to drive for the time being.

Elaine's car was as good as new and sitting outside the house, a young mechanic from the garage had brought it back and taken the courtesy car in exchange. Elaine had every intention of returning the journal with the car, but in the event, she had forgotten to give it to the lad and it was still sitting on the hall table.

When she rang work to keep them updated, she got the impression that Trish felt that Elaine was taking advantage. In an effort to appease her, Elaine had offered to do some work from home. Apparently, James was to be in her area researching a story and he could bring some manuscripts to her.

Elaine was in two minds about working from home. On the one hand, being very committed to her job and was keen to get back to it as soon as possible. On the other hand, Elaine had carved out a comfortable routine which mainly consisted of sleeping and reading. There was no need to go out as her friends did all the shopping for her. It had got to the point where she had no desire to do anything else. Although she depended on friends to keep her supplied with food, she had started to find herself resenting their visits because they distracted her from a tight routine. So far, she had remained civil but Elaine had barely stopped herself from snapping at Mrs Williams for bringing her a hot casserole that she felt was going to take her too long to eat.

Elaine started to regret having given out spare keys to Mrs Williams and Barry, it had meant that the strategy she had recently adopted of ignoring the door had been foiled in their cases. Elaine knew of course that her various well-wishing visitors only had her best interests in mind, but she felt their concern cloying and their chatter irrelevant.

The doctor's instructions had given her a welcome delay in having to think about getting back to normal life; over the next few days, she left her phone switched off and even bolted the front door for hours at a time.

It had been weeks since Elaine had taken a bath, but recently she had been economical with showering too. Today, she made an effort as she expected the manuscripts to be dropped off soon. She was aware of a stale odour about her person and she didn't want that to be the subject of office gossip or banter. As she wrapped a towel around her head, Elaine glanced at herself in the steamy mirror, she frowned at the image and wiped the glass with a cleaning cloth. Her shoulders were bony with two prominent lumps at the top. Ribs were clearly visible where they had not been before. Elaine peered at her face rubbing her hand over her cheeks as she did so, her eyes were hollow and her cheek bones sharp. Quickly dressing, Elaine went to the kitchen and poured herself a pint glass of cold milk. The cold creaminess tasted good; it reminded her of something but she couldn't quite put her finger on what. Maybe a farm visit during her school days she wondered but the actual event eluded her.

As Elaine headed upstairs to the attic, the doorbell rang. An intense wave of irritation coursed through her. She turned and saw a figure waving through the glass of the front door, it was obvious she had been spotted, so she couldn't retreat undetected. Reluctantly, she went to the door and opened it.

James stood smiling on the doorstep a bulging document wallet in his hands. "Lainey! How are you, mate?" He waved the document holder at her. "I've posted most of the stuff to you online but there are still some gems that arrive with snail mail as you know, I didn't want you to miss anything."

Elaine opened the door wide. "Come in! Good to see you. I haven't opened my e-mail in weeks, I dread to think what there is to go through in there." She genuinely was pleased to see James, the sight of him reminded her of who she was. All her life she had been brought up to have a strong work ethic. Elaine's parents, though kind, had always ensured that the first thing she did when she got home from school was homework, only after this was done was, she allowed to see any television, or when she was older, go out with her friends. Her room had always been neat and tidy, glancing around she was now embarrassed at the coffee stains up the stairs. Mrs Williams had offered to help with the cleaning but Elaine had rather ungraciously declined.

James accepted Elaine's offer of a coffee, they sat in the lounge with it and chatted. James told her about the story he had been researching, mid-sentence Elaine sprang up and went into the hall, she brought back the journal having dug it out from under a pile of junk mail. "This might interest you," she said to James, "it was left in the courtesy car I never got to use, remember I had a bump in the car on the way to work?"

James nodded, "Yes, I wondered if that had anything to do with your fall?"

Elaine shook her head, "I don't think so, anyway, have a look at it." She handed the notebook to James. "I haven't had chance to look at it in detail, but I think it belonged to the professor you are researching."

James opened the book. "Beautiful hand writing, I've seen it before, hang on." James put the book on his lap and fished in an inside pocket, bringing out an envelope, he compared the writing on the address with that in the notebook. "It's the same without a doubt! That's interesting."

Elaine sat forward in her seat. "Where did you get the letter from?"

"A friend of the professor gave it to me. He was concerned about the change in behaviour in the months leading up to his death. The friend was hoping I could shed some light into why there was such a stark decline. He felt there had been something worrying the professor but the police weren't interested since there was no evidence of foul play. The friend suspected blackmail or something." James flicked through the pages. "I think this is going to be very valuable, can I borrow it?"

"Of course!" Elaine nodded. "Maybe you're the best person to have it if you're in touch with the friends and family. I had meant to give it back to the garage but now I'm glad I didn't." Elaine knew that James would treat it with respect and ensure it was returned into the right hands when he was done with it.

"The entries go back four years but it looks as if they start getting shorter just under a year ago, perhaps, he got ill at that point, I can't see any mention of that though." James turned to the most recent entries. "They get shorter and shorter towards the end." He looked up and smiled. "Sorry, this must be boring for you, I'll take it away and study it."

Elaine had been fidgeting; the call of the attic was strong. "No, it's not boring but I should get on, let me know what you find out, I would be interested." She stood up.

James copied her. "Of course." He put the journal under his arm and went out to the hall. "E-mail me when you want me to bring some more work for you, I'm out this way at least twice a week."

After James had gone, Elaine wondered if she had been rude in bundling James out of the door quite so quickly, he hadn't seemed put out but it was hard to tell with such an easy-going character. Elaine didn't ponder for long; the call of the attic was strong and all thought of James's feelings disappeared from her mind before she was on the third step of the staircase. The coffee mugs stayed where they had been left with several other dirty ones on the coffee table.

Chapter Thirteen

The documents that James had brought lay on the coffee table untouched. Elaine fully intended to get to work on them each morning but she somehow got diverted every time and took the easy option of holing up in the attic with her book.

This morning, she was determined to make a start on the work. Iris wound herself around Elaine's ankles in an effort to get noticed. Although she had been well fed and looked after the cat was missing her normal lap time stroking.

"It's your own fault, puss, if you won't come up with me, I can't be in two places at once!" Iris yowled as if she understood, her furry eyelids were half closed giving her a slightly resentful look. Elaine filled up the cat bowl with Iris's favoured food, there was some left for her from when Mrs Williams had been looking after her. It struck Elaine that she was like one of those bad parents who lavish material goods on their children but too little attention.

Elaine's own childhood had been good. Her mother was the sort to bake with her and find interesting things to do after school, her father chose to work near to home in order to have more time with Elaine and her mother. The three of them always did something active at the weekend; walking, cycling or going with her father to his triathlon events. The happy childhood had ended with university. Elaine's grandmother had died shortly after Elaine's father and in what seemed like a very short space of time, although in reality it was over two years, Elaine's mother had reunited with an old school sweetheart. A perfectly nice man, but Elaine had found her mother's new relationship hard to swallow.

All of a sudden, the thought of getting down to work exhausted her, all Elaine wanted to do was climb up into her little nest and escape. Realising that her hand was sore, Elaine looked down and saw that she had been biting her thumb quite hard, she could see the indentations of her own teeth. Wearily climbing up the stairs, she attempted to get Iris to follow but gave up when she saw the attempt was useless.

As soon as she opened the book, her energy flooded back. It felt like throwing back the curtains. The light from the skylight reflected on the pages and radiated out as if welcoming her. Elaine felt a sense of belonging. The whimsical thought had often occurred to her, who was to say that the world of the story was unreal, and everyday life 'real'. Maybe it could be the other way around? At this moment, she felt this more than ever.

Over the next few days, Elaine didn't answer the door at all. On one occasion, there was a note shoved through the door, it was scribbled on the back of a till receipt, recognising the writing immediately, she realised that Barry must have brought supplies, they were on the doorstep. Elaine knew that Barry was often short of cash and she felt a pang of guilt as she tore into a loaf of bread, she resolved to pay him as soon as possible, she would go over to The Carter's and leave the money with Holly. Iris peered into the shopping bag as if checking to see if the cat food was there.

"Don't worry, puss, you haven't been forgotten." Elaine felt a fresh pang of guilt when she realised that the cat food was the expensive one.

The crumbs from the bread lay where they fell on the doormat. Normally, Elaine would have cleared them up immediately, in fact, normally, she would not have dropped the crumbs in the first place, she had always considered there was a right and a wrong way to do such things. Now tidiness no longer seemed to matter and eating was a necessity, not a pleasure.

Looking at the time, Elaine decided that she had a good few hours before The Carter's called last orders so she went up to the attic to read a chapter first. Before she knew it, she could hear the sound of letting out time, there were one or two regulars at The Carter's who, despite all entreaties, would insist on shouting their jovial goodbyes to each other. Elaine gathered herself together and went downstairs, she looked at the time and realised it was too late to take the money over now. Grabbing her purse, she opened the front door in the hope of intercepting Barry. Barry was nowhere to be seen but she noticed a Mercedes parked right up close to her car. The close parking was no problem as she had no intention of going out any time soon. As she started to go back inside, Elaine saw a man open up the car remotely, there was a beeping and all four indicators flashed for a couple of seconds. The man was talking to a friend.

The friend stopped short. "You're surely not going to drive, are you?"

The Mercedes owner looked familiar, Elaine was sure she had seen him in the Carter's being a bit of a pain, he laughed. "Don't be such a bore, I'm fine."

The friend looked doubtful. "I'll get us a taxi."

"Oh, for God's sake! You're going to have to grow some balls if you want to be involved in this deal, the rules are there for the idiots who can't judge for themselves. You'll be treading a fine line if you come in with me but at the end of the day, we won't be hurting anyone will we? Just relieving them of a bit of cash and giving them something to focus on."

The friend still hung back. "Are you sure it's legal?"

The car owner shook his head. "Look, if you're getting cold feet, let's call it a day. I know plenty that would jump at the chance."

"Is it legal?"

"Look, I don't pretend to be anything that I'm not, if some people are stupid enough to make the wrong assumptions, then maybe they deserve to be fleeced."

"Stupid or desperate?" The friend was starting to step back now.

"The way I see it, I'm selling hope and what I give them certainly won't do any harm, in fact, I really do believe that the placebo effect is very powerful, so what if conventional medicine is doing the majority of the work? What's the harm in creaming off a bit of the profit for ourselves?" The owner of the car was round by the driver's door now. "Hell, I work hard for what I get, you've no idea how difficult it is dealing with all those vain and neurotic women."

He opened the car door. "Are you in or out?"

The friend opened the passenger side and got in.

The driver smirked. "I've got a couple of crates of Merlot I 'acquired' at home, why don't you come back and help me with a bottle or two while we talk about specifics?" He climbed into the driving side and slammed the door.

"Iris!" Elaine stopped the little cat from shooting out of the front door as she went back inside, she was unsettled by the conversation she had heard.

Chapter Fourteen

Laura waited in the manager's office, her arms tightly folded across her chest; she told herself that she must remain calm and polite. It was understandable that she should be picked up on the mistake, but the shop was so busy in the lead up to Christmas and she had been so tired.

The manager smiled as she sat down, she smoothed her skirt and reached for a notepad. Clear blue eyes regarded Laura not unkindly, but it felt like a judgement nevertheless.

"What's up, Laura?" The manager's familiar tone was unexpected.

"Besides being the single parent of a seriously ill child, you mean?" The words were out before Laura could stop herself, she drew her lips inward and clamped her teeth on them.

The manager took her glasses off. "You have a great deal on your plate at the moment, I know, and if there is anything we can do to arrange your shift patterns or give you time off for appointments, you only have to ask, you know that?" Laura nodded.

"This is something different though, Laura, and it's very unlike you. I have to be honest if it had been anyone else, this incident would have led to severe measures but you have been a good and reliable employee for so long."

"It was just a mistake; I was distracted." Laura realised how weak that sounded.

The manager put her glasses back on and referred to her notes for a moment and frowned. "This is just not the sort of thing you would do though, Laura. We're all human and of course anyone can make mistakes, but you are far too experienced to allow this to happen."

Laura had been at the end of her shift, she remembered she only had about ten minutes to go and she was eager to get away that night, she had a pile of work to get through at home and she wanted to avoid getting stuck in the rush hour traffic. Lilly had been going to a friend's for the night and it was a good opportunity to get some work done. The home working had not been going as well as she had hoped. The data entry did not require good typing skills, but the internet connection was slow at home and that had been holding her back.

It was a rule at the supermarket that you were not supposed to serve friends and family, the temptation to defraud was deemed to be too great. There was a fine line however as to who this rule included. If the rule had been strictly adhered to, then that would mean that no supermarket employee would get served, after all they were all colleagues. It was embarrassing to refuse to serve neighbours who were not really close friends but who you were on friendly speaking terms with. In these cases, there was a certain flexibility.

Laura had been surprised to see Dr Sharmer in the queue, *he was quite a long way from home,* she thought, although in truth, she didn't really know where he lived, she only knew where the practice was. He had instantly recognised Laura and engaged her in conversation straight away. Laura had seen the two boxes of Merlot in the trolley. He had wheeled the trolley through her checkout in a casual way as he talked. At first, Laura had assumed he was going to mention them at the end of the transaction, she could have entered them without swiping anyway, Laura had no idea what stopped her. The manager was right, it was unlike her; normally, she would have had no trouble at all in bringing the omission to the attention of the customer, she was skilled in doing this so that no embarrassment was caused and without the slightest hint of accusation. In Dr Sharmer's case, it was different. He had kept the conversation flowing throughout, his voice full of authority and resonance. There had been no opportunity to slip a word in and she had felt too awkward to challenge him at any point.

The manager waited whilst Laura gathered her thoughts together, although Laura felt no direct pressure, she felt she owed some sort of reasonable explanation but she had none to give. "I'm sorry, I really can't explain it myself. I had no intention of doing anything dishonest. I did know the customer but we had no 'arrangement', I promise you."

"I believe you, Laura." The manager nodded in encouragement.

"I had intended to add the items on at the end. I admit I did see them in the trolley, and then afterwards, when I realised my mistake, I just couldn't bring myself to shout after him. I know I should have reported the error straight away; I honestly don't know why I didn't." Laura's voice began to crack.

The manager stopped her. "I'm duty bound to take some action, Laura, but in the circumstances, I think that putting you on a limited re-training schedule will be sufficient. As I said before, you have worked with us for many years and have always been one of our best colleagues, I don't think it would be in anyone's best interests to take it any further than that."

"Thank you so much." Laura could hardly get the words out; she realised she had come far too close to a possible dismissal. The thought of the implications of that filled her with horror and the relief of such a positive outcome was immense.

When she got home, Laura tried to hide her agitation from Lilly but as usual, Lilly had a kind of internal 'mood barometer' and spotted Laura's distress straight away.

"Bad day at work, Mum?" She put her skinny arms around her mother and caught her in a surprisingly strong grip. "I hope you haven't been letting those ratbag customers get to you!"

Laura always found it difficult to hide things from Lilly, she wasn't a very good liar at the best of times but she couldn't let her know the full story. "Just a little problem with the till being out that's all, it was ok in the end." She hugged her daughter back and planted a big kiss on her soft downy cheek.

"Another batch of supplies has come." Lilly pointed to a box in the corner. "I haven't looked to see what we're having tonight though." She limped across to the box and peered in, as she did so she bent down and rubbed her leg.

A cold wave coursed through Laura's veins. "Your leg, is it hurting you?"

Lilly straightened immediately and shook her head. "Just a bit stiff after ballet that's all." She saw her mother's look of concern. "No, it's not hurting, I'm fine."

Unconvinced, Laura ordered her daughter to sit down on the sofa, she took the gazelle like limb on her lap and ran her hand over it. The lump was no smaller, in fact, it seemed a little more solid than before. Laura wondered if this could be a sign that it was changing, maybe it was reacting to the therapy. Maybe it was like a fever that had to reach a crisis point before it started to wane? Laura fought the conflict inside her, was she doing the right thing?

The phone rang just as Laura stood up, she managed to get to it on time. "Hello?"

Laura grimaced. "Hi, Trish, how are you?"

"Oh, you've been getting them, how are you finding them?"

"They are quite pricey, yes but the convenience is great, isn't it?"

"No, yes, I know you're a good cook of course but you have a very busy life, don't you?"

"Lilly? Yes, she's doing well she…"

"No, she isn't due an appointment at the moment."

"Three months."

"No, I don't think it's worth phoning them, they will get in touch when they need to."

"No, don't do that, I can sort it myself." Laura's voice was sharp.

"No, sorry, I didn't mean to snap." Laura was aware of the big favour her sister was doing in signing up for the meal plan, she was also aware of how much she needed her help with this, she could barely afford the payments at the moment, if Trish dropped out then that would bump the price up considerably, so much so that she might have to discontinue it herself. Dr Sharmer had hinted that the cost therapy itself could only be kept as low as it was because of the income from the dietary services.

"Would you and Rob like to come over for a meal one night, I know Lilly would love to see you?"

"Yes! Of course, I would too."

"No, of course, we'll fit around your schedule."

Laura always had to tiptoe around her sister. Trish had been her only support when she had been carrying Lilly, Laura had been forced out of the family home at the time and had not spoken to her parents since. What she had done had sent shock waves through the family whose old-fashioned view on morals stemmed from their strict 'Daniel's Brethren' faith.

'Daniel's Brethren' was a sect which has existed in the area for hundreds of years, although curiously, it hadn't spread further than within a two-hundred-mile radius of the small Cotswold village where it had originated. Despite the small number of adherents, the devotion of the followers was strong and the basic tenets of the faith had remained relatively undiluted since it arose in the mists of time. The sect lived by a strict code of morality. Witchcraft and sorcery, including astrology were abhorrent and modern science was treated with great suspicion. It was said that the cult began with a single family who had been persecuted for their unorthodox lifestyle.

Although Trish paid lip service to the faith, she did not share the very narrow views of her parents and she had provided a shelter for Laura. The price Laura paid for this was that she forever after would have to concede the moral high ground to her sister.

"Saturday night, it is then." Laura forced a smile. "See you then. Bye, Trish, bye."

Lilly grimaced at her mum. "Why did you say I'd love to see her?"

"Scamp!" Laura said with mock severity.

Chapter Fifteen

Elaine grabbed a tin of baked beans out of the cupboard, she pulled them open and ate some straight out of the tin; she had intended to cook a proper breakfast, she had woken up ravenous, but she couldn't be bothered in the end. As usual, she had seen to Iris first, the cat was just finishing off the last of the luxury cat food that Elaine had spooned into her bowl, she began licking her paws but had one eye on Elaine as she did so. Elaine couldn't help but feel judged in some way. Scooping the little cat up, she headed to the attic; as she reached the top stair, Elaine felt Iris stiffen, she put her down and the cat immediately shot down a flight again, sitting on the landing below she glared back up at Elaine.

"Ungrateful, Puss." Elaine tutted.

Iris slunk off into the bedroom tail all a twitch.

Hours later, Elaine heard a tapping on the door, she nearly ignored it but she remembered Barry and the money she owed him, she really couldn't let it go another day, it wouldn't be fair. When she got downstairs, she saw a blonde head through the glass. A pair of amber eyes peered through close up magnified by the pattern in the glass. Elaine opened the door to find Sylvia beaming at her.

Elaine stepped back. "Come in!"

Sylvia enfolded her in a hug. "Elaine! You're all skin and bone, you haven't been looking after yourself."

"I'm fine." Elaine felt rattled by her friend's concern, she squashed the feeling, she knew that Sylvia had a kind heart and didn't deserve to be snapped at. Normally, Elaine would have been delighted to see her friend, she didn't know why she felt so antisocial.

"I'm going to make you a cup of tea and we're going to have some of these doughnuts I've brought." Sylvia ushered Elaine into the lounge and sat her down. Elaine stayed there impassive, she knew she should help with the tea, after all Sylvia was her guest not the other way around, but she felt exhausted.

Sylvia placed the box of doughnuts on the table and opened the lid. There were two glazed rings and two shiny cream filled ones with glossy pink icing, white chocolate shavings and strawberry pieces on top.

Elaine realised she had had nothing to eat or drink since the half can of beans, she practically ate the ring doughnut whole, she was halfway through the cream filled one when she realised that she had been ignoring Sylvia.

"Good choice then?" Sylvia laughed. "I rather hoped that they would be your favourites!"

"Sorry." Elaine spoke through a mouthful of crumbs.

"Don't be! I'm glad you're enjoying them." Sylvia glanced around the room. There was no judgement in her expression but Elaine felt ashamed of the state of the place anyway.

"Sorry, I haven't had time to clean up." This didn't ring true even to Elaine herself but Sylvia showed no sign of incredulity.

"If there's anything I can do to help."

"No!" Elaine cut her short and then regretted the fierceness of her response. "I'm sorry, I've been a bit wound up lately, there is something you can do actually, I owe someone some money for shopping, could you pop across to The Carter's and leave it with them for me?"

Sylvia licked a blob of cream filling off her top lip. "Sure! Course I will, but why don't you come over with me afterwards and we can have a bite to eat?"

"No, Sylv, I'd rather just stay here and rest up."

Sylvia tried her best to persuade her friend to come out but when she realised that Elaine was not going to be persuaded, she suggested that they eat in together. Sylvia offered to get in a take away but Elaine wouldn't hear of that either. When Sylvia tried to press the point, Elaine got agitated so Sylvia changed the subject. "How's the work going?"

Elaine buried her face in her hands. "I haven't had chance to get to it, *please* don't nag me!"

Sylvia leaped over to Elaine and put an arm around her. "Hey now, Lainey, I didn't mean to hassle you, there's no rush to get it done; we just thought you'd be raring to get to it that's all. Don't you worry, you take as long as you like getting better. Maybe working from home is not the way to go?"

Elaine shook her head. "No, I need to get back into it, I just can't seem to get started."

Sylvia patted her back. "Wait until the doctor signs you as fit, it'll be easier when you're back in the routine."

Elaine took her hands from her face and looked up. "Actually, he said I was fit to come back last week but I haven't got organised."

Sylvia stared in disbelief. "But that's not like you at all! Remember that time when you dragged yourself in with full blown flu? We had to force you to go home in case you gave it to the rest of us! What on earth is the matter, lovely?"

Elaine shook her head, droplets appeared on her eyelashes. "I don't know, I just don't know, I feel so weak." She began to sob in earnest.

"You're depressed, that's what it is; I can see we're going to have to take you in hand." Sylvia kissed the top of Elaine's head.

Elaine pulled away. "I just want to be left in peace!"

Sylvia looked stung by the ferocity of the words but she was undeterred. "You let it out my, lovely. I can tell you though, we're not going to leave you to stew here any longer. You need to get down to that doctor and tell him how you feel and I'm sure he'll extend the sick note. Then we're going to get you through this one way or another, don't you worry. It's not surprising you are feeling low, you've gone through a lot in recent years, and it's bound to come out somehow. Maybe the fright of your fall was the last straw?"

Elaine fell on Sylvia's shoulder sobbing; she couldn't explain to herself why she felt like this but she did know she just wanted to escape the feeling.

Eventually, Elaine allowed herself to be packed off to bed with a hot milky drink. The warmth of the bed felt delicious and she fell almost immediately into a deep sleep. Her dreams were vivid and memorable. In one, she was milking a dun-coloured cow, she was near the edge of a forest, the two children were collecting hen's eggs from under the hedgerow which formed a boundary to their vegetable garden. In another, she was talking to the elderly gent she had seen collapsed in the park. He had kind sad eyes, he was trying to warn her about something, he had told her not to make the same mistake as he had, Elaine struggled to know what he meant. The elderly gent had shaken his head and said something about the bookseller not wanting to sell him the book in the first place but that he had pressed him.

Elaine woke to the smell of bacon frying and the sound of someone singing an 'Adele' song; she wasn't alarmed, she reasoned that an intruder would be unlikely to be making so much noise. As she dragged herself to consciousness, Elaine recognised the voice. It was Mrs Williams. Throwing her dressing gown on, Elaine went downstairs. Iris was sitting in the middle of the kitchen and licking her paws and Mrs Williams was tending three pans on the cooker, she had a frilly pinafore covering her ample form. Iris gave a trill of greeting when she saw Elaine but didn't move position.

"Hello, dear, I hope I didn't alarm you; I'm just cooking breakfast."

Elaine thought the explanation a little redundant but asked, "Why?"

"Your nice friend, Sylvia, had been on to me; she says we need to cosset you a bit that you're feeling rather down in the dumps."

Elaine wanted to scream that all she wanted was a bit of peace and privacy, but she managed to contain herself.

Mrs Williams was filling the teapot and didn't see the scowl. "Holly will be round later to make you lunch and James and Sylvia are coming back this evening to see you." Elaine felt a wave of panic engulf her, she felt trapped and manipulated.

"These eggs were laid fresh today." Mrs Williams took two plates from the oven and set them on the kitchen table, she piled them high with bacon and sausages and placed two fried eggs on each, the yolks were the colour of sunflowers.

Despite herself, Elaine sat down to join her kind neighbour, the breakfast tasted delicious and she had finished it before Mrs Williams was half way through hers. "It's so kind of you to do this for me, but I really must get on I've got work to do upstairs." She lied.

"Of course, my dear, you go off and do that and I'll wash up and leave the way clear for Holly." Without a second thought, Elaine went off to the attic; Iris scowled at her as she went.

Elaine barely heard Mrs William's cheery goodbye as she called up to say she was leaving. Hearing the door shut, Elaine realised she had not replied but the momentary disquiet this caused her soon passed.

It seemed like only minutes, although in reality, it was four hours later, that Elaine's peace was broken into once more. Holly had let herself in and was calling up the stairs. Elaine tried to ignore her but she persisted. Reluctantly, dragging herself downstairs Elaine tried to look as if she was pleased to see the cheery Landlady.

"I've brought a couple of fresh ham rolls." Holly held out two cellophane packages. "I thought we could have lunch together."

Elaine sighed. "I'm busy at the moment; I can't really stop what I'm doing."

"Well, whatever you're doing, you still need to eat." Holly was not accepting a refusal; her tone was gentle but firm. "I won't stay long, I promise, I have to get back, so Alex can go off to Bookers."

Elaine could see that it would be quicker not to argue, she reluctantly made a cup of tea and they sat at the kitchen table to eat the rolls.

As soon as Holly had gone, Elaine went straight upstairs, she had marked her place in the book with the crumpled golden bookmark, she could see that she was two-thirds of the way through.

A feeling of dread hit her, what was she going to do when she reached the end? She couldn't imagine life without the book. *I will start again from the beginning,* she thought.

Elaine heard the doorbell ring but she ignored it. The ringing carried on for several minutes until eventually it stopped. It was just beginning to get dusk outside, Elaine looked up through the skylight, the clouds were a soft pink above. *Thank goodness they've gone.* Moments later it seemed, she heard a key in the lock. Furious, she ran downstairs. Barry was peeping around the door looking embarrassed.

"What on earth do you think you're doing letting yourself in like this?" Elaine hissed.

Barry held his hands up and looked behind him to where Sylvia and James were standing, they were shuffling about glancing at each other. "Sorry, Elaine, but Sylvia asked me to let her in, she was worried about you, we all were."

"For heaven's sake, I'm not a baby." Elaine flung the door open with such force that it crashed against the hall table. "I suppose you all better come in."

Barry stepped back. "I won't if you don't mind, I've got a pint on the bar but I'll pop back tomorrow to see if you need any shopping?"

James held up the bag he was carrying. "You sure you won't stay for curry? There's plenty for all."

Barry shook his head. "No, I'll get off." His voice sounded sad.

Sylvia bent to stroke the cat.

James held the bag towards Elaine. "This might need reheating." She took it from him silently and went into the kitchen. Sylvia looked at James and shrugged.

Elaine opened the packages and put the oven on, a fragrant spiciness filled the kitchen. Iris came weaving around her ankles, it was time for food.

"I've brought some wine." Sylvia put a bottle of Merlot on the kitchen table.

Elaine forced a smile and nodded.

James stood in the kitchen doorway and shifted from one foot to another. "I'm sorry for the invasion, we've been concerned about you. We don't want to be nosey but we couldn't just leave you to get on with things alone; to be honest, we felt you needed a bit of company."

Elaine sighed. "No, it's me who should apologise, I've not been myself and I know you are both just being kind, but I feel as if my life isn't my own at the moment. I do appreciate your concern though and I'm glad you haven't given up on me."

The atmosphere broken; the three friends were almost back to normal. They took the piping hot food into the lounge and shared it out. Sylvia chatted about what had been going on in the office and James told them about the latest stories he had been working on.

The wine slipped down well and Elaine started to relax and enjoy the evening.

James slipped out to The Carter's for another bottle, when he came back, he poured some for the other two. "I'm driving, so I'll not have any more." He sat down, and looked towards Elaine. "The journal you gave me is intriguing; it was definitely Professor Cambwell's. I've been writing a piece about him. His brother said that I could use it in my research but I don't intend to quote from it I feel it's far too personal for that."

Sylvia pushed the cat away from her plate with gentle hands. "What have you found out about him?"

James frowned. "Well, as you know, his field was English Literature but he was also very interested in old books, he had quite a large collection. His latest find seems to have been an anomaly. Although the book cover was several hundred years old, the contents were modern in character."

Elaine started to take an interest. "What do you mean?"

James continued. "Well, the contents took the form of a novel which as you know is a modern construct. It was possible to roughly date the calf skin binding, but the pages were apparently impossible to pin down. The gilding however seemed to tally with the date of the cover which intrigued the professor. He was unable to find the publisher in any records either, it seems as if they never existed."

Sylvia stroked the cat who had been rubbing against her ankles. "Did the journal give any clue about any illness he might have had?"

James shook his head. "Not directly, but it does seem that his health was deteriorating. The early entries are very detailed and they largely outline the research he was doing into the book. The later entries are very sketchy and even the handwriting deteriorates."

"But he doesn't mention a particular illness?" Sylvia ran her hand over Iris's back, who was clearly enjoying the experience as she rolled over to expose her belly front legs curled up.

"No, he doesn't but he does refer to his obsession."

Elaine's attention was drawn by this. "Obsession?"

James nodded. "Yes, at first, he was just interested in the book as an object and his research centred on finding out its origin, later he became engrossed in the story itself. The thing that interested him was it was a modern plot which belied the ancient binding. He says that he could closely identify with the story and he became totally immersed in it."

Elaine frowned. "I suppose you think that's funny?" She slammed her wine glass down on the table and stormed out of the room.

"Elaine?" Sylvia called after her and stood up trying not to frighten the cat as she did so.

James got on his feet and called out. "What's the matter, what did I say?" They looked at each other in disbelief.

Elaine had escaped to the attic but she could hear what was being whispered in the hall two flights below.

"We better go, I'll wash up first; perhaps, we should leave a note?"

"I don't understand, what was it that I said?"

"I don't know but I think she is seriously unwell; did you see how thin she's become and the circles under her eyes?"

"Yes, she's looking awful, and the state of this place, she's normally so neat and tidy."

"Do you think she's depressed?"

"It's got to be something like that, but it's come on very suddenly; it might have been the bump she had on her head, she was unconscious for a couple of days, wasn't she?"

"I think she was going a bit strange before that to be honest, remember you saw her sitting in the car at lunch time and she said she had been for a walk?"

"Yes, we wondered about that at the time didn't we, that was quite unlike her. We should convince her to see the doctor again, her behaviour just hasn't been normal."

Elaine had been sitting on the top step leading into the attic biting her thumb, it was bleeding now. *So, they've been gossiping about me for a while?* She thought to herself. She couldn't contain her anger any more, she screamed down at them. "Get out! What gives you the right to talk about me like that? You're no friends of mine, I can see that now, get out!" Iris shot off out of the cat flap and Sylvia looked up in anguish.

"Elaine, we're just concerned about you that's all, come down and talk, tell us how we've upset you please."

There was silence upstairs. Eventually, the two baffled friends let themselves out closing the door behind them with great care. A little while later, the cat flap opened and closed and Iris padded almost silently up the stairs.

Elaine leant over the book, the blood from her thumb staining the pages as she did so.

Chapter Sixteen

Laura had planned the trip to London months before, she had bought advance train tickets for Lilly and herself, and they had both been really looking forward to it. The plan had been to go to the Science Museum for most of the day and then stop for a pizza on the way home. Now, it looked as if the pizza idea would be out, so far, they had stuck to the meal regimes rigidly and Laura was reluctant to deviate from the routine. It was clear that Lilly was bitterly disappointed by this and she was now having an uncharacteristic teenage sulk. Laura wavered in her resolve.

On the one hand, she didn't on principle want to give in to teenage tantrums, on the other hand, Lilly had been so good and so compliant about the regime that she really deserved a little treat.

It was fear that a small deviation might undo all the good that had been done so far which still stopped Laura from relenting. Dr Sharmer had been clear, the food plan must be followed to give Lilly's immune system the best chance but he hadn't said what the effect of a small digression would be. Laura phoned the surgery but Dr Sharmer wasn't available to advise and the receptionist wouldn't give out his e-mail address. In the end, Laura had phoned Trish to see what she thought. To Lilly's delight, Trish managed to convince Laura that one pizza could not do any harm, especially if it was accompanied by a healthy salad.

They spent most of the day in the Science Museum; afterwards, since it was such a nice day and Lilly's leg was holding up well, they decided to walk back to Paddington through Hyde Park. As they came out of the Science Museum, Laura noticed a group of children in wheelchairs being loaded into a small bus with the logo 'Sunshine Charity' on the side panel, they didn't seem to be with their parents and the carers looked tired and disengaged. Putting her arm around her daughter, she realised how lucky they were to be able to share a day out together like this.

The low evening sun lit up the Albert Memorial as they reached the top of Exhibition Road. Walking past the Peter Pan Statue in Kensington Gardens, Lilly laughed at Laura as she recoiled in horror from the brown rats, bold as you like, begging for scraps along with the squirrels. They crossed over into Hyde Park at the Serpentine Bridge and were both fascinated to see the Egyptian geese perching high up in the trees.

As they headed towards Paddington Basin, they wound their way through a residential area, they turned into Connaught Square where Laura immediately felt an irrational guilt when she saw two policemen with machine guns standing casually in a doorway. Lilly was delighted and stared open mouthed.

"Don't stare!" Laura whispered through her teeth.

This precipitated a giggling fit from Lilly and Laura bustled her onwards. As they got closer to Paddington, the grand houses gave way to small shops and cafés. They turned left into Spring Street; the shops were painted drab greens and browns.

Lilly stopped in front of a dingy tan fronted shop which advertised Chinese medicines. "That's the address on my medicine containers."

Laura frowned. "No, I don't think so, love."

Lilly was insistent. "It is, Mum, I'm sure, I've read the address several times, I always wondered where it was."

There was a small warehouse attached to the shop, the whole frontage of this was painted matt black. On the windows, there was an advert for a massage service.

"It must be a distribution centre." Laura peered in the window, there were old-fashioned supermarket shelves closely packed inside. She stepped back from the window. "Come on, let's find this pizza place."

Just around the back of Paddington Station, they dropped down to the canal, the area was in stark contrast to the place they had recently been a few streets away. Expensive apartments lined the waterside and houseboats painted in extravagant colours bobbed about on the water.

They found the pizza place and it wasn't long before they were guiltily tucking into their meal. As always, they ordered one Neapolitan and one Hawaiian, split them and shared half each.

Laura felt it was like old times, Lilly was her usual happy self, but more than that, she had regained an extra sparkle. The strict food and exercise regime seemed to have taken their toll, it was clear that they just hadn't had enough fun lately.

Laura had insisted that they had a salad to accompany the meal, it was her attempt at balancing out the bad effects of the pizza. Lilly had never been too fond of 'greenery' as she put it but even this she was wolfing down with relish.

On the way home, the train was packed with people and although they had pre-booked seats, there was a young couple sitting in their places. Laura hated confrontation but she was keen to get a seat for Lilly.

"Excuse me, I think you're sitting in our reservations."

The couple looked up briefly and shrugged, they made no attempt to move.

Laura knew that there were no seats further up the train as that was the way they had come in, they had only just got to the train in time so they had to hop into carriage K and walk through.

"Would you mind moving please?" There was still no response.

Lilly shook her head. "It's cool, Mum, we can sit in the vestibule on our bags."

Not wanting an argument to spoil a nice day, Laura capitulated and they found a little corner next to a boy who was sitting with his legs stretched out listening to rap on his headphones.

"It's like camping." Lilly laughed.

As the train moved off, the draught from the window got colder and colder. Laura tried to close the window tight but it was jammed about two inches open.

"Never mind, Mum, it'll take the smell of those banana skins in the bin away." Lilly wasn't letting it get her down.

Throughout the journey, they constantly had people climbing over them to get to the toilet.

Some scarcely held back their irritation at the human obstacles.

"You'd think we were sitting here out of choice." Laura muttered. Lilly didn't answer, she had fallen asleep on her mum's shoulder and was drooling slightly. This made Laura see the funny side of the situation and she chuckled to herself.

As the train approached their station, Laura gently woke Lilly. "Time to wake up, sleepyhead."

Lilly woke with a start and moved to get up. "Ouch!"

"What is it?"

Lilly grimaced. "Cramp, I can't get up!" She gripped her leg with both hands and leaned forwards breathing rapidly.

"Can I just get to the bin, please?" A woman stood over them frowning.

Something clicked inside Laura and she released a stream of vitriol at the woman, the woman retreated in alarm. Lilly found this hilarious and managed to stand up and lean against the door, the worst of the cramp was abating.

"Go, Mum!" she chuckled as the train glided into the station. "I'm impressed!"

As the train stopped, a kind man opened the door and held it for them and they climbed out onto the platform, Lilly was still hobbling.

"Let's just sit on this bench until the feeling comes back in your leg properly."

Lilly made no protest as she limped over to the metal seat and flopped down. "It's much better now actually, just pins and needles." She said still rubbing her leg.

"We're in no rush." Laura assured her.

The train moved slowly off, still tightly packed with passengers travelling further down the line. As the rear first-class carriage passed, Lilly jerked her head and pointed at a window.

There was a man with half the carriage to himself holding a wine glass, his mouth a thin tight line, his eyes glazed. "That's Doctor Sharmer, look, Mum."

Laura looked in the direction of Lilly's gaze, it was definitely him, what a coincidence, she thought but she found it troubling to see him with a glass of wine, it didn't seem appropriate somehow.

"I hope he's not going to a consultation in that state." Lilly snorted.

"At this time of night?" Laura shook her head but gazed in the direction of the retreating train.

"No, it's probably the end of a long day for him and he's just winding down with a glass of wine on the way home. Doctors have stressful lives you know and they need to relax when they can."

Lilly pursed her lips. "Oh, he was relaxing alright." She flexed her leg. "I think, I'm good to go."

Laura was still looking into the distance at the train's red lights, she turned back and smiled.

"Are you sure?"

Lilly got up and performed a quick *bourrée* to demonstrate.

Laura grinned. "Don't overdo it." She gave Lilly a feather light push. "And don't show off!" Lilly made a cheeky face and skipped off towards the ticket barrier.

Laura trotted after her. "Just what do I have to do to tire you out, you little rascal?"

They had left the car parked in the station car park. It was a bit of an expense but Laura had not wanted Lilly to have to walk too far at the end of a long day out. She remembered her own childhood days out when she and Trish had to walk home instead of getting the bus. They had always been tired and crotchety by this stage and the day had inevitably been spoilt by squabbling followed by a good telling off.

Laura remembered that she had invited Trish around for a meal, she didn't relish the prospect. Although they no longer squabbled, Trish could never quite get out of big sister mode and Laura found it wearing. Still, Lilly always managed to lighten the tone; Laura sometimes reflected on the fact that Lilly invariably behaved in a more adult way than she did herself.

Chapter Seventeen

Elaine stared at the blood dripping down on the pages, she grabbed a paper tissue and dabbed at the stain but this only made it spread further over the page. Sobbing she ran down to the bathroom and ran her thumb under the cold tap until it stopped bleeding. Feeling a soft and furry pressure against her ankle, she looked down to see Iris peering up at her.

"Oh, Puss." Elaine picked the little fluff-ball up and held her close. Iris responded with a trilling noise and rubbing her head hard into Elaine's shoulder. Tears wetted the top of the little cat's head. Elaine felt weary, she wrapped her thumb in a tissue, plodded into the bedroom and burrowed under the bedsheets without even changing into a nightdress. Iris curled into a contented ball against the small of Elaine's back, only her loud purring broke the silence.

Elaine had not closed the curtains, so she was awoken by a shaft of sunlight falling across her pillow. Iris was still at her back but as soon as Elaine opened her eyes, the cat leaped to the floor with a surprisingly heavy thud. Elaine smiled to see Iris stretching out her front paws, bottom and tail aloft. A tiger like yawn revealed sharp white little teeth.

Swinging her legs off the bed, Elaine enjoyed a stretch too. "Come on then, Iris, we better get you fed." The cat sprang up and shot downstairs meowing in anticipation. Elaine watched as the bowl was cleared after which Iris discretely slipped out of the cat flap on a private errand.

Elaine downed a glass of water and ripped off a small hunk of wholemeal bread which she munched on as she went upstairs, she headed straight into the attic. A paper tissue was still lying on the book covered in blood. Tutting at her own stupidity, Elaine took it off and examined the page; the page gleamed back at her as clean as ever, there was not one spot on it. Elaine opened the tissue; there was blood all over it. *That's not possible*, she thought to herself, she was sure that the book had been stained the night before, she remembered making the stain worse by rubbing it. Elaine stroked her fingers across the page, it felt silky smooth like satin, she could smell the fresh blood on the tissue at the side of the book; on an impulse, she bent her head down to sniff the book, it smelt of wild cherry blossom. Closing her eyes, Elaine was transported back to her school holidays when the three of them used to go hiking in the Cotswolds, they always stayed at the same farm, Mum and Dad slept in a barn conversion and she was allowed to stay all by herself in an attic above the stable block. The track leading to the stable block was lined with wild cherry and once, when they had gone there in spring, the trees had been in full bloom, the smell had been intoxicating. In the barn conversion, there was a wood burning stove; one Christmas time, they had stayed there and burned logs from one of the felled trees, the farmer said the tree was cut down because it had canker. The smoke from those logs was sweet and reminiscent of spring.

Tears fell onto the book and rolled straight off like liquid mercury.

Elaine heard a knocking on the front door, she hobbled downstairs expecting to see James or Sylvia but when she got to the door, she saw Holly's face smiling through the glass. As she opened the door, Holly's smile turned to a frown. "You've been crying."

Elaine shook her head as she stepped back to let her visitor in. "It's nothing, I'm just feeling sorry for myself that's all."

Holly suggested they go shopping together, just for groceries; reluctantly, Elaine agreed and on the way to the big Tesco on the outskirts of town they chatted.

Elaine looked down at her thumb and started picking at it. "This may seem like a silly question." she began. Holly gave a slight shake of the head as she watched the traffic.

Elaine continued. "But do you think that it's possible for a place or a thing to be affected by events in the past and kind of hold an echo of those events? No, don't answer, it sounds ridiculous!"

Holly shook her head. "I don't think it sounds ridiculous at all; in fact, I'm sure that it happens all the time, you know, some places have good atmosphere and some bad. It's hard to put your finger on how or why, but I strongly believe that events leave some sort of imprint. The universe is a strange place, energy is matter and matter is information. Doesn't the written word leave a trace of what has been before? What's stranger than that when you think about it? Sunlight from millions of years ago has left energy trapped in the form of fossil fuel, that's incredible too. Why do you ask?"

Elaine stared out of the window for a moment. "I don't want you to think I've gone totally mad."

Holly giggled. "I'm sure I won't, believe me, I hear some very strange stuff from behind that bar, so whatever you say, it probably won't be the most outlandish thing I've heard this week!"

Elaine still hesitated. "It's the book I'm reading." Holly glanced towards her nodding encouragement before she turned back to watch the traffic. "I think it's trying to tell me something."

Holly glanced again and smiled. "Isn't that what books are supposed to do?"

Elaine looked down at her knees. "I knew you'd think I was potty."

Holly shook her head. "No! I'm sorry, I didn't mean to make fun of you, I'm interested honestly."

They had reached the supermarket car park now and Holly slid into a parking space, she turned to give Elaine her full attention.

Elaine bit her lip. "Well, the book draws me. At first, I was just absorbed in the story, but it's got to the point now that all I want to do is to be reading it. It's as if nothing else matters. It calls to me, Holly, all the time."

Holly nodded. "I know what it's like to get immersed in a book, you just don't want to put it down do you? Reading is such a great escape, that's why I only dare to read when I'm on holiday."

Elaine banged her fist on the dashboard stopping Holly short. "No, you don't understand! Will you please listen!"

Holly sucked her lips in and looked straight ahead.

Recognising how rude she had been Elaine continued. "I'm sorry, I'm not myself, Holly. I've been so full of anger, I don't know why. I think the book is taking me over, it's all I care about. It's more than that though." Holly waited.

"I don't know how to say this, but the book has some very strange properties. It's as if whatever happens to it, it always comes out on top. It seems to drain my energy and use it to renew itself."

Holly nodded. "Do you think it means you harm?"

Elaine was encouraged by the positive response. "That's the strange thing! I get a strong feeling that it's trying to warn me, or protect me in some way. I honestly don't think it wants to hurt me."

Holly's deep chocolate eyes showed no signs of scepticism or mockery, she regarded her friend for a moment. "Would you like me to take a look at it?"

Elaine looked puzzled for a moment and then nodded.

Holly continued, "My mum's family were Romany and she taught me to be open to things we don't necessarily understand. I don't follow all her ways but I do think that I have a certain sensitivity to things that not everybody has."

Elaine clasped Holly's hand. "Thank you, for not dismissing my ramblings out of hand. I've felt so alone lately, Holly; the book has been my only refuge." Even as she said it, Elaine realised that this wasn't true; she had had people running around after her since her fall, they had all been so kind to her. "That sounds awful! You have all been so good to me and I've been treating you appallingly. I don't deserve such good friends."

Holly clasped her other hand around Elaine's. "We're glad to do it, and don't worry we know that this isn't 'you' at all; I think the knock you had took more out of you than you thought, the main thing is to get you better, however long it takes."

Elaine drew back and looked down at her feet. Holly cocked her head trying to catch eye contact again. After a moment's pause, she swung around and grabbed the shopping bags off the back seat. "Come on, the sooner we get the shopping done the quicker we can get back and look at the book together."

At this, Elaine looked up and smiled, the passing cloud of a frown disappearing.

Holly had to get back to The Carter's for opening time, so they didn't tarry long in the supermarket. There was no queue at the checkout so they were back well in time.

After storing the fresh groceries in the fridge, Holly followed Elaine up to the reading attic. Iris, who had been making much of Holly; recognising her as a provider of treats, skulked off at this point.

Holly sat at the desk and laid her hands flat on the open pages, she closed her eyes for a moment.

"There is a lot of energy, I can feel it." She closed the book and held it to her chest; she was silent for what seemed like minutes. Elaine did not disturb her but watched closely, her friend's expression changed to one of deep sorrow. When at last Holly opened her eyes, Elaine could see there were tears in them. Holly put the book down with great care as if laying a baby in its cradle, she turned to Elaine and stared. "I'm getting a very strong feeling; I've never felt anything like this before. It's as if a profound torment and a fierce anger are trapped inside and need to be released."

Elaine gasped. "So, I'm not imagining things?"

"I don't believe you are, the feeling is so powerful, I don't know how you kept it to yourself for so long."

Elaine shook her head. "I don't think I feel what you do, Holly. It's different for me; at first, it was just a normal compulsion to read, it's only lately that I can feel that something's trying to communicate with me. I thought it was all in my head."

Holly gazed at the book, "The question is, what do we do about it? We need to be very careful."

Elaine agreed. "The first thing is to find out as much as we can about the history, perhaps that would give us a clue about how it came to be so charged with…" Elaine struggled for a word.

"With power, I suppose. Will you help?"

Holly snorted. "Of course! You don't have to ask. I think we're going to need advice though; I have the feeling we can't do this on our own."

Holly had to be at The Carter's to open up but she managed to persuade Elaine to go over there with her, so that they could plan what their next step would be. They could talk privately as there were few customers in yet. They decided it would be a good idea to ask the seller if he had any provenance for the book. Elaine thought it was unlikely but that it was worth a try, she suggested James as a better source of information since he was not only an expert investigative reporter but also interested in old books.

"James might be sceptical about the idea of there being a strange force involved though, mightn't he?" Holly queried.

Elaine frowned. "You're right, but he is quite open minded and besides, there may be an alternative explanation, so it would be good to approach the problem from different viewpoints." Elaine could feel her old enthusiasm flowing back; for the first time, she felt ready to get going again and resume normal life.

Chapter Eighteen

Elaine phoned work when she reached home. "I'm going to see the doctor tomorrow and see if he will let me come back into work on Monday, I'm feeling much better now." She had got Trish on the other end of the line, and had met with a cold response.

"Sorry it's been so long; it's taken longer than I thought to get back on my feet."

"Yes, I know, it's put a strain on the rest of the team, I'm really sorry about that. I honestly didn't mean for it to go on so long."

"Yes, thanks, Trish, I appreciate that, you've been very understanding. I hope to see you on Monday then, I'll let you know if it's anything otherwise."

"No! I am fully expecting to be in, it's just a formality seeing the doctor."

"Yes, thanks, Trish, bye…bye."

Elaine grimaced as she disconnected the call, she looked in her contacts and texted Sylvia.

Can you talk?

Sylvia texted back straight away.

Hang on, I'll pop to the loo.

A minute later, Sylvia called. "Hi, Sylv, listen I just wanted to say sorry about the other day."

"Yes, I hope to be back on Monday, gosh that news travelled quickly!"

"Listen, can you and James come round for a takeaway tomorrow night? There are things I need to tell you."

"Great, shall I ring James or are you going to arrange it with him?"

"Ok, that's great, I'll wait to hear from you."

"Yes, you'd better get back before Trish gets suss. See you soon, bye."

Iris was standing in the doorway to the kitchen, staring cannily up at Elaine.

Elaine bent down to stroke her, "Have I been neglecting you, little puss? Don't worry, I'm more myself now." She picked the cat up and made fuss of her,

Iris responded with a chainsaw purr and rubbed her head into Elaine's shoulder with an almost fierce affection.

Elaine decided to start going through some of the work that James had brought home for her, including a short break for lunch, she spent a good four hours on it; by the time she finished, she had made sound inroads and felt pleased with herself. Iris had kept her company throughout, alternately curling up in a little ball on the sofa, her eyes thin green slits, or vigorously washing from head to toe.

After a bite to eat, Elaine decided she had earned some reading time, she took the kitchen timer from on top of the fridge and set it for an hour. Elaine was determined not to let herself get seduced into reading far into the night as had been her habit of late; she wanted to build up a sleep credit before Monday to make sure she was fresh to go back to work.

Iris followed Elaine up to the first landing but stopped there. Elaine continued up and turned to see the cat glaring up suspiciously. "It's ok, puss, I'm only going to be a little while and then I'll be back down to spoil you."

Iris yowled and stalked off into the bedroom.

Holly had left the book closed on the desk but had forgotten to put in the bookmark; it didn't matter as Elaine knew where she was up to. As she leafed through to find her place, something caught her eye on one of the preceding pages. As the light from above caught the page obliquely, she could see faint gold writing reflecting in one of the margins, she had not seen this before. The writing was hard to read, the script was gothic looking, but with some manipulation of the angle of the light, she could make it out.

Protect yourself my beloved. Let not this anger destroy you. A vessel must be found to contain the evil that has been created. Only then will it be attenuated.

This was all that she could make out; Elaine searched through the pages to see if she could find other pages with the strange text, she tried different angles of light but there was no sign. Turning back to the page she had just been looking at, she held the book up to the light again but couldn't see the script. Elaine held the book close to the angle lamp and searched but there was no trace of the bizarre writing. Could she have imagined it? No, she had definitely seen it, she was sure.

Unsettled, Elaine read for a little while, at first, her heart wasn't in it but she soon found the old enthusiasm and before long, the kitchen timer alarmed. Just as she was about to set it for another hour, Elaine stopped herself, she wavered, *just one more hour and I'll stop,* she thought to herself. Just then, she heard a plaintive meow from down below and she remembered her promise to the cat. Another hesitation, *the cat won't really know,* she thought to herself, it would be silly to be influenced by that. Setting the timer again, she settled herself down to read a little more but she found she couldn't concentrate, it wasn't just the misgivings about the cat which made her uneasy, it was something else that she couldn't put her finger on. The disappearing writing had worried her and she had the strange feeling that it was addressed to her. Putting the crumpled bookmark in place, she closed the book and went downstairs. Iris was ecstatic circling around Elaine's feet in a figure of eight as soon as she had reached the bottom step of the attic stairs.

"Are you trying to kill me or what, puss?" Elaine laughed.

Iris looked up with guileless green eyes and trilled.

Over the next couple of days, Elaine managed to keep a disciplined schedule of work and finished off all that James had brought her. The completed work was piled in orderly stacks on the coffee table. Sylvia had rung with an update on the arrangements for Friday; Elaine had insisted on providing the takeaway this time but Sylvia was going to bring wine with ginger beer for James who would do the driving. They were to meet in The Carter's Arms as Sylvia was coming straight from work and they didn't know how bad the traffic was going to be.

Elaine went over to the pub early on Friday evening, she wanted to catch Holly when she was less busy to see if she had had any more thoughts about the book. As Elaine sipped her pint of blonde, Holly joined her at the table with a cup of tea. Holly talked about her grandmother and the wisdom she had passed down to her. Elaine had had no idea that Holly had such a colourful background.

As Elaine had come in, she had recognised the man sitting with a friend on the corner table, she was sure it was the same man who parked his Mercedes outside her house. As Holly was deep in conversation he walked over to the bar and started to drum his fingers. Holly sprang up and skipped behind the bar smiling. "What can I get you?"

"A bit of service would be nice." He smirked around the room looking for an audience then his eyes lit on Holly's cup of tea. "Not a very good advert for the brewery, are you? Can't you stomach your own beer?"

Holly laughed but Elaine could see she was rattled. "I don't drink it when I'm working, what would you like, same again?"

"No, I've had enough of that swill, give me a double Laphroaig quarter cask." He turned to his friend and shouted across to him. "Are you having another of those or would you like a malt?" His friend came across to the bar to avoid shouting. "No, a pint of gold will be fine." He flickered an embarrassed smile towards Holly who had carefully placed the Laphroaig on the bar. Holly immediately started pulling a pint of the gold. The first man took a sip of his whisky and pulled a face.

"How long have you had that on the shelf, it tastes like bloody phenol!"

Holly spoke in even tones. "It does have a distinctive taste but it's a newly opened bottle and our last delivery was two weeks ago."

"Well, I'm not drinking that." He wiped his mouth with the back of his hand. "I want it changed."

The friend took a sip of the whisky, "It's fine, Alan, I'll have it, let me get you something else." Mercedes man turned to his friend with a cold hard stare. "I said, I wanted it changed."

Holly smiled at the friend. "Don't worry, I'll change it." She turned to the first man. "What would you like instead?"

"Give me a double Glenfiddich," he growled.

"Would you like to try it first?" Holly's voice remained calm and friendly.

"Don't treat me like a complete idiot! I know how it's supposed to taste!"

"Yes of course but a taster will just make sure you're happy with it." She poured a small amount into a sherry glass and handed it to him.

"I'll taste a bit of all of them then and I won't need to buy one." He laughed at his own joke and looked around again for appreciative spectators.

Holly's clear blue eyes took on a steely look as she stared at him unblinkingly, he downed the sample and looked into the empty glass. "That'll do, I suppose."

Holly poured him a double and put it on the bar, she took the Laphroaig away and was about to throw it down the sink when Mercedes man's friend stopped her. "Don't waste it, I'll buy it!"

Holly regarded him, he looked apologetic. "You can have it if you want, but I won't charge for it, your friend hasn't paid for the round yet, by the way."

"I'll settle up; I probably owe him a round somewhere along the line I suppose."

By this time, there was a small queue of regulars waiting to be served, so it was a few minutes before Holly sat down again with Elaine.

106

"Your tea has gone cold now." Elaine pulled a sympathetic face.

"Hazard of the job." Holly grinned.

"How do you remain so calm when you're faced with such rude behaviour?" Elaine shook her head in wonderment. "Didn't you feel like just throwing him out?"

Holly gulped her cold tea and frowned. "That's something that my grandmother taught me too; being travellers, the family faced a lot of prejudice and abuse. She always said that it's the abuser which loses their dignity not the victim. She also said that revenge is possible but it is not to be considered lightly because it can damage both the seeker of the revenge and the target of it. Justice is better left to higher powers."

"The Crown prosecution service?" Elaine raised her eyebrows.

Holly laughed. "No higher than that!"

"God?" Elaine smiled in embarrassment.

"Whatever you want to call it." Holly nodded. "Revenge is all about making the powerless feel powerful. If you know you have access to great power, but choose not to use it, then getting your own back becomes less important."

Elaine took a sip of beer as she struggled to follow what Holly was getting at.

Holly smiled, "He'll get what's coming to him sooner or later. Believe me, messing me about on the bar is the least of his misdeeds. That man is a thoroughly nasty piece of work from what I've heard. Anyway, less of my rabbiting, let's talk about your book."

Elaine was intrigued and wanted to hear more but she could see from her friend's demeanour that the matter was closed for now, besides she was keen to tell Holly about the strange things she had experienced.

Holly showed no sign of incredulity or surprise when Elaine told her about the 'hidden' script but took all that Elaine told her in a matter-of-fact way. Elaine was glad that what she was saying was accepted so readily; of late, she had doubted her own sanity at times, she felt that she could be quite open and unburden herself to her non-judgmental friend.

As arranged, James and Sylvia met the other two in the pub. The traffic had not been too bad according to James, so they were in good time for Elaine to phone through an advance order to the takeaway. Sylvia ordered a glass of Merlot and James a can of ginger beer.

James looked uncomfortable as he sat down with his back to the door. "I'll go and pick up the order when it's ready, there's someone over there that I don't want to be noticed by."

The others knew better than to quiz him about this but Elaine decided she would ask him to explain later when they were in private.

Later, when they were tucking into their Thai Curry back at her house, Elaine asked James who he had been trying to avoid.

"It was the chap in the corner with the moustache and the loud mouth." James paused to finish a mouthful. "I've been investigating a health food racket and it looks as if he is the central figure. The trouble is, that as far as I can see, he is doing nothing illegal. He's making a lot of money out of therapies and supplements that are composed of cheap, ready to obtain ingredients. He's targeting sick and vulnerable people and conning them into thinking his products will help them but he's charging high prices for things that anyone could readily obtain from elsewhere. It may not be illegal but what he'd doing is highly immoral in my opinion, particularly since I think he may even have children on his books."

Sylvia slammed her fork down on her plate. "That's awful, how can he live with himself, is there nothing he can be 'got' for?"

James shook his head. "All his stuff seems to be compliant with the food safety act, and not liable to come under medicines legislation. He has a clever marketing technique which ensures that people come to him willingly in the belief that he can help. He doesn't claim anything about 'cures' in his marketing material but he manages to imply that his products will be therapeutic and this is enough to fool people apparently. He can be charming in his one-to-one dealings with people, especially women."

Elaine laughed. "He wasn't at all charming with Holly earlier, in fact, he was a real pain in the neck."

Sylvia nodded. "Yes, Holly was telling me, I told her I would have thrown the drink over him and she said that that would have been playing into his hands. I've been thinking about it and she's right, negative deeds only lead to future suffering, whereas good deeds lead to future happiness."

Elaine agreed. "Let's hope that man gets his karma before long then. Do you know what his name is James?"

James nodded swallowing his mouthful. "Yes, it's Alan Sharmer. He calls himself Dr Sharmer. That's another thing, he can't be touched because he has actually got a PhD, so he's eligible for the title but he had no medical training whatsoever."

The talk passed on to other things. Elaine wanted to mention the strange happenings with the book but she didn't think that James would be a receptive as Holly had been, she was doubtful about how Sylvia would view it too. Before long, however, James brought the subject up himself albeit indirectly.

"I've been researching the Professor Cambwell story," he took a swig of his ginger beer, "you know, the gent who was found dead in the park?"

Elaine moved to the edge of her chair; Sylvia nodded.

"Although there was no foul play suspected, the exact cause of death couldn't be determined. His friends and neighbours say that he became very withdrawn in the months prior to his death but there was no indication of suicide."

"Maybe his heart just gave out?" Sylvia pulled a sad face.

James shook his head. "That would have shown up on the post mortem. There was no sign of heart disease. His next-door neighbour was also a close friend, he said that the professor had become obsessed with the book he had acquired. You'll remember he wrote about it in his journal?" James looked across at Elaine as if evaluating her reaction, when he saw that she seemed interested he continued. "The neighbour let me read the professor's notes on the book and it seemed that he had thought it was linked it to a terrible event which occurred just outside the town walls over four hundred years ago. The professor had got the information from the National Archives in records from the King's Justices."

Sylvia put her fork down. "Do you mean the book was five hundred years old? I thought it was a modern one from what you said before."

James held up his hand. "No that's just it, the calf skin cover was from that period but the pages themselves were a mystery, he was still trying to find out how the two came together. The link to the historic event came from the inscription on the flyleaf which detailed the persecution of an alchemist Benedict Auber whose wife and children were brutally murdered in Landown wood."

Elaine started at the mention of the name. "That name is so familiar; I don't know where I've heard it before but I feel as if I know him."

"Maybe he was a character in a book," Sylvia suggested, "sometimes when the characterisation is so good, you feel as if the people in a story are totally real."

Elaine screwed her eyes up. "No!" She paused to think. "No, I'm sure that I have seen him, maybe on TV?" Elaine paused again and then shook her head. "No, it's gone, I can't think where I've seen him."

James smiled. "I expect it will come back to you when you're least expecting it."

"Maybe, it was in a former life." Sylvia sounded serious.

James nodded. "Or perhaps, you've tapped into some collective consciousness, a meme from an earlier time."

Elaine had little idea of what James was talking about but it seemed new age enough to encourage her to mention the disappearing writing. "Do you think that we can detect echoes from the past sometimes?" She addressed the question generally.

"Well, we've had recording devices for over a hundred years now, so yes." James was about to carry on when Elaine interrupted him.

"No, that's not what I mean, well I don't really know what I mean, but do you think that places or objects can hold a feeling, an atmosphere perhaps?"

"In a supernatural way, do you mean?" Sylvia asked.

Elaine bit her lip. "Kind of, I suppose."

James continued. "I didn't mean to be flippant; I was going to say that there are a lot of things we don't understand, but we do know that things can be recorded by known technology, what's to say that nature doesn't record things herself and that sometimes we can detect these imprints in the universe's energy fields?"

"So, you don't think it's so farfetched then?" Elaine sucked her bottom lip.

James and Sylvia both shook their heads. "Not at all!"

"No!"

This gave Elaine the encouragement she needed to tell them about the writing she thought she had seen. Both Sylvia and James wanted to know more, so Elaine brought the book down for them to look at again. Iris shot out of the cat flap as soon as Elaine brought the book down the first flight of stairs, Elaine pointed out to the other two that the cat seemed to have a fear of it, she also told them about Holly's impressions.

During the course of the evening, the three gradually came to conclusion that there was a deep mystery involved. Neither James or Sylvia felt any particular emotion when examining the pages, they could find nothing strange about it other than the fact that it seemed so immaculate for such a well-read volume.

It was Sylvia who first suggested that it was not impossible that Elaine's book could be one and the same as the one Professor Cambwell had described. James had told them that the professor's book could not be found, James himself had made extensive efforts to unearth it with no result.

Sylvia's suggestion was a watershed; from then on, the three of them were fired up with enthusiasm to investigate further, they all agreed that Holly would be a useful ally in their quest for an explanation.

Chapter Nineteen

Laura was on an early short shift on Saturday, so there was plenty of time to prepare the meal for Trish and Rob. After the pizza lapse, there had been no deviation from the meal plan and Laura was sticking to it today too; she had bought fresh vegetables and extra Quorn 'steaks' at work to supplement the ingredients that had been delivered. They would have fresh fruit for dessert. By and large, the meal regime had been easy to follow, the food was tasty and appetising, Laura had lost weight through it she was sure, her waistband was definitely looser. Losing weight had not been the aim, but Laura felt she could afford to shed a few pounds, her main concern was Lilly who was skinny as it was, she was keeping a careful eye on her. So far, Lilly was full of energy and bounce which was reassuring.

As the two of them were preparing the vegetables, Laura pondered what to do about wine.

Normally, she would have bought a bottle for an occasion like this, but all alcohol was ruled out of the dietary scheme, of course, this didn't affect Lilly who wouldn't have been having any anyway, but Laura did miss the occasional relaxing glass of red.

The first thing that Rob did when he came through the door was thrust a bottle of Merlot into Laura's hand. Trish was carrying a huge bunch of freesias, Laura caught a whiff of the heavenly scent as she pecked her sister on the cheek.

"They're beautiful!" Laura took the bunch and fumbled on the hall table for a vase, as she did so the letter rack fell over spilling out the contents. "Let's get these in water, Trish, you're so kind, you know they are my favourites!"

Trish sniffed. "They were on offer anyway."

"Well, they're gorgeous, thank you, and thanks for the wine, Rob."

Rob smiled. "I know we're not supposed to have it with this new food arrangement, but I reckoned a glass each wouldn't harm."

Trish frowned. "It's not meant to be followed slavishly surely? A bit of common sense needs to be used, doesn't it?"

Lilly laughed. "I know, Mum and I had a pizza the other day, we weren't going to tell you." She shot a cheeky grin at Laura who responded with a raised eyebrow warning.

"Well, it's not me that told you to follow the diet anyway, I don't see why you feel you need to hide it from me." Trish glared at Laura.

Laura could feel an argument brewing. "Oh, it's just Lilly being dramatic, you know what teenagers are like." She blinked an almost imperceptible apology at Lilly.

Lilly had already gauged the way things were going and she understood that she needed to provide an 'escape' for her mum, she threw her arms around Trish. "I was only joking, Aunty Trish; I know you wouldn't deprive your favourite niece her little treats."

Trish had stiffened as soon as Lilly hugged her and she shuffled as Lilly held on tight, she raised a rigid arm to stroke her niece's head. "You're my only niece, aren't you? But no, you're right, I would fully approve of such a brave young lady receiving a little treat."

Lilly roared with laughter as if her aunty had told her the best joke ever, she released the bear hug. Immediately grabbing, Trish's hand, Lilly dragged her into the dining room. "Look, I decorated the table, do you like it?" The dining room table was a picture; Lilly had used a pink sheet as a tablecloth and in the centre was a group of origami swans. There were four place settings and at the left of each fork was a napkin, cleverly folded to resemble a ballerina. Trish looked genuinely delighted. "Still keen on 'Swan Lake', I see." Trish's gaze flashed to Laura momentarily, Laura could detect a hint of sadness in her eyes.

During the meal, it was mainly Lilly and Rob who did most of the talking with Laura and Trish joining in when they were addressed directly. Rob was a great joker and Lilly a responsive audience, so the conversation flowed easily and pleasantly.

At the end of the meal, Trish and Laura washed up whilst Rob and Lilly played Jenga on the coffee table in the lounge.

Trish took out a clean tea towel and began drying. "What's the latest on Lilly's treatment?" Laura checked the shine on a Pyrex dish she was rinsing. "Oh, it's fine, she's still getting the pills delivered every week and going to the exercise classes and apart from the pizza we've been keeping to the food plan faithfully."

Trish nodded. "Sorry, I meant the hospital treatment; has she got a date for the operation yet?" Laura looked away and focused on the dishes. "If the tumour recedes, an operation may not be needed."

Trish looked puzzled. "Are they giving her chemo then?"

"No, we're watching and waiting at this stage." Laura scrubbed a pan hard.

Trish piled up the clean plates and put them away in the cupboard. "Isn't that unusual with childhood cancers?" She measured her words carefully. "Is that what the consultant advised?"

Laura rinsed the pan in hot water. "Dr Sharmer is confident that the treatment he is giving will do the trick."

Trish put down the tea towel. "Dr Sharmer, he's the homeopath. I was talking about the hospital consultant, what does he say?"

"It's a woman actually, Miss Maitlin."

Trish supressed an impatient scowl. "Sorry she, what does *she* say?"

"She understands, she's a mother too."

Trish was getting visibly annoyed by now. "What's that supposed to mean?"

Laura, aware that Trish's childlessness was a sore point, rushed to make amends. "Sorry, Trish, that was a stupid thing for me to say. What I meant was that she understands that I don't want to rush into anything."

Trish went over to close the kitchen door checking Lilly and Rob were still occupied with the Jenga game as she did so. "For goodness' sake, Laura, you're not choosing a new outfit; this is Lilly's future health we are talking about. Surely, the sooner she gets surgery, the better chance she has of a good outcome?"

Laura slammed the washing up brush into the bowl. "You're not listening! I told you that surgery may not be necessary!"

"Says who?"

Laura didn't reply.

Trish stood in front of her sister and looked her directly in the eye. "Says who, Laura?"

Laura hesitated. "Well, Miss Maitlin, didn't say it in so many words but that's what she meant."

"You need to go back and talk to her again, Laura, and get this clarified. Would you like me to come with you?" Trish's voice softened. "Listen, I know how it is in these places, it's hard to take all the information in at once, that's why it's a good idea to have an extra pair of ears."

Laura looked at her sister with glistening eyes, she tried to speak but it came out as a croak.

Trish put her hand on Laura's arm. "Please let me come with you to the next appointment." Laura nodded silently.

"When is the next appointment?" Trish waited for a reply.

"I'll phone the hospital tomorrow, I promise." Laura avoided her sister's gaze.

Once Laura had regained her composure, they stepped out into the hall on their way back into the lounge. There was a sound of crashing blocks and Lilly's delighted laughter. Trish noticed the fallen letter rack, and conforming to her character, she moved to put it straight.

"Leave it, I'll do it." Laura's tone was sharp.

Trish was surprised by the strident command, she passed to the spilled letters to Laura, as she did, she stopped and stared at the post mark on one. "This is over two weeks old and you haven't even opened it." She shuffled through the pile. "This one's a month old. Laura, these look like hospital letters, what's going on?"

Hearing the raised voice, Rob wandered out into the hall. "She's thrashed me yet again, steady hand that girl." He laughed. "Or maybe, it's me that's got a shaky one." He stopped; his warm grey eyes regarded Laura with concern. "What's up?" He looked from Trish to Laura and then back again.

Just then, Lilly came bouncing out. "Are you two having an argument again? How can washing up be controversial?" She raised a finger to her cheek. "Come to think of it, there are numerous potential points of contention associated with that exercise, I can understand how you could come to blows."

Rob roared with laughter, he gathered the two sisters one on each arm and shepherded them into the lounge. "You two sit down and I'll make us a nice coffee to round off the lovely meal."

He hesitated. "Ah, I forgot, coffee's not allowed, is it? Herbal tea?"

"Coffee." Trish asserted inviting no argument.

Laura nodded meekly.

Lilly followed Rob out into the kitchen to show him where everything is.

Laura and Trish went into the lounge, Trish still had the letters, she thrust them into Laura's hand. "You need to deal with these, open them." It was more an order than a request.

As Trish had suspected, the letters contained appointments for Lilly to attend clinics, they became increasingly pressing in tone until the last one informed Laura that her GP would be contacted. Sure enough, there were letters from the GP in the pile. When pressed, Laura admitted that she had been ignoring phone calls from the surgery.

"Why?" Trish was genuinely upset. "This is just madness, Laura. What on earth possessed you to ignore all of these?"

Laura was twisting a paper tissue in her hands, she used it to wipe the tears from her cheeks, her voice was tiny when she answered. "I was scared." She blew her nose. "I was scared that things would get out of hand, that I wouldn't get to have a say in Lilly's treatment. That they would take her away and bring her back a hollow shell of the child I knew."

"But that's madness, you risk her being taken away more by doing this, you'll have social services on your back if you're not careful, causing medical treatment to be withheld is considered a form of abuse."

Laura began sobbing in earnest now, Trish pulled out a fresh paper tissue and handed it over, she shuffled closer to Laura and put her arm around her shoulders, it made an awkward picture but Trish's voice softened. "Don't worry, we'll make this right. You always were a head in the sand sort of person, weren't you? Remember when your hamster died when you were eight? You hid it at the back of the cage for three days before we discovered it." This was Trish's attempt to lighten the mood but it had the opposite effect, Laura broke into a fresh fit of sobbing.

"Shush." Trish was whispering now. "They'll hear you in the kitchen, you don't want to upset Lilly, come on, dry your eyes. Don't worry, we'll work it out."

Right on cue, Rob came in, carrying a tray of coffee and a milkshake, Lilly was close behind him.

"Hey, what's going on here?" Rob's voice was gentle.

Lilly went straight to her mum and hugged her hard.

Trish fumbled for the letters and scurried away to return them to the hall table. "It's just me and my big mouth again, love, I just can't help being the big sister."

Lilly had noticed the letters. "You opened the mail, Aunty Trish?"

Trish had the grace to look guilty. "I'm sorry, Lilly, I need to learn to mind my own business, don't I? I'm sorry I upset your mum."

Lilly shook her head. "No, I'm glad, I knew they were there, and I knew what they were, but I didn't know how to ask Mum about them."

Laura looked up, her tear-filled eyes were full of remorse. "Oh, Lilly you're such a little trouper, I had no idea!"

"It's ok, Mum, but can we go back to see Miss Maitlin? I'm not scared and I really like her."

Rob looked at Trish for explanation. "Can someone please tell me what's going on?" It fell to the fourteen-year-old to paint an accurate picture.

"Mum is scared that I'm going to get my leg chopped off if I go back to the hospital, she's hoping that the lump will go away of its own accord if I live a healthy lifestyle."

Rob was open mouthed with disbelief. "You mean she's not having any treatment?" He addressed his question to Laura.

"She's having alternative treatment; non-invasive therapy, the doctor calls it."

Rob frowned. "Which doctor?"

"You could call him that!" Lilly quipped.

Laura looked from Rob to Lilly and back again nonplussed. "Dr Sharmer, he's got a private practice in town."

"Is he qualified?" Rob looked worried.

"Yes, he has certificates." Laura's voice was querulous.

Lilly started to speak but thought better of it.

Rob looked in her direction. "What were you going to say, Lilly?"

"Nothing, it's ok." Lilly glanced at her mum and smiled cheerily.

Trish stepped in. "No, come on, I know you have something on your mind, now's the time to get it out into the open. Mum only wants what is best for you, she won't be cross, will you, Laura?"

Laura looked in danger of weeping again. "Of course not! Come on, tell us what's bothering you please."

Lilly swallowed. "I'm not afraid that you'll be cross, Mum, I just don't want to upset you." She paused and looked over at Rob. "It's just that I think Mum is wasting all this money on a quack cure when I could be getting the best treatment at the hospital."

Rob nodded. "What makes you think that the private doctor is no good?"

Lilly glanced across at her mum. "Well, he's not a medical doctor for a start, he might know a lot about homeopathy but he's not been to medical school."

Rob looked at Laura. "Is this right?"

Laura was puzzled. "He has certificates on the wall."

Lilly's voice was gentle. "Mum that doesn't mean anything, you can buy phoney certificates online."

Rob agreed. "She's right, there's a whole industry around producing these things, the websites are quite open about it and they're quite professional too, there doesn't seem to be any secrecy needed. Having said that the certificates could be quite genuine."

Lilly shook her head. "Well, he's not on the GMC list, I've checked."

Laura shook her head. "GMC?"

Rob filled her in. "General Medical Council."

"But how did you know what to do, love?" Laura was open mouthed.

"It's easy, Mum, you can just google GMC and you get on to their website, then you can check any one to see if they are registered. Miss Maitlin is on there; it even tells you when she qualified and when she went on to the specialist register."

"That child amazes me sometimes." Trish addressed no one in particular.

Lilly reddened. "I didn't want to sneak behind your back, Mum. You've been working so hard to pay for the private treatment; I know the sacrifices you've been making. I hated to think that you were being ripped off and I just had a bad feeling about Dr Sharmer."

Laura kissed the top of Lilly's head. "I think I need to start listening to you, don't I? I'm sorry, I forget that you are growing up into a sensible young lady." She turned to Trish and Rob. "I'll contact the hospital on Monday and get an appointment."

Trish closed her eyes, and nodded, Rob squeezed Laura's shoulder.

"Have you been getting in debt to pay for the treatment?" Trish tried not to be strident in questioning. "We can help you if you have, but maybe you should consider withdrawing from the plan?"

Laura nodded. "I think you're right, Trish, but I've signed an agreement to stick with the whole course, I'm not sure I can get out of it."

Rob stepped in. "We'll see about that! It's not like a phone contract, there must be a way of withdrawing without penalty. I'll help you with that."

"Mum?" Lilly fixed her clear blue eyes on Laura. "Don't worry." Laura patted Lilly's hand.

"No, I mean it, Mum, don't worry whatever, because I'm not."

Laura stared back at her daughter and an unspoken communication passed between them, she nodded slowly and then hugged the child close. Trish and Rob looked on in silent comprehension.

Chapter Twenty

Elaine's first day back to work was uneventful, she had expected a cold shoulder from Trish because she had been away for so long, but Trish seemed preoccupied with other things and said nothing about the long absence.

Sylvia had written a little welcome back note and put it on Elaine's desk, other than that, the desk was exactly as she had left it.

As Elaine took her sandwiches out of her bag to put in the tea room fridge, she thought about the book that she had left behind, it had been very difficult not to pack it in her bag to take to work, the thought of being without it for the whole day filled her with dread but she knew that she must wean herself off the obsession.

All through the morning, Elaine found herself losing concentration and thinking of ways to leave work early in order to get home to read. At ten o'clock, she went to the tea room with Sylvia and they sat and drank coffee together.

Elaine kept her voice low. "I was expecting a tongue lashing from Trish but she's been very reasonable."

Sylvia chuckled. "Yes, you'd expect her to be right on to you as soon as you stepped through the door, wouldn't you? She's been preoccupied lately; I think there is some illness in the family."

"I don't know much about Trish's family, do you?"

Sylvia shook her head. "No, she's pretty close about personal things, it's hard to get anything out of her. I know she visits her parents at weekends and that she's married but that's about it."

"Maybe we should ask if she needs any help?"

Sylvia looked at Elaine in mock horror. "You can risk getting your head bitten off if you like but I'll stand back so I can pick up the pieces afterwards!"

"Oh, she's not that bad." Elaine laughed.

Sylvia nodded her head with theatrical emphasis. "Oh yes, she is!" She sipped her coffee.

"Anyway, how are you feeling on your first day back?"

"To be honest, I just want to be at home, I want to get back to the book."

Sylvia raised her head. "It's really got a grip on you, hasn't it?"

Elaine lowered her eyes. "I feel so pathetic admitting it, but yes, it has."

Sylvia regarded her friend for a moment, her amber eyes full of concern. "Why don't you come and stay with me for a while? It might help in breaking the habit."

Elaine felt her heart thumping and her breath combing in short gasps at the thought of being separated from the book like that, it was as if her blood was running cold. "No!" She almost shouted. "Sorry, I mean that's very kind, but I couldn't leave Iris alone like that."

"I'd forgotten about Iris; couldn't she come with you though?"

"I'd be too afraid she'd wander off and get lost, she's a very outdoorsy cat." Elaine's answer came in a flash.

"What if I take charge of the book instead then?"

Elaine could feel an unreasonable anger rising up in herself, she knew that Sylvia was only trying to help but she was irritated nevertheless. "I can't, I can't let go just yet. I need time, Sylvia, I can't cut it off just like that, I need to do it gradually."

Tess, who had been tidying around the sink turned around to face Elaine and Sylvia, she looked worried. "Sure, it should never have been sold to you in the first place but you are the very image of her."

Sylvia frowned as if she hadn't heard properly. "Of who?"

Just then, Trish came into the tea room, anxious to change the subject Elaine turned her attention towards her. "How are things with you, Trish?"

Trish faced the sink. "Better now we have a full complement of staff again, I was starting to think that you weren't coming back."

Sylvia shot Elaine a knowing look, Elaine smiled back at her. "Yes, sorry about that, Trish, I'll do my best to catch up with the work."

Trish continued making her coffee but gave no reply. The other two decided it would be politic to end their coffee break and return to work at this point. They both looked towards the sink to acknowledge Tessa but she was no longer there. Elaine thought nothing of this because Trish did tend to command everyone's full attention and she concluded that Tessa had slipped quietly out when Trish had entered the room.

For the rest of the day, Elaine tried her best to keep from thinking of the book. At five, though she couldn't wait to get home, she resolved that she would cook an evening meal and spend some time playing with Iris before retiring to her reading room. As soon as she set foot inside the house, Elaine's resolve vanished and almost before she has taken off her coat, she fed Iris and shot upstairs. Once in the attic, all the feeling of panic disappeared and a calmness flooded through her. Opening the book was like entering a fertile valley after trekking through wilderness, this was where she wanted to be, she never wanted to leave this place.

Elaine's peace was soon shattered, a knock came at the front door and she knew she couldn't ignore it. Reluctantly, she went down and opened the door. Holly was standing smiling on the doorstep. Elaine threw her arms around her. "Holly, I need help, I can't do this on my own."

Holly needed no explanation; she knew exactly what was going on. "I'll help, but you must trust me, Elaine."

Elaine nodded. "I will, I mean I do, but it's as if all my strength leaves me."

Holly laid her hands on Elaine's shoulders and looked her straight in the eye. "I am going to look after the book for you, you can come to see it but I'm going to take it away from you at least for the time being."

Elaine's gasped for breath. "No! I can't be without it, I can't."

"You can and you will." Holly's voice was firm.

"Please, Holly, that's too much to ask."

Holly squeezed Elaine's shoulders. "You have to trust me, Elaine."

Elaine watched as Holly took herself upstairs and went into the attic, she came down with the book.

"Don't take it away, I'll ration myself, I promise." Elaine's voice was tremulous.

Holly spoke slowly and clearly as if to a child. "Elaine, I have to take it, but you can come and see it at any time so long as you understand that you can't be alone with it. This is the only way you will be able to cut your dependency."

Elaine reluctantly allowed Holly to take the book away but she felt utterly bereft when it had gone, she went into the attic and it was as if the light had been taken away and there was a huge empty void in its place. After a few minutes, Holly returned, Elaine hoped that she had brought her treasure back but Holly just assured Elaine that she had found a safe and secure storage place.

"You can come to see it any time, it's in the safe but there will always be one of us available to get it out for you."

Elaine hated the thought that she had to be supervised to see what was in fact, her own property but she managed to grasp the wisdom of the arrangement.

Holly continued. "We need to find out more about it and why it has this power over you. Where did it come from did you say?"

Elaine described the location of the shop.

"We'll start by going there to see if the shop owner knows anything but you won't be free till Saturday, will you?"

Elaine was still dazed and preoccupied. "No, I can't really take time off work."

"We'll leave it until then then. Are you going to be, ok?"

Elaine's voice was like a thread. "Yes, I'll be fine."

When Holly had gone, Elaine could not settle, she went into the attic again, she felt as if someone had died. Iris bounded up the stairs after her and leapt onto the desk purring, after sniffing every corner, she lay down and began to clean herself.

The presence of the cat filled the yawning emptiness to a degree but Elaine felt a wave of weariness wash over her, she knew she should eat but she didn't have the will or the energy to prepare a meal so she dragged herself to bed and fell into a deep sleep.

The book was just out of her reach, she tried to get closer to it but every time she drew near, she found it has moved again. There was a huge oak bench, she could see the book the size of a postage stamp on the centre of it. All of a sudden, the book seemed huge, bigger than herself but then it shrunk again before she could hold on to it.

Hearing her name being called, Elaine turned and recognised a familiar face, familiar and strange at the same time. "Elaine?" His voice was full of sorrow. "It is time for us to part."

Elaine didn't understand. "Do I know you?"

The man's grey eyes were filled with compassion. "No, but I know you, or one who came before you. It is time for me to go back to find her. First, I must right the wrong I have started. I need you to help me."

Elaine was still confused. "How can I help you?"

He stepped towards her. "You must help me find the vessel, an unrighteous bearer of the burden I have created with my hate and anger." The man began to weep. "I was consumed by hatred and wanted revenge but I was unable to control that which I generated. The fire of my anger has consumed that which it should not, and there must be an end to it."

"How can it be ended?" Elaine felt she knew what he meant.

"You know what you must do." He seemed diminished.

Elaine struggled to find him. "Don't go, I need you to explain, please."

He was gone and Elaine was left alone in the cavernous room in front of the oak table. The book started glowing and then it was aflame. Before long, the whole table was on fire, the room was full of smoke but Elaine had no difficulty breathing, neither did she feel any heat from the flames. Something made her reach out to touch the blazing book, her arm caught fire immediately but all she felt was a tingling sensation. The skin on her arm started to evaporate and she fell backwards onto something soft, there was whiteness all around her.

Elaine's arm felt heavy, she raised her head to see Iris curled up on top of the duvet on her right-hand side. Elaine extracted her arm from under the sleeping cat and the pins and needles made her wince, she lay there planning her next move. She would have to burn the book to be released from its power, the very thought made her panic. Knowing she would never be able to do it herself, she decided that she would have to ask Holly, but even the thought of that made her heart pound. Elaine could feel her temperature rising, her counterpane wet with perspiration.

In the shower, she thought up a plan of action, she would go to work as normal, then ask either Sylvia or James to phone Holly and instruct her to incinerate the book. It occurred to Elaine that Holly may not take instructions from them but she would cross that bridge when she came to it.

Elaine felt a heavy weight in her chest as she drove to work, it was the same feeling she had had when she was going to her father's funeral, a bleak aching deep in her soul.

James was already at his desk when she arrived in the office, he looked up and smiled as she approached but he immediately went back to studying his notes, he called her attention to them.

"I've been looking through the professor's papers and he had actually found out quite a lot about the history associated with your book. There was man of learning; Benedict Auber who some of the townsfolk believed had found the secret of turning base metal into gold. He was hounded for the secret but of course he wouldn't or couldn't divulge it. His wife and children were captured in an attempt to force him into giving his secret but it all went wrong and they ended up suffocating in a well."

Elaine listened but seemed to be thinking about something else.

James continued. "Strangely enough, the wife's name was Elaine. The tragedy seems to have cost Benedict his sanity, he became a hermit and no one dared to go near his dwelling, anyone who got close would hear him ranting and raving swearing revenge. Nobody knew how he got food or fuel but he survived for years after and there were always signs of smoke coming from the chimney until one day there was an explosion which destroyed the building and Benedict was not seen again."

Elaine had a faraway look. "James, would you do something for me?"

James nodded. "If I can, what is it?"

"I need you to get Holly to burn the book."

James looked aghast. "Burn it? But isn't that a bit drastic?"

Tears were streaming down Elaine's cheeks. "I think, it's the only way."

Elaine explained that she would never have the strength to do it herself and after a while, he agreed to contact Holly. Elaine overheard the conversation and it was clear that Holly was very unwilling, she took a lot of persuading during which Elaine had to fight with every ounce of strength to stop herself wresting the phone off James and telling him to stop. When the deed was done, Elaine tried to concentrate on her work but all she could think about was the destruction of her treasure.

Elaine's heart was even heavier as she made the journey home, she dragged herself through the front door. The house seemed empty despite the fact that Iris came gambolling up to her purring. As she fed the cat, a knock came at the door, Elaine could see Holly through the glass, a sense of dread hit her like a sledgehammer blow. Opening the door, she found it hard to read Holly's expression.

Holly stood on the doorstep with her mouth open and a blank look on her face. "I couldn't do it," she said.

Elaine was relieved yet frustrated. "What you mean you couldn't bring yourself to put it in the fire?" She stepped back to let Holly in.

"No, I got a good fire going in the garden incinerator and put the book in but it wouldn't burn. I tried barbeque fluid and everything. I covered it with wood and that all burnt but not the book itself. That's not all though, Elaine, it's not even singed, there's not a mark on it!"

Elaine stood staring for a moment. "That's impossible."

Holly nodded. "I know, if I hadn't seen with my own eyes, I wouldn't believe it."

They went into the lounge to sit down, both speechless. Holly regained her composure first.

"We have to find a way to dispose of the book, Elaine, there's something very unnatural going on and I don't like it. Maybe the bookshop would take it back."

Elaine looked up. "That's a good idea, we could ask anyway. We'll go on Saturday to see if he'll take it back, I don't see why he wouldn't, he didn't want to sell it to me in the first place and if he gets it back for nothing, then he'll make a nice profit in selling it again."

Holly shook her head. "Elaine, I don't want to leave it until Saturday I have a bad feeling about it and I think we need to act quickly."

"I need to come with you though, the shop owner won't know who you are, he has a better chance of remembering the sale if he sees me. The problem is that I don't feel I can take the day off work since I've only just gone back after so long." Elaine bit her lower lip.

Holly nodded. "Ok, I suppose, it will have to be Saturday then; I'll keep it locked away in the safe till then."

Elaine ran her tongue around her lips. "Perhaps, I could have it here for a while?"

"Not a good idea!" Holly frowned.

The next day, Elaine turned up at work early, she had found it difficult to sleep all night, so at four o'clock, she decided to give up on sleep altogether and set off for work after feeding the puzzled and slightly indignant cat. The office was quiet when she arrived and Elaine managed to get a lot of work done before the rest of the staff came in. Sylvia and James were the first into the office and this gave Elaine the chance to tell them about the plan to return the book to the shop and why. James was as incredulous as Holly had been but for some reason Sylvia showed little surprise when told about the book's resistance to fire, she agreed that the book needed to be taken as far away as possible though.

It was ten o'clock before Elaine realised that Trish had not come into work; she mentioned it to James who told her that there had been a phone call saying that she wouldn't be in.

"That's unusual for Trish." Elaine looked surprised.

126

James agreed. "Yes, I've never known her take a day sick in all the time I've been here."

Sylvia corrected them. "She's not sick, she said she was going to a hospital appointment with her sister and her niece, she's taking it as annual leave."

Elaine had an idea. "James, you finish at one today, don't you?" James nodded.

"Do you think it would be ok for me to go home early since Trish isn't around? I was in early and I can make up the rest of the time tomorrow."

"Fine by me." James looked across at Sylvia who nodded in assent.

Elaine contacted Holly by phone and arranged for them to go to the bookshop that afternoon. Holly sounded relieved at the plan. When James heard the arrangements, he offered to go with them as Elaine had been secretly hoping. Sylvia looked slightly disappointed to be left out but she showed no signs of irritation.

Holly met the other two at Elaine's house, she had the book carefully wrapped up and packed in a strong shopping bag.

The old-fashioned bell clanged on the shop door. The shopkeeper didn't look up as the three of them went in, all they could see was the top of his head and the long curly locks hanging down like a lion's mane. Holly placed the book on the counter in front of him, he stared at it for a moment and then silently looked up at Holly.

Elaine was the first to speak. "I don't know if you remember me but I bought a lovely old book here a few months ago."

The shopkeeper regarded her with hooded eyes. "I get hundreds of customers every week." Holly and James exchanged sceptical glances.

Elaine smiled. "Yes, of course, but I thought you might remember the book?"

"It's a little late to express dissatisfaction with your purchase now if, as you say, you bought it months ago."

"No, I'm far from dissatisfied. It's the most wonderful book I have ever had, it's totally captivated me and…" Elaine found herself lost for words, the shopkeeper was looking at her, his dark blue eyes full of comprehension which made her even more tongue tied. "I'm sorry, this was a mistake, I was going to ask you to take it back but I was wrong, I can't give it up."

Holly stepped in. "Elaine, you must, remember we agreed it was for the best." She appealed to the shopkeeper. "She doesn't want the money back. It's a very special book and we were hoping you would know what to do with it."

"No."

Holly frowned. "No what?"

"No, I don't know what to do with it."

Holly was exasperated. "But you're a bookseller, couldn't you take it back to resell it?"

"I didn't want to sell it in the first place, I don't know how she persuaded me."

"Well, then take it back!" Holly was visibly annoyed.

James put his hand on Holly's shoulder, he turned to the shopkeeper. "The book has a very interesting history, I'm sure you know its provenance."

The bookseller addressed Elaine as if James didn't exist. "I will take it back and resell it one more time but you must help me to find a rightful buyer."

Holly relaxed. "Someone who will appreciate it?"

Ignoring Holly, the man continued. "You know what I mean, don't you?"

Elaine saw an expression on his face which reminded her of something she couldn't put her finger on but it made her feel calm and in control. "I think, I do." she struggled to remember but couldn't quiet. Picking up the parcel, she held it to her chest and touched her face to it. Slowly and painfully, she released it and gave it to the bookseller, he took it off her and nodded. Elaine indicated to Holly and James to follow her as she walked out of the shop with reverential steps; they followed obediently.

Chapter Twenty-One

Laura had phoned Doctor Sharmer's surgery and got through to the receptionist, who when she heard that Laura wanted to terminate the plan became very cold. At first, Laura was accused of putting her child's health at risk but when she explained that she was going to concentrate on the hospital treatment, for now at least, she was told that the contract that she signed was binding and that either six months' notice must be given or she would be liable for a large penalty payment.

Today, Trish was coming round to go with Laura and Lilly to the hospital. When Trish arrived, Laura told her about the conversation on the phone and her worries about the continuing payments. Trish immediately phoned Rob to tell him, filling him in with as many details as she could.

"Don't worry about the finance, Laura, Rob will sort it out, it may take a little while but he'll stick at it, he's furious that they are as good as extorting money out of you, he won't let the matter rest. For now, all we have to think about is getting Lilly to her appointment and paying close attention to what they tell you at the hospital." Trish sounded like a school mistress but Laura knew that sisterly rivalry was out of the picture at the moment and Trish genuinely was out to help both Lilly and herself.

As they drove to the University Hospital, Laura kept a close eye on her daughter but she could detect no hint of nervousness or unwillingness. In fact, Lilly seemed more upbeat than ever.

Laura wasn't sure if this was an act or if Lilly was genuinely excited to be going to the hospital, either way Lilly spent the whole journey chatting about one thing or another.

Trish was first out of the car when they reached the hospital car park. "I'll go and get a ticket," she said as she sprang out of the car.

Lilly climbed out more slowly, Laura helped her out with a hand under the armpit. "You alright, love?" She said as she steadied her skinny legged daughter, she reminded her of a fawn struggling to stand for the first time.

Lilly gritted her teeth. "Just a bit of cramp, Mum, don't worry."

Laura kissed the top of her head. "I'm your mum, it's what I do!"

Lilly rolled her eyes at Trish who was sticking the parking ticket on the windscreen by now. "She's such a fuss pot!"

Trish defended her sister for once. "It's her job to worry, she's your mum, and aunties have the right to be fuss pots as well, so be warned!"

"You're ganging up on me now!" Lilly grinned at them both.

In the paediatric unit, the nurse immediately recognised them, dimples appeared in her dark rounded cheeks as she flashed a brilliant smile. "Lilly! Good to see you how's de ballet going?"

Lilly hugged her, she had to bend slightly to touch cheeks as she was a full head above the nurse despite the fact that they were both wearing flat shoes.

Lilly went off happily to have her bloods taken, she had never minded needles, unlike Laura who hated the sight of them.

Trish and Laura sat in the waiting area until Lilly returned. Laura glanced at her sister. "Thanks for all your support."

Trish waved her hand as if brushing away a fly.

"No, Trish, I mean it, you didn't tear a strip off me for ignoring the letters, I've been an idiot but you didn't make me feel bad about it."

Trish smiled. "Like I normally do, you mean?"

Laura hesitated. "No, it's me, I can be oversensitive I know. I always feel I have to go it alone and I shy away from criticism to a ridiculous degree."

"Don't we all?" Trish stared down at her hands clasped tightly in her lap.

"Trish, I've never needed anyone like I need you and Rob now."

Trish looked up, her dark brown eyes reflected a mixture of affection and embarrassment.

Wordlessly, they hugged each other in a way which might have suggested to an outsider that they were both wearing body armour. After a moment, Trish coughed and brushed imaginary hairs from her lap. Laura fiddled with her handbag and looked over towards the corridor.

After what seemed like hours, Lilly came back down the corridor holding a pad on her arm, she was grinning broadly. The nurse opened the consulting room door and looked in then she nodded at Laura. "You can all go in now."

130

Laura felt as if her heart had dropped to the ground, she looked at Trish who was gathering up her things.

Lilly grabbed her mum by the arm. "Come on, slowcoach." She chirped.

Miss Maitlin was sitting at her desk typing on the keyboard whilst looking at the screen, she stopped as soon as they came in. "Lilly! It's so good to see you, please sit down." She indicated the chairs and glanced at Trish.

Laura sat down. "I've brought my sister, Patricia with me to help take notes, if that's ok?"

Miss Maitlin smiled and nodded. "That's an excellent idea if you don't mind me saying, sometimes in these situations, there is so much to take in that details can be lost on the way."

Trish took out a reporter's pad and a pen, she sat on the edge of the chair.

Laura fiddled with the clasp on her handbag. "We've missed a couple of appointments, I'm sorry about that."

Miss Maitlin was reading the notes on the screen a faint frown moved over her face like a passing cloud. "Well, it's good that you're here now but can I ask what the delay was?"

Laura looked ashamed and uncomfortable and hesitated to answer, so Trish stepped in. "It was fear, doctor, fear of what was going to come next."

Miss Maitlin smiled across at Lilly. "Hospitals can be scary places, can't they? But there's no need to be afraid, you'll be very well looked after here."

Lilly shook her head and was about to speak but Laura put her hand on her arm. "It was me."

She said, "I was the one who was afraid, but I had no right to interrupt Lilly's appointments." Laura glanced at Trish who was looking away.

Miss Maitlin continued, "We need to get things moving now anyway, I'll get Lilly booked in for surgery but it should only be an overnight stay two days at the most."

Laura stared wide eyed. "Surgery?"

Miss Maitlin's voice was gentle. "Yes, the biopsy showed that the lesion is a soft tissue sarcoma called a myxoid liposarcoma, the sooner we resect it, the less damage there will be to the surrounding tissues. As long as we are happy that the margins have been cleared," she hesitated and looked towards Trish, "when we are happy that the whole lump has been removed, we can review the case and decide on the form of further treatment if any."

Lilly reached across and squeezed her mother's hand; Laura placed her other hand on top of Lilly's.

"Do you have any questions you want to ask me, Lilly?" Miss Maitlin glanced at Laura.

Lilly nodded. "Is it going to affect my dancing?"

"You are going to have to go easy with it for a while after surgery, but as soon as the tissues are healed, there's no reason why you shouldn't start introducing it again gradually."

"Will there be a big scar?" Laura gripped Lilly's hand tighter.

"There will be a scar, but I will try to make the incision along the natural curve of the muscle to minimise the appearance. There are very good products now which are quite effective at concealing such things if you feel self-conscious. Most of my patients say that once the scar is fully healed, they never even think about it."

Laura could see the surgeon's face through a buzz of static, she seemed very far away and her voice echoed around the room. Laura heard voices but couldn't understand what they were saying.

Miss Maitlin was on the phone. "Hello, this is Cara Maitlin calling from Paediatrics, I'm in consulting room five. A patient's relative has fainted…yes, thank you." Trish held Laura's head and Lilly was still holding onto her hand.

'Mum, are you ok?'

Miss Maitlin reassured Lilly as she poured a cupful of bottled water. "It's ok, your mum has just fainted, the crash team will be along in a minute and they'll check her over. Don't worry, this sort of thing happens surprisingly often."

A nurse came into the room wheeling an equipment trolley, a second one followed with a tall stand on wheels, a bag full of clear liquid hung from a hook on the top. A third woman also stepped into the room, she had a white lab coat and carried a stethoscope around her neck.

The first nurse knelt down and spoke to Laura who was now sitting up. "Can you tell me your name?"

Trish rushed in with a reply. "Her name is Laura Palmer, she used to faint a lot when she was at school."

The nurse politely ignored Trish but Miss Maitlin pointed out that Laura needed to answer for herself.

Laura's voice was weak as she replied, "Laura, Laura Palmer."

"Have you had anything to eat this morning, Laura?"

"A slice of toast."

"I'm just going to take your blood pressure." The nurse slipped a cuff around Laura's arm and it seemed to automatically inflate. "Do you remember what happened?"

Laura frowned, "I started to feel peculiar and then everything went fuzzy. I fell off the chair." She looked across at Lilly.

The nurse took a note of the reading. "Did you hit your head at all?" She glanced at Miss Maitlin who shook her head.

Laura frowned again, "No, I don't think so."

The woman with the stethoscope took the cup of water proffered by Miss Maitlin and offered it to Laura who took a couple of sips.

"How are you feeling now, do you think you can get up to sit on the chair?" Laura nodded and carefully stood up and eased herself back onto the chair.

After more questions and checks, the crash team were no longer needed, but it was decided that Laura might be better waiting outside with Lilly whilst Trish took down the details of the next steps in Lilly's treatment.

They were all quiet on the way home. Trish drove and Lilly played a game on her phone, Laura just looked out of the window.

When they got home, there was a letter on the doormat, it had been hand delivered there was no stamp on it. Laura opened the letter straight away; she felt the colour drain from her face as she read it.

Trish took hold of Laura's arm. "Sit down, you're looking pale again, what's the matter?" She took the letter as Laura sat down on the second step of the stairs. Trish scowled as she read it.

"Threatening legal action? We'll see about that!" Trish took her mobile out and began to key in a call.

Lilly, who had been in the lounge, poked her head around the door. Trish paused, "It's ok, Lilly, it's absolutely nothing to worry about, Uncle Rob will sort this out for us."

Lilly sat down on the stairs next to her mum. Laura had been biting the edge of her thumb, she was blinking back tears. "It's fine, Lilly, Trish is right; Rob will be able to help."

Trish's call connected. "Rob? Thank goodness you're in the office. We've just got back from the hospital and there was a threatening letter from Dr Sharmer's clinic on the doormat, it has a very nasty tone…Yes, I'm starting to agree with you about him being a quack…Can you phone them and see if you can get any sense from them? Thanks, Rob. So, you think that Martin could help? You've already contacted him? Great, I'll leave you with it then." Trish put her phone away. "Rob is going to phone them up and try to sort it out, his friend Martin is a solicitor and he's asking him for advice, between the two of them we'll get something done."

Laura nodded. "I haven't got that sort of money, Trish, it looks as if I'm tied into the plan, there is no way I can buy out of it. I didn't know that clause was there when I signed the agreement." Trish lay her hands on Laura's shoulders. "Listen to me! This will be sorted out, I promise. You two have enough to worry about at the moment, so leave this all to me and Rob. Any communications you get from the clinic need to be passed on to me, ok?"

"I can't help but worry though, Trish."

Lilly put her arm around her mum. "Uncle Rob will sort it, Mum, I'm sure, he will."

Trish stayed to make lunch for them all and ensure that Laura was calm before leaving.

After lunch, Lilly and Laura watched 'Frozen' on DVD after which Laura went into the room with the computer to spend a few hours doing data entry as part of her home working. Lilly had changed into a loose track suit and was practicing her ballet moves, the 'Step by Step Guide to Ballet' was open on the floor beside her and she was using the back of the sofa as a barre. A knock came at the door. Lilly skipped through to the hall to answer it, as she opened the door, she saw two men standing on the doorstep, the larger of the two had a thick bull neck and his bald head was shiny with sweat. "Is your mother in?" He pushed the door open and both men stepped inside.

Laura was already emerging from the other room. "Can I help you?"

The second man showed her a piece of paper, the cuff of his wax jacket was frayed and greasy.

"We've come to assess the value of assets on the premises, we have reason to believe that you intend to default on your loan."

The first man had invited himself into the lounge and was staring at the television, his heavy boot entrapped a corner of Lilly's book.

Lilly bent down to pick the book up. "Excuse me!" The man was as oblivious as if she had been a fly.

Lilly turned to where the book had been open, there was a picture of a dancer performing a *retiré,* the imprint of a sole made a dark greasy smear across the dancer's leg. Lilly, normally a self-controlled and easy-going child, began to sob.

Laura dashed through to the lounge. "What on earth is going on?"

The first man smirked at his companion. "That's it, turn on the water works, we've seen it all before. You should have thought of the consequences before you got your friends to start throwing their law books at us." Laura was puzzled.

The second man explained. "Our office has been having phone calls telling us that we can't hold you to a contract you signed of your own free will. If you are trying to force us to let you out of the agreement, then we will need you to pay the loan back straight away."

Laura frowned. "The loan is entirely separate from the contract."

"All the same business, actually." He folded his arms and stuck out his belly.

"But one is a health clinic and the other is a pay day loan company."

"All the same business." He spoke the words slowly as if talking to a young child, then he snorted in derision and shook his head at his colleague. "We've seen what we need to see, nothing of much value here anyway." He stomped out into the hall, and followed the other man through the front door. He turned to face Laura once more and spoke in a low voice, "Call off your stroppy friends or you'll be seeing us again very soon."

Chapter Twenty-Two

They walked along in silence for a while, Elaine led, Holly and James followed. The route that Elaine took was the path next to the main road, the path was narrow and the traffic was heavy so they wouldn't have been able to hear each other anyway.

When they got to the edge of the park, Elaine turned to speak. "What's the plan now, guys?"

Holly looked at her watch. "I'm on shift in half an hour, so I'll have to go back to The Carter's."

Elaine nodded. "I was just thinking that I fancied a pint, how about you James?"

"Excellent idea!"

It was only a ten-minute walk to The Carter's from there, as they approached the underpass, they saw two men coming the other way. "Not the sort you want to meet in a dark underpass." James quipped to the others under his breath.

The men were sharing a joke, Elaine heard a snatch of conversation as they passed.

"Scared the crap out of them, they won't cause no more trouble."

"Nice little earner for us though for ten minutes work." The men didn't seem to worry about being overheard.

When they arrived at 'The Carter's', Barry was sitting at the bar talking to Tim, Holly's husband, in hushed tones.

Holly went round to the back of the bar and gave Tim a peck on the cheek. "What's up?" She looked from Tim to Barry and back again.

Tim and Barry gave each other knowing looks and Tim glanced over to the corner table where a bald man with a dark moustache was sitting.

"That man over there." Tim talked quietly.

Holly nodded. "He's been in before, he's a real pain."

"He just had two friends with him, not the sort you'd think he'd normally associate with, so I was keeping an eye on them. Money was exchanging hands and I wanted to make sure there was nothing illegal going on." Tim nodded at Barry. "Baz went to sit at the table next to them with his back to their table so he could listen in."

Barry took up the tale from there. "The two heavies were bragging about a job they had done, paying a visit to a woman who is in debt to our friend over there. The language they were using to describe her was not very choice. From what they said they had deliberately set out to frighten her, and matey there didn't pull them up on it at all." Barry held his pint to his chest. "He's a nasty piece of work, I know him of old. I do a few jobs for him from time to time but he's tried to involve me in some dodgy stuff over the years and I stay well clear of that."

"He's one of the few customers I'm always glad to see the back of." Holly said as she stood the two pints of 'Gold' she had been pulling on a bar towel, she went round to the front of the bar to take them to Elaine and James who were settled on the big square table next to the darts board.

Elaine took a long sip. "Delicious! I'd forgotten how much I've been missing my beer."

James smiled. "It's great to see you looking so much better, Lainy, you're getting your old spark back."

Elaine nodded. "I feel as if a huge worry had been taken off me, thank you for your help with all this, I know I've been a pain recently and I'm sorry for that."

James protested with a mid-gulp gurgle and Holly shooed away an imaginary fly and began to protest but Elaine cut her short. "No really, I literally haven't been myself lately but I'm on the way back now I know it."

James put down his pint and licked his lips. "So, the bookseller will sell your book on then, will you get the payment and he takes a commission or what? How is it going to work?"

Elaine peered into her beer. "I don't want anything for it, I don't care about that but a buyer must be found."

James frowned. "What? That book is worth a packet, isn't it? You want to make sure you don't lose out too much. Do you want me to go back to the shop and clarify the arrangement?"

Elaine shook her head. "The money is the least important aspect in this, honestly, James."

Holly somehow understood. "I know what Elaine means, James, the book has an unearthly power but like fire, that power must be harnessed or it will destroy indiscriminately."

A light came into Elaine's eyes. "That's exactly it, Holly, you understand, don't you? I can't explain it, but I know that there is a way to lay the book to rest, it craves something and only when that craving is satisfied, will it stop wreaking havoc on those who come into contact with it."

"The shop owner seems unaffected." James said pensively. "I still think it might be worth going back to get more information out of him, would you mind if I went to see him, Elaine?"

Before she could answer, their attention was drawn by a commotion at the door. It was Mrs Williams looking for Barry.

"Barry! Can you come and help?" There was panic in her voice. "My hens are all over the road, they got out after the gate was broken."

Barry sprung up straight away followed by Tim who indicated to Holly to take over the bar.

James and Elaine followed leaving their pints on the table.

Mrs Williams lived on the end terrace, Cotswold Street was truncated by the bypass which was up a high bank and edged by fencing which provided a sound barrier. The fencing became post and rail further away from the houses.

Mrs Williams showed them where the hens had got through. Barry told her to go and get the corn bucket and the others climbed over the fence and up the bank, when they got to the top, they saw a huge articulated truck. Elaine feared that they would find the hens flattened on the road. The door of the lorry was open and the driver was a large man with a pony tail and elaborate tattoos up both of his arms which were bare to the shoulder. On the opposite side of the road was a lady in a battered dark green fiesta, the fiesta was stationary and had its hazard warning lights on. The lorry driver tiptoed around a small flock of chickens his muscled arms held in a balletic pose; he made gentle shooing movements with his hands. Barry went to the back of the fiesta to hold up the traffic. James and Tim went the opposite side of the flock, James took his jacket off and held it like a toreador and edged closer to the birds. Meanwhile, Elaine stood at the top of the bank making the noises she had heard Mrs Williams use at feeding time. At first, the lead hen, a portly Buff Orpington, eyed the three men beadily, then slowly, in her own good time, she decided to stroll back to the top of the bank followed by the others. Mrs Williams was at the bottom of the bank shaking the feed can. Their adventure over the hens ran down the bank and followed the sound of the food back into the garden and to safety.

Mrs Williams had been close to tears but now her creased shiny face was radiant as she secured the gate behind her and shouted towards the embankment, "Thank you all, you've been so kind, I thought I'd lost my chickens for good."

James held his hand high to the lorry driver who had swung back into the cab, the driver nodded in return and continued on his way. In moments, the bypass was back to its normal busy flow.

James and Tim slid down the embankment followed a little later by Barry, they joined up with Elaine and Mrs Williams.

Tim put his hand on Mrs Williams shoulder. "Are you ok? You had quite a fright."

Mrs Williams nodded. "I'm fine now, thanks to you all, but yes, I was in a bit of a panic and I didn't know what to do."

"How did they get out?" Elaine was eying the gate.

"I had two men come into the back garden uninvited, they just walked in and they must have seen me at the back there weeding. One of them started poking at my wall with a trowel pulling bits of mortar out, they said that the whole wall needed repointing. I asked them to leave and they wouldn't. They said that they would do the job at a good price but that they needed a three hundred pounds deposit to buy the materials. I told them that I didn't have that sort of cash and that I didn't want them to do the job anyway. They wouldn't take no for an answer, they said there was a post office up the road and I should go and get the money out."

The other four looked at each other In indignant anger. Barry ran his hand over the wall.

"There's nothing wrong with it, they were trying to con you."

"I know." Mrs Williams continued. "They said I could be in big trouble if a bit of brickwork fell off and hurt a child. They even suggested that I might end up in prison for negligence.

That's when I told them to leave or I'd call the police. They still wouldn't leave and I was quite frightened by then, so I went inside and locked the door. I tried to phone the police but I was shaking so much and I couldn't remember the non-emergency number. I heard them leave then. They must have kicked the gate open because when I eventually got up the courage to go out, it was all broken, flat on the pavement. It opens inward see, so forcing it to open the other way broke it clean off its hinges."

"We should tell the police; do you think you could describe the men?" James took out his mobile.

Mrs Williams drew James and Elaine to the side. "I don't want to involve the police, they probably wouldn't do anything and anyway," she drew them further away, "they went into The Carter's afterwards, I saw them through the bedroom window. They left after about half an hour but I don't want it to reflect badly on Holly and Tim."

Tim was examining the gate, he called over to them. "It's wrecked; don't worry, I'll soon fix you up with a new one."

"That's kind." Mrs Williams hesitated.

Elaine could see she was uncertain. "What's up?"

Mrs Williams took a paper tissue from up her sleeve and blew her nose, her China blue eyes were rimmed pink. "Jack made it when we were first married."

Barry saw the problem immediately, he stood next to Tim and looked down at the splintered wood which had been tied up with bailing twine. The brace and stile had rotted through and the hinge side was just a mass of shards, three of the rails were broken in two, this had clearly taken more than one boot kick to accomplish. "A fine gate like this should be restored not replaced." Barry's voice was light as if it would be an easy task. "I can do that; we might need a temporary replacement while it's in my workshop though."

Tim nodded. "I'll sort that out." He turned to the other three. "Your pints will be getting warm, you get back, I'll secure this as best I can for the minute and then I'll bring a pallet over from the brewery to swap with it for a while."

Mrs Williams rooted in her apron pocket and brought out a small purse. Taking a twenty pound note out she handed it to Tim. "Please, put this behind the bar for you all to have a round on me for your trouble."

Tim folded it back into her hand. "I wouldn't hear of it and neither would the others." Elaine and Barry both nodded in agreement.

"After all you've done for me," Elaine protested, "I'm only too glad to be a tiny bit of help to you."

When they got back to The Carter's, Holly had covered the beers up with mats. Tim disappeared round the back to sort out a pallet, Barry downed his pint and followed.

Elaine was very quiet; James could tell she was affected by what has happened to her neighbour, he attempted to change the subject. "So, do you feel better now we've got your book sorted out?"

Elaine was pensive. "It's not quite sorted out yet. I still need to be involved, but I know where it has to go. It's just a case of getting it there." James looked puzzled.

Elaine smiled. "I'm sorry, I'm talking in riddles, aren't I?"

"It's probably me being thick."

Elaine shook her head. "You're going to think I'm mad if I tell you what I'm thinking."

James sat forward in the seat. "Try me."

"Well, I think the men who upset Mrs Williams are the same ones who were with that man in the corner."

"That's not mad, I was thinking that myself." James took another sip of beer.

"I think they need teaching a lesson." Elaine lay her hand flat on the table.

James sprung back in his chair and held up his hands like a shield. "Woah now! I don't think we should go there."

Elaine clarified. "No, I don't mean we should get the heavies in."

"That's good because I don't happen to have a whole bunch of bruisers to call upon!" Elaine laughed. "Anyway, this is the bit where you are going to phone the men in white coats."

"Go on." James sat forward again.

Elaine stared at him. "I think the book has the power to punish them."

James didn't react at first, he took a slow draught of beer and then regarded Elaine. "Are you saying that we should go back and retrieve it from the shop?"

Elaine shook her head. "That's not it, what I was going to say is that I want them to end up with the book somehow."

They talked for some time about how this might be accomplished, they both agreed that the best way would be to get them to believe that the book was worth a lot of money. James felt that the men's fondness for confidence trickery might be a way to draw them in. James showed no sign of scepticism about Elaine's idea. When Holly came over for a chat as she was collecting glasses, she took to the idea straight away, it was as if she and Elaine had a secret understanding which needed no verbal expression.

It was Holly's idea to get Barry involved, although he had no liking of the men, he had some association in that he had done odd jobs for their friend. It would be easy for Barry to get talking to them socially. James also suggested that Sylvia might be a useful accomplice, with her blond hair and winning smile, she would have the ability to charm the louts and have them rolling over like pit bull puppies.

Elaine was hesitant about drawing Sylvia into the plan. "I wouldn't want to risk putting her in any danger."

Holly laughed. "She's made of tougher stuff than you think! But I agree, we'll have to be careful and make sure they don't think that she's fair game." Elaine shuddered at the thought.

Chapter Twenty-Three

"The operation should only take an hour or so but Lilly will stay in recovery for a while before she comes back to the ward." The nurse waited for a response from Laura.

Recovery, the word was a comforting one Laura thought, as she tried to form a pattern of events in her mind.

The nurse continued. "You needn't worry, it will be a straightforward operation, I know the waiting is difficult, but Miss Maitlin is very thorough and she is very optimistic of an excellent outcome."

Optimistic, the word jarred, it made Laura think of her colleagues who spend far too much of their hard-earned money on lottery tickets.

"Do you have anything you want to ask me?" The nurse's kind brown eyes were fixed on Laura; Laura could see herself reflected in their depths.

"When will we know if it has spread?" A scene from a film came into Laura's mind where scores of nameless insects suddenly appear swarming in different directions.

The nurse took Laura's hand. "There's absolutely no reason to think that it has, going by the MRI results, Miss Maitlin is quite confident of that. The tumour will go to histology, it will take about a week and then we will know if it is completely excised." The nurse squeezed Laura's hand. "It will be! The sarcoma will be characterised with immunohistochemistry; that is, investigated to see exactly what type we are dealing with. If molecular biology is needed, then we'll have to wait a bit longer."

"Why would it need the biology?" Laura felt a panic rising again.

The nurse rubbed her thumbs across the tops of Laura's hands. "Don't worry, it's all about seeing exactly what type of growth it is, so we know exactly what treatment, if any, we need to use."

Lilly had been given her pre-med, she lay on the trolley smiling happily. It was the first time Laura had seen her so relaxed since the men had come barging into their home. Their intrusion had a profound effect on Lilly, where she had seemed not to be worried about her leg before, now she never stopped fretting about it.

"You mustn't worry about me, Mum, go and get yourself one of those double choc muffins from the Starlight restaurant while you're waiting."

The Starlight restaurant was Lilly's favourite place in the hospital, open for both staff and patients. It was on the seventh floor of the main section of the hospital, there were floor to ceiling windows on two sides and you could see for miles over the city and beyond to the rolling downs. There was a main section where you could get full meals or perhaps just salad or soup but there was also a small café section which specialised in hot drinks and snacks.

Laura stroked Lilly's forehead. "You are such a sweetie, here you are looking after me when it's you that's lying on a hospital trolley."

"I'm not scared, Mum; I know Cara will look after me." Miss Maitlin was always Cara to her patients.

Laura watched Lilly being wheeled into theatres, she wasn't allowed beyond the automatic double doors leading to the theatre reception area. There was a shiny leather couch just outside the entrance, she sat there and waited.

"Would you like me to get a plaster for that?" The smiling brown-eyed nurse was bending over Laura, her ample figure nipped in by a belt giving the impression of a comfy mattress.

Laura looked up in puzzlement, she followed the nurse's gaze to her own fingers, she had bitten her nails until they bled, and crimson drips were forming at the tips. Laura could do nothing but stare at them. The nurse fetched a small envelope and peeled back two sides to reveal a snow-white pad. Pressing it to Laura's fingertips, she squeezed tight for a minute or two. Carefully peeling back the dressing, she checked to see if the bleeding had stopped, then she took out a plaster and skilfully applied it to Laura's finger, she repeated this on two more and then satisfied with the result she sat down next to Laura.

"Lilly is going to be at least an hour, I know the waiting is awful, why don't you go and grab a coffee?"

Laura didn't want to leave her vigil but something made her get up, maybe it was Lilly's words or perhaps the nurse's smile, she decided she would just go there for a half an hour at the most, at least she would be able to honestly tell Lilly that she had gone that way.

The restaurant was quite busy, there were no tables completely free so Laura went to a four-seater with just one lady occupying it. "Is there anyone sitting here?"

"No, please sit down." The woman's golden hair shone like a silk curtain in the sunlight as she turned back to look at the view.

Laura sipped her coffee and stared down at the muffin, she had no idea why she had bought it, and there was no way she could eat in the circumstances.

"Looks delicious, I should have got myself one." The blonde lady had turned her attention to Laura's muffin.

"Would you like it? I haven't touched it." Laura pushed the plate towards her neighbour.

The woman protested, mortified that she had caused an embarrassment, but in the end; the muffin was exchanged with the recipient who insisting on paying for it. Laura was secretly relieved, she had very little spare cash for anything at the moment and she had regretted the impulse buying of a cake she knew she couldn't possibly eat.

Laura explained her promise to Lilly. "I more or less promised my daughter that I would come here once she had gone into theatre. She loves it here, it's a magical place to her."

The woman, who introduced herself as Sylvia, totally understood that Laura's appetite had left her, she cut a small slice of the muffin and pushed it towards Laura.

"Just take one mouthful and then you will be able to tell your daughter truthfully that you had some muffin with your coffee."

Laura dutifully obeyed although even that small mouthful was hard for her to swallow.

"Are you visiting someone in hospital?" Laura dabbed at her mouth with a napkin, her hands shook as she did so.

Sylvia's golden curtain swung gently. "No, I'm with a friend who has come in for a follow up scan, she had a nasty fall six weeks ago and it's taken her a while to get over it, she's on the mend now though. I'm just here for moral support."

Laura pushed her chair back. "Your friend is lucky to have you watching out for her. It's been lovely talking to you, I must go back now."

Sylvia got up too. "Listen, why don't I come with you to keep you company?"

Laura hesitated. "But your friend."

"No problem, she's going to text me when she's out, so I can wait for her anywhere."

As they headed out of the café, Sylvia came to an abrupt halt next to one of the tables. "Tessa! What a coincidence to see you here."

An older lady smiled back at her. "I'm here once or twice a week volunteering." She nodded to Laura who was edging away. "It's a difficult time for you, my dear, but all will be well in the end."

Laura felt repulsed by the woman's kind words and walked away without replying. Sylvia followed her after a few brief words with the kindly Tessa. Catching up with Laura, she apologised. "Tessa means well, I hope she didn't upset you."

Laura tried to stop the words coming out but she was powerless to control her own tongue. "How can she possibly know my situation? She should mind her own business."

Sylvia didn't reply but laid a gentle hand on Laura's arm as they navigated the hospital corridors.

Once they reached the corridor outside of theatres, the two of them sat down on the leather sofa and talked. Laura's mind was not on the conversation but she was glad of the soothing effect Sylvia's presence had on her and the anger she had felt just moments before dissipated. Sylvia told Laura about her sick friend's uncharacteristic behaviour and how she had been worried about her. Laura told Sylvia about Lilly's leg and how brave she had been until the incident with the men. Sometimes friendships can be forged in the blink of an eye and this was such an occasion. When Sylvia received her friend's text and had to go to meet her, she felt a bond had grown between Laura and herself, she couldn't bear never to know how Lilly's operation went.

"Are you on Facebook?" Laura dabbed at her phone.

Laura nodded. "Laura Palmer."

"I'll send you a friend request, don't worry if you don't want to accept, you don't know me from Eve, but I really want to know how your daughter gets on. Sorry I have to go and meet Elaine; I wish I could stay with you longer."

Laura smiled. "Thanks for sitting with me it was a big help. Good luck with your friend." She watched her new acquaintance disappear along the corridor, flaxen mane swinging with every step. She felt waxiness on her lips, Laura realised she was chewing on the plasters which the nurse had put on for her. Had

Lilly made it to recovery yet? Laura imagined a lifeboat full of rescued travellers pulling into safe harbour, somewhere along Cornwall's rocky coast perhaps. Laura and Lilly had been to St Ives every year from when Lilly was seven. They stayed in a cottage owned by a family Laura used to clean for before she got the job in the supermarket. The owners only charged Laura a token rent for the week, and in return, Laura always gave the cottage a good clean, this included washing all the curtains and scrubbing out the kitchen cupboards. They were both quite well known in the village, and even from the age of seven, it was safe for Lilly to go down to the jetty to watch the fishermen tending to their lobster pots whilst Laura was busy. Most of the time was spent together though, walking along the beach or up across the green. The highlight of the week was to treat themselves to a pasty each, they would spend all week deciding which bakery to go to. Laura longed to be there now, with not a care in the world, away from hospital appointments and money worries.

The theatre doors swung open and the smiling nurse came padding out. "The operation went very well; Lilly is just having a slice of toast and she'll be back on the ward very soon." Laura stared silently at the nurse.

"Do you know the first thing she asked?" Laura's face was blank.

"How's my mum? That's the first thing she asked me." The nurse smiled so broadly that her face creased up and her rounded cheeks almost made her eyes disappear until only the sparkle remained.

Laura felt something happen to her lower lip, it was as if it no longer belonged to her face as the muscles pulled it this way and that. A tidal wave rose in her chest and she began to sob.

The nurse held Laura tight and let her continue, she knew better than to tell her not to cry. By degrees, the sobbing got less, as Laura drew away from the nurse, a long string of mucus remained attached to her shoulder. Laura fumbled for a handkerchief and dried her face, the nurse laughed.

By the time Laura had been to the ladies' toilet and rinsed her face, Lilly had returned to the ward and was already half sitting up in bed playing with the television remote. The walls around the ward were painted with stylised forest scenes in vibrant blues, greens and purples. The bed screens were thin wooden panels on wheels which were covered with a riot of pictures, Minions seemed to predominate but there were also plenty of amusing cats, puppies and ponies with implausibly long manes and tails.

Laura was amazed to see how alert Lilly was, she had expected her child to be surrounded by a mass of tubes. Instead, Lilly had a single intravenous line attached to a long orange pole which sprouted from a bright yellow hub. Radiating from the hub were five curved legs each of which had a comical looking green and red wheel at the end.

Lilly grinned up at her mum. "The nurse said I might go home tomorrow."

Laura bit her lower lip and stroked Lilly's forehead. "I don't think so, poppet, I think you must have got confused, maybe you were still woozy from the anaesthetic?"

"No, that's what she said." Lilly's attention was on the television screen.

"Don't get your hopes up, sweetheart, it may take a while." Laura was anxious that there were no false expectations.

"Did you go for a muffin while you were waiting?" Lilly flicked a glance at her mum.

"I did!" Laura said truthfully.

Lilly focused her attention on Laura's face. "Really? Did you actually eat it?"

Laura looked sheepish. "Well, actually I shared it, but the bit I had was delicious."

Lilly looked ready for a cross examination but she was interrupted by a movement to the left.

Miss Maitlin approached Lilly's bed; she was still in scrubs. "How are you feeling, Lilly?"

Lilly switched the television off. "I feel great, not sore at all!"

Miss Maitlin smiled. "Good, just to warn you though, there will be some discomfort once the painkillers wear off." She looked towards Laura. "We'll send you home with a supply of oral painkillers which she should take at least for the first few days."

"How long will it be before she can come home?"

Miss Maitlin turned back to Lilly. "As soon as she has seen the physio in the morning."

Laura stared open mouthed. "Tomorrow?"

"Yes, there will be follow up clinics of course and she will have to stay off school for a couple of weeks. There is no reason why she can't do the exercises that physiotherapy give her at home." She patted Lilly's hand. "She's a bright girl, I've every confidence that between the two of you, our instructions will be followed to the letter."

Laura was puzzled. "But the treatment?"

A light of understanding came into Miss Maitlin's eyes. "Once we have the results from the lab, we will know for sure but for the moment, we will watch and wait. I very much doubt if Lilly will have any further trouble, the tumour was fully encapsulated and we excised it completely." Lilly saw Laura's expression of puzzlement. "So, it's all out and won't come back?"

Miss Maitlin laughed. "That is about the sum of it, Lilly. You will have to have six monthly checks for quite an extended period but apart from that, you can get on with your life and try not to worry."

After the doctor had gone, Lilly asked Laura if she minded if she turned the television back on. They sat watching in companionable silence. There was an interview with a professional dancer. "I bet Cara could have been a dancer if she hadn't been a doctor." Lilly nodded at the screen.

Laura had to smile. "She has got very good deportment, hasn't she?"

Lilly's eyes still didn't leave the screen. "I bet she works out."

"I wouldn't be surprised although she must have a very busy life, I wonder if she has time." Laura stole a surreptitious glance at Lilly's dressing.

Lilly turned to her mum. "I can't wait to get back to my ballet classes."

Laura caught her breath. "Now, don't get your hopes up, we don't know what you will and won't be able to do after the operation. We have to take it one step at a time." She was anxious to avoid disappointment for Lilly.

"Oh, Mum, you are such a fuss pot, you heard what Cara said, I can go back to school in a couple of weeks. If I'm ok to go to school, then I'm surely alright to go to ballet."

"It's different, love." Laura's voice started to waiver. They both let the subject drop.

In the event, Lilly was right. The physiotherapist gave them detailed instructions about the exercises that Lilly needed to do, she also gave an information pack for Laura to give to the school and any exercise class instructors, including ballet. The information pack detailed which movements should be avoided and for how long.

Chapter Twenty-Four

Sylvia was all for the plan that Elaine and Holly had in mind, she was keen on a bit of adventure, James was less keen about her getting involved and insisted that he or Barry should always be close at hand during any interactions with the two men.

Sylvia didn't really understand why Elaine and Holly wanted them to get the book, she knew that the thing had caused Elaine a lot of trouble, but the two thugs didn't seem the literary types, and she wondered what the attraction would be for them. When Elaine pointed out that the book was a valuable one, Sylvia conceded that they probably would be keen to sell it on the black market but she still didn't really understand why Elaine would want them to profit from it.

James, Sylvia and Elaine discussed the matter over lunch in the tea room. Sylvia, as usual, thumbed her phone as she picked at a tuna salad. "I'd hate to think of them ending up on top financially. I know you're not bothered about getting the money for it, you just want it gone, but I can just imagine them gloating over it afterwards."

Elaine spun her noodles on a fork. "The book has the power to bring them down, I know it has."

Sylvia looked up from her phone. "I know you feel it's brought you bad luck but those two oafs are so thick skinned, it would probably make no difference to them."

"It feels right to try." Elaine sounded apologetic. "I know it sounds strange but I feel as if I'm being guided."

James peeled the top off a yoghurt and stirred it with a spoon. He could see that Elaine was getting embarrassed and wanted to change the subject. "How did your appointment go yesterday, Elaine, are they happy with your progress?"

Elaine smiled. "They were very pleased, so much so that they've signed me off now. I don't have to go back for any more checks. They said there had been a vast improvement compared to last time."

"That's brilliant." James glanced from Elaine to Sylvia.

"It is good news, isn't it?" Sylvia continued to scroll on her phone. "Great! Laura has accepted my friend request, now I can PM her and find out how her daughter is."

James and Elaine looked at each other in puzzlement and then back at Sylvia.

"Oh, she's someone who I met when I was waiting for you in the hospital." Sylvia addressed Elaine. "She was waiting for her daughter to come out of an operation, and the poor thing was so worried. It sounded as if she had been through a bad time lately too."

James laughed. "You make a friend wherever you go, don't you? How many Facebook friends have you got now?"

"I can't help it; I start chatting to people and get interested in their stories." Sylvia tapped a message into her phone. "This lady seemed as if she needed support, she said her sister normally came with her to the hospital but she had been called away on an emergency involving their mother."

"You've got a kind face, that's why people open up to you." James scraped the yoghourt from the bottom of the carton.

Sylvia put her phone down and folded her hands in her lap. "Right then, what's the plan with those two men?"

James looked at Elaine.

Elaine shrugged. "I don't think we have a plan but I thought we could somehow engineer to have them overhear a conversation about a valuable book we knew was available for far less than it was worth, maybe if you could get into conversation with them Sylvia and let them think they were getting information out of you?"

James took a swig of water. "It's all a bit vague though, how do we get them to overhear this conversation? We don't know where they will be, I haven't seen them in 'The Carter's' before."

"I've seen their friend a couple of times though and by what Holly said, he's a regular visitor." Elaine bit her lip.

"Perhaps, we could get to them through him then?" Sylvia offered. "Would Holly be able to tell us when the best time would be to catch him at the pub?"

Elaine nodded. "I'll ask her. I think he's often there on Friday nights, I know his car and I've seen it parked quite often when I come home."

"We will have to get the shopkeeper involved in this; I went to see him on Monday but he wasn't very forthcoming; he said he would only deal with Elaine." James lent across and threw his empty yogurt pot in the bin.

Sylvia nodded. "I suppose that's only right as she is the owner, after all he doesn't know you, and you could be trying a scam yourself."

Trish came into the tea room to put on the kettle, she eyed the others and slammed her mug on the work surface.

"Time to get back to work," chirped Sylvia flicking a glance at the clock.

As they returned to their desks James spoke under his breath. "Trish is in a particularly bad mood today."

Sylvia answered quietly. "I think she has family problems."

Elaine nodded. "Her niece has been in hospital." Elaine patted her empty pocket. "I've left my phone on the table in there, I'll just go back and get it."

As Elaine went back into the tea room, she realised that she hadn't washed her coffee mug either. Trish was in conversation on her phone. Elaine smiled as she reached across to retrieve her things. Trish was too deep in conversation to acknowledge her.

"I really wanted to be with Laura when Lilly was having her operation, I feel it was very unfair of you to not to let me know that your 'emergency' was a false alarm..."

"Yes, of course you can call on me any time you need me, it's just that you didn't really need me, did you? You were perfectly fine, but Laura and Lilly did need me..."

"Mother, I've asked you before not to call her that, she is my sister and whatever your relationship is with her, I want to stay in touch with her and be there for her..."

"Yes, of course, I'm there for you, Mother, you know that, please, calm down, have you taken your inhaler this morning?"

"Of course, I care, please don't upset yourself, Mother...hello?" Trish looked at the phone in frustration and slammed it on the table.

Elaine dried her mug and put it carefully in the cupboard, she glanced at Trish and wondered whether to say anything, but Trish was deep in thought, so Elaine just quietly left the room and went back to her desk.

Moments later Trish came bustling through the office. "I have to take half a day annual leave, sorry it's short notice, can you cover the phones, Sylvia?"

Sylvia looked up in astonishment. "Of course, Trish, is everything alright?"

Trish was half way out of the door. "Probably, I'm not sure." She was gone before she could elaborate.

The rest of the afternoon passed in a relaxed atmosphere. Although everyone was doing their work, there was time in between to make pleasant conversation. James and Elaine decided that it would be ok to leave work an hour early and head for the bookshop before it closed, they would both make the time up later. They drove separately and parked in Cotswold Street where Elaine left her car and transferred to James's car. He drove to the town centre and parked in the main car park, they walked to the shop from there.

The shopkeeper was not in his usual place behind the counter but was at the far end of a row of bookshelves facing the arched window. The sun streamed through the window and illuminated long wavy hair like a halo. He turned around quickly as they entered the shop, he seemed taken aback and almost agitated by their presence.

James took the initiative. "Hi, we've come to clarify the arrangements for the book we brought in the other day." His voice was assertive to the point of stridency.

The shopkeeper had regained his composure, he regarded James for a moment, his dark blue eyes full of distain, and he turned to Elaine. "I have already told your friend that I will only deal with you regarding this matter."

Elaine smiled apologetically at James and then addressed the shopkeeper. "Of course, I understand you want to do things properly." She turned to James. "Do you mind?"

James stared at her for a moment and then realised she wanted to speak privately. "Of course, I'll go and browse."

Elaine waited for the shopkeeper to speak, it was almost as if he didn't need to say anything, his gaze reminded her of the night sky, there was such a depth to his expression.

"You have a plan." His quiet utterance was more a statement of fact than a question.

Elaine faltered. "It's the start of a plan but there are a lot of details to fill in."

A slight smile crossed his face like a passing cloud. "The details will look after themselves, all you need to do is to identify the correct recipient."

"I think, I have." Elaine paused. "Well, there are two of them actually."

The shopkeeper frowned. "There can be only one."

"What?" Elaine was confused.

"Let me show you." He led her to his desk and opened the top drawer from which he took out a box file. Inside there was a document written in Gothic script on what looked like velum. Elaine tried to read the script but apart from the fact that text was very faint, it seemed to be written in Latin. She looked up in puzzlement.

The shopkeeper stared back at her. "Aren't you going to read it?"

Elaine shook her head. "I don't read Latin, I'm afraid." She felt irrationally sheepish.

He raised his eyebrows. James looked across from the other side of the shop. The shopkeeper glared back.

"It talks about the fifth generation."

Elaine was clearly meant to understand this but she was still perplexed.

The shopkeeper rubbed a hand over his bushy eyebrows and talked slowly as if to a small child. "After the tenth generation, the last decedent will be found and the final retribution will be wrought."

"Where did this come from?" Elaine pointed at the document.

"It came from a reliable source." He seemed annoyed at the question. "But you talk of two where there can only be one, are you sure you have got it right?"

Elaine shook her head. "No, I'm not sure at all, I'm only going by gut instinct but I felt led in that direction."

"Instinct is a good place to start." He hesitated. "No doubt, the correct course will become clear."

Elaine looked thoughtful. "I'm wondering how we will bring the book and the men together. Greed will make them curious, of course, but how will we guide them to it without them becoming suspicious?"

"Have no fear, the book will draw them to itself." The bookseller glanced at James, who was examining a bookshelf on the far side of the shop. "Your friend, does he know the entities we are dealing with?"

Elaine looked across at James. "I haven't spoken to him about it in detail, but he's sympathetic and I trust him."

The shopkeeper pursed his lips. "Your other friend, the woman, she was here with you last week."

Elaine nodded. "Holly?"

"She seems to have insight; I think she could be instrumental in fulfilling our purpose."

"Holly has a lot of deep wisdom; she was far more aware of the power of the book than I was."

"We must take advantage of that; will she be willing to help?" He raised his bushy eyebrows.

Elaine smiled. "I'm sure, she will."

"Good."

Elaine became thoughtful again. "How will you know who the men are, we don't want the book to get into the wrong hands?"

"It will be obvious to me, and don't worry, it can remain obscure for long periods until the time is right, the book can hide itself." The bookseller paused when he noticed that James had come within earshot.

James gave an embarrassed smile and turned away again.

"Your friend is a sceptic."

Elaine bit her lip. "He's a journalist, so he has to be up to a point, but he had an open mind and he won't make any difficulties, I'm sure."

"I wish I could share your faith in him, he troubles me." He turned back to her. "All you need to do is get the men into the shop, I will know how to transfer the book into their ownership." The bookseller was unwilling to go into more detail in James's presence, so the conversation came to an end. It wasn't until they were outside of the shop that Elaine was able to tell him what had been said. The bookseller was right, James hinted that he was uneasy about the arrangements but that he understood that it was entirely Elaine's business what she did with her own property.

The following Friday, Sylvia and Elaine arranged to meet in The Carter's; as usual, Barry was around. Barry had been helping Tim out in the brewery and was enjoying a pint afterwards, he sat on a high stool at the bar chatting to Holly. Barry knew about the arrangements they were trying to pull off, so he was primed not to have it out with the two men about the broken gate. In any case, no one had seen the men since.

Holly was certain they would be in tonight through and luckily, although Holly insisted that it was more than luck, they did turn up. They sat at the corner table by the door and the shorter of the two went to the bar to order a couple of lagers. Holly had texted Elaine to tell her when the men arrived, she and Sylvia were waiting for the cue at Elaine's house across the road.

The men had hardly started on their drinks before Elaine and Sylvia breezed in and ordered a bottle of wine and two glasses. Holly served them politely and turned down the background music.

Sylvia stood at the bar and perused the empty tables. "Let's sit over there, that's a cosy corner." She pointed at a table right next to the two men.

As Sylvia sat down, she flashed a brief charming smile at taller of the two men, he looked astonished but didn't smile back.

Elaine and Sylvia chatted about the events of the day to each other. Elaine told her about the robin that she had found on the doormat and how she wished that her cat wouldn't bring hunting spoils home like that. In reality, Iris had never caught anything faster than a catnip mouse. They chatted about work and made it obvious that they worked in a large publishing house, they didn't think that simply mentioning 'Kessler and Drake' alone would be enough to spark the interest of the men, although the name would chime with anyone who was keen on books.

Sylvia leant across the table towards Elaine and spoke in a careful stage whisper. "Do you remember the book collector I was telling you about?"

Elaine nodded. "Oh, yes, the American who's got more money than he knows what to do with?"

"That's the one." Sylvia took something out of her handbag and slid it across the table to her. "That's his card. He's interested in a particular book and I know he'll pay tens of thousands for it."

Elaine flipped the card between her fingers. "Do you know where the book might be found?"

"That's just it! I've seen it in the bookshop in Market Street, you know, the one with the car manuals in the window?"

Elaine shook her head. "I'm not sure if I've ever been in there."

"To be honest, I don't think the shopkeeper knows what he's got." Sylvia continued. "He would have sold it to me for a few pounds there and then but I didn't have any money on me and he doesn't take credit cards."

Elaine took a long sip of wine. "You need to get back there tomorrow then and snap it up."

"Should do but the thing is, he will remember me, and if he thinks I'm keen to buy, he could realise there's value in it and up the price."

Elaine licked the corner of her mouth. "I see what you mean. Do you want me to go in and buy it?"

Sylvia took a pen out of her bag. "Would you?" She took the card back off Elaine and wrote on it. "I'll write the details on here, the title is 'Feral Justice'. The shop isn't far off the bypass." Elaine took back the card, studied it for a while, and then put it down on the table. "I'll go after lunch tomorrow; I'd go before but I have to take the car for servicing in the morning."

"No problem, I can't imagine that a few hours would make any difference." Sylvia sipped her wine.

Elaine topped up both their glasses. "It's been a long week, it's good to relax, isn't it?"

"It so is!" Sylvia agreed, she flashed a brilliant smile at the table next to them.

Chapter Twenty-Five

Laura had expected Lilly to have to stay in bed for weeks after the operation, so she made Lilly's bedroom into a comfortable little den. Trish bought a small flat screen television and Rob had fixed it to the wall opposite Lilly's bed, they had also bought a small sofa futon which just fitted nicely into a corner next to the bedroom door although it was a bit tight when extended. Lilly loved the bright pink sofa, it matched the colour of her bedroom walls, and the whole look was finished off by two large butterfly cushions in the same shade, these had been given to them by one of Laura's colleagues.

Everybody had been really kind when they heard about Lilly's operation. Laura had not admitted to anyone how she had been getting into debt, and she never asked for help but the small kindnesses which people had shown had been a big support. The one source of help which would have been automatic in other families was not forthcoming however. Laura's parents were stony silent even though Trish has told them of the seriousness of Lilly's condition. Laura unfortunately overheard Trish telling Rob how her mother had even alluded to the possibility that the predicament was brought on by Lilly having been born 'out of wedlock'. Although this was slightly upsetting to her, Laura was not surprised by the reaction, it was no less than she had come to expect over the years since Lilly's conception. Trish on the other hand had been a pillar of support, and the normal 'big sister' bossiness had not been evident of late. Laura and Trish's relationship had become closer than it had ever been. Trish had arranged to take time off work to be with Lilly once Laura herself had to return to work.

For the moment, Laura had been able to take compassionate leave but she couldn't afford to do that for long.

As it turned out, Lilly was not confined to bed after the operation, in fact the opposite was the case, and she had been told to keep mobile to help the healing process. The bedroom refurbishment didn't go to waste though as Lilly spent every possible moment in her 'den' and was delighted to have somewhere private to take her friends when they visited. There were plenty of school friends popping by to see how she was getting on, they kept her in the picture regarding vital news from school such as Miss McNamara's latest hideous outfit and the like.

Laura had visitors too, several of her colleagues had brought meals that they had prepared to save Laura cooking, and there was a steady and plentiful cake supply.

Laura was expecting a new visitor this morning, the lady she had met in the hospital had kept in touch via Facebook, she was going to pop by to bring a newly published ballet book which she had acquired through her work, the book was not yet out in the shops and Lilly was very excited about it. Laura didn't like to tell the friend that her sister Trish also worked in publishing and could also possibly have sourced the book. Upon reflection, Laura realised that this was not the sort of thing that Trish would think to do anyway.

As it happened, Trish and Rob were also visiting when Laura's Facebook friend was due, Trish had brought a batch of freezer meals which she had prepared herself so that Laura wouldn't have to worry about shopping and cooking for a while. The meal packages had ceased to arrive since Laura had tried to withdraw from Dr Sharmer's scheme, and there had been multiple letters asking for more money for what they termed an exit fee.

Trish gathered her bags together. "Come on, Rob, we should leave before Laura's friend arrives, we need to get back anyway."

"There's no need really." Despite her words Laura was relieved, there has been many occasions when she had lost friends due to Trish's abruptness.

Trish and Rob were just going out of the front door when Trish was stopped in her tracks.

"Sylvia, what are you doing here?"

Laura was puzzled. "Do you two know each other then?"

Sylvia laughed out loud. "We've worked together for years! Who would have thought it? Goodness, it's a good job I'm not pretending to be off sick, isn't it?"

Trish didn't laugh but she wasn't hostile, she stepped back to let Sylvia in and then hovered in the doorway as if uncertain how to proceed. Rob diffused the situation by asking if Laura would like him to make a hot drink for her guest, this led to an impromptu afternoon tea fuelled by the abundant supply of cakes which had been brought by other visitors. As soon as Sylvia met Lilly, there was an instant rapport. "You look so much like a friend of mine." she gasped. Sylvia had brought a big box of Belgian chocolates, somehow, she had guessed right that they were Lilly's favourite, and they all had a couple each at Lilly's insistence.

Sylvia had objected. "They are for you and your mum; you don't want to be wasting them on me!"

Lilly shoved the box across at Sylvia and the others. "I'll be as big as an elephant if I eat them all myself, I'd never dance again!"

An awkward silence followed but Lilly didn't appear to notice, she was too busy studying the card from the chocolate box. "What are these things called?" She waved the little card in the air.

The others started to answer but realised they couldn't.

Laura laughed. "Don't worry, Lilly's a master of difficult questions, are they called menus?"

Rob interjected. "I don't think so, I think they are called key cards but I'm not certain."

This satisfied Lilly who wafted it in front of her nose. "Even the card smells delicious!"

Sylvia smiled. "I'm glad you like them, Lilly. It's really nice to meet you and to see how well you are doing."

Rob munched on a praline. "How do you two know each other again?" He looked from Laura to Sylvia and back again.

Laura licked her fingers. "We met in the hospital in the Starlight Café. We just got talking. Sylvia contacted me on Facebook." She looked towards Sylvia. "I confided in her about my problems with the private clinic."

Sylvia nodded. "I don't like the sound of it. They seem to be preying on people at a time when they are vulnerable."

Rob reached across and took another chocolate. "I agree with you, Sylvia. We went along with the healthy eating plan at the time because we thought we were helping Laura. Looking back on it we ought to have known better. The scheme is very expensive for what you actually get." Trish glanced at Lilly who seemed unconcerned. "We didn't realise at the time how much Laura was paying for the treatment plan either, it was only when I quizzed her about the second job that it all came out."

Sylvia frowned. "Will you be able to get any of your money back, Laura?"

Rob spoke for her. "I've been looking into it and unfortunately, she paid up front for a six-month course. I have been making headway with the exit fee though. Laura signed the contract which did mention there would be a financial penalty for withdrawing from the scheme but the clinic would have to take legal proceedings to reclaim the money should we refuse to pay. I do have some leverage, in that they put themselves in the wrong by sending the two men around to threaten Laura, and they know it, a solicitor's letter was enough to quieten them down."

Lilly caught hold of her mother's arm. "Those men won't come back will they, Mum? I didn't like them being here."

Laura hugged her daughter. "Don't worry, they won't be bothering us again; Uncle Rob is making sure of that."

Lilly scowled. "I bet the Velcro was for a gun."

Laura leaned back and studied her daughter's face. "Velcro?"

Lilly nodded. "Yes, he had it on his shoulders, I bet it was to keep a gun in place, he looked like the sort of man who would go around shooting birds." Laura looked nonplussed.

Lilly continued. "The man who stood on my book, he had Velcro on the shoulders of his jacket." A slow comprehension unclouded Laura's face. "He was a nasty piece of work, he seemed to enjoy frightening us but don't worry, neither of them will be back, they won't upset us anymore."

Sylvia looked puzzled. "Who were the men? Did they threaten you?"

Laura stroked Lilly's head. "They came because I cancelled the treatment at the clinic. They said they were looking for assets because they thought I'd default on the loan."

"It was my fault." Rob explained, "Perhaps, I went in too heavy handed with the solicitor's letter."

"They said that they'd be back." Lilly looked fearful again.

Trish took charge of the situation. "Lilly, we'll make sure that those men get a very clear message that if they bother you again, then there will be serious consequences for them."

Sylvia tried to make sense of what she had been told. "You took out a loan?"

Laura looked embarrassed. "Just a hundred pounds to top up the savings I had, I thought it would save me money, there was a time limit on the introductory offer. The trouble is, with the interest, I now owe five hundred."

Trish scowled. "I wish you'd approached us for help on that, Laura, those pay day loans are invidious."

Rob put a hand on Trish's knee. "Come on, now, you know it's not always that easy, love."

Sylvia took out her bag. "You have to get rid of that loan as soon as possible, Laura, it's just going to get worse otherwise. Let me transfer the amount to your account and you can pay me back as and when with no interest of course."

Trish looked ruffled. "We can sort out family problems ourselves, thank you, Sylvia, there's no need for you to play the great bounty queen."

Rob stood up. "It's a very kind offer, Sylvia, thank you." He glanced at Trish with a certain fierceness. "Trish's family are rather proud but I'm sure she didn't mean to sound ungrateful." His gaze remained on Trish as he emphasised the words.

Sylvia's cheeks had flushed giving her the appearance of a painted porcelain doll. "I'm sorry, it was insensitive of me, I didn't mean to give offence." She stuffed her purse back into her handbag.

Laura's bottom lip quivered. "It's so kind of you, Sylvia, but Trish is right, you hardly know me, it wouldn't be right."

"I should have been in the hospital with you on the day of the operation." Trish spat the words out. "If mother hadn't called me on one of her false alarms, then I would have been."

Laura tried to appease her sister. "She told you she had fallen and she couldn't get up. You thought she had broken her hip; you had no choice."

"Yes, and when I got there, she was sitting drinking a cup of tea and watching Countdown having sent the ambulance crew away." There was no trace of humour in Trish's tone.

Rob went into the hall to fetch his and Trish's coats. "Come on, Trish, I think we should head off home, we'll be back soon, Lilly." He patted the top of her head and smiled.

Trish made a polite but brusque exit. Laura, Lilly and Sylvia were left to retrieve the lost light hearted atmosphere.

"I'm sorry about my sister, Sylvia, she can be rude sometimes but she's protective of me and she's always been there when I needed her." Laura's voice was thin.

"There's no need to apologise, Laura, I know Sylvia well from work and yes, she can be fierce but I realised a long time ago that there's another side to her." Laura waited for Sylvia to continue.

Sylvia saw that further explanation was expected.

"A colleague of mine, well actually, she's a friend, the one I was waiting for in the hospital when we met, she went through a rough time when her father died. Neither of us, that is my colleague nor I, had worked at Kessler and Drake for long. Elaine went a bit off the rails with the loss of her father and started having lots of time off work, the standard of her work went right down too. Since she was still in her probationary period, management wanted to let her go but Trish fought tooth and nail for them to give her another chance. Elaine never knew anything of this and Trish never gave any indication that she had helped her but basically Trish saved her job."

Laura smiled. "I don't think many people see that side of her, it's nice to think that some people see through the bossy outer shell."

A knock came at the door, Lilly drew in a sharp breath. Laura went to answer the door and Lilly called out. "Be careful, Mum."

Laura called back. "It's ok, pet." She opened the door with the chain on at first and then seeing the postman she opened the door fully and took a large parcel off him.

"It's just some more home working materials." Laura told Lilly as she came back into the lounge.

"Mum, can I go and watch TV in my room?" Lilly still looked shaken.

Laura helped Lilly up the stairs and got her settled comfortably before leaving her to rest in her cosy new den.

When Laura came downstairs again, Sylvia was already getting her things together in the hall.

"I must go and leave you to get on."

Laura was crestfallen. "Do you have to go?"

Sylvia shook her head. "No, I've got plenty of time but I know you must have lots to get on with." She glanced at the parcel.

Laura sighed. "I suppose, I do actually but I was enjoying your company so much." They both went back into the lounge in unspoken agreement.

Sylvia studied Laura's face carefully for a moment. "Listen, can I give you that money without Trish knowing or would you feel it to be disloyal to her?"

Laura held up her hand in protest. "You are so kind, Sylvia, but honestly, it wouldn't be right."

"But you're working all the hours to get this debt off your back and it's just getting bigger." Sylvia protested.

Laura agreed. "I know and I'm really worried about it but I honestly couldn't take your money."

Sylvia frowned but then her face cleared and a faraway look came into her eyes then, as if she had suddenly realised where she was, she looked back at Laura and smiled. "I understand, still it was worth a try. Maybe I could help in a more practical way though." Laura listened with interest.

Sylvia treaded carefully. "I couldn't help notice how jittery Lilly was when the postman came to the door."

Laura nodded. "Yes, she's not normally like that, I think she's still feeling weak after the operation, and the two 'bouncers' barging their way in last week really upset her."

Sylvia drew her lips tight. "I'm sure it wasn't legal what they did."

Laura continued. "Rob is trying to sort them out, hopefully we won't see them again."

"I have a friend in work who is a reporter. He has various contacts. Maybe he would be able to find out a bit more background about them which might be useful in getting them off your back." Sylvia acquired the faraway look again.

Laura shook her head. "I wouldn't want to antagonise them; Rob has already stirred them up in the first place."

Sylvia reassured her. "James is very discreet, don't worry, they would never connect any investigation with you, you can rest assured."

Laura looked at her friend's clear blue eyes and was instantly reassured. "I'm pretty sure they work for Dr Sharmer, I can give him the address of the clinic for a start."

Sylvia looked puzzled. "Dr Sharmer?"

"Yes, he runs a private clinic specialising in alternative non-invasive therapies, I took Lilly to him thinking that we could avoid surgery that way. Trish found out though and made me see that I was burying my head in the sand."

Sylvia sat forward in the chair. "Where is this clinic exactly?"

Chapter Twenty-Six

Elaine knew that the bookshop opened at nine o'clock but she wanted to contact the bookseller before then to clarify a few things; she phoned the shop at eight-thirty, fully expecting to be unsuccessful the first time but the phone was answered straight away.

Elaine was taken aback. "Hello? Yes, hi, this is Elaine Wood. I called in at the shop yesterday…"

"Yes, it's all going to plan, the men have taken the bait…"

"Yes, I'm pretty sure they are interested, we left some details on a card, supposedly the name of a rich client, Holly, the landlady of The Carter's who you've met, saw one of them take the card whilst we were both away from the table…"

"No, you shouldn't have any trouble recognising them, they both have very short haircuts and are thick set. One wears a green jacket with Velcro on the shoulders, the other one wears a dark blue fleece. They may not both come in together though, of course…"

"Ok, just one thing though, the story is that you don't take credit cards…"

"Yes, I see what you mean, that wasn't such a good idea, was it? My friend wanted to give a plausible reason for not buying the book straight away but it might limit how much they will spend…"

"Yes, ok, I'll pop around this afternoon to see if they turned up. Thanks, see you later, bye."

Elaine felt relieved to have spoken to the shopkeeper, all was going to plan so far, and she hoped that it would continue to do so.

Holly had been keen to come with Elaine and was free in the afternoon, so just after two, they set off together to the town centre. They cut through the park to take the longer but more pleasant route to the shops. The trees were stark and bare of foliage, their branches stretched upwards like skinny fingers reaching to the slate grey sky.

"That's the bench where I saw Professor Cambwell." Elaine pointed to a park bench next to some shrubbery.

Holly went over to the bench and lay her hands on it. "I can feel it." She said closing her eyes.

Elaine approached with caution. "What do you feel?"

"The peace." Holly nodded as if answering an invisible speaker. "There's an energy in this place, but it feels as if there has been a resolution, a 'letting go' of some sort." Holly opened her eyes and her gaze met Elaine's. "I can't explain it, but the feeling is very powerful."

Elaine looked at the bench, she walked to the spot but she felt nothing but a little sadness. At length, they carried on their way to the bookshop.

The bookseller was at his usual place behind the desk engrossed, he looked up when he saw Holly and Elaine and almost smiled, it was the nearest thing to a cheery greeting either of them had ever seen from him. "You'll be pleased to know that things went according to plan this morning."

Elaine stepped forward. "The men came for the book then?"

The bookseller nodded almost mischievously. "They did, but by the time they got here, I'd already sold it."

"What?" Elaine was taken aback.

He continued. "As soon as I opened up this morning, a bald suited gent with a black moustache burst in and asked about the book. He knew exactly what he was looking for, so it was clear he was part of the gang."

Elaine frowned. "I think I know who he might be but I wasn't expecting him to get involved."

"I told him that it had been reserved by phone and that the buyer would be in later on. I gave the option of first refusal if they failed to turn up but he was having none of it. I mentioned the sum that 'I had been offered' and he doubled it there and then, he even had the cash with him." Elaine glanced at Holly who was standing next to the counter both hands pressed flat on it, her eyes closed. Elaine focused back on the bookseller. "Had you been offered a sum already?" The bookseller snorted. "You don't know much about sales technique, do you?"

Elaine's smile was thin. "So, no then?"

His mouth formed a perfect round. "No."

"How much did you get for the book?" Elaine felt she needed to nurture his responses.

"Five thousand pounds." He retreated to the back of the counter, unlocked a drawer and pulled out a large roll of bank notes. "It's all there, I've counted it." The smile finally reached his eyes.

Elaine stood aghast, she turned to Holly but Holly had not been following the conversation and was oblivious.

"The two men you describe did come in, but later. The man who purchased the book was in a great hurry to get out of here, he wouldn't even let me package it properly." Elaine was still dumbstruck.

The bookseller continued. "The two men were angry that the book had been sold already although they didn't suspect that I had been expecting them. They complained amongst themselves that their boss had sent them off on an unnecessary job. They claimed if it hadn't been for that they would have beaten the other buyer to it."

Elaine turned to Holly. "That's astonishing, isn't it?"

Holly was still leaning on the counter; she looked up as if in a dream and stared blankly. "Sorry?"

Elaine repeated what the bookseller had said and Holly agreed that the plan had worked remarkably well but she still seemed preoccupied.

Holly turned to the bookseller. "The book will return here once more."

He nodded. "I know but this will be the final shriving."

Elaine was puzzled.

Holly explained. "The reason the plan went so well was that it wasn't really our plan at all." Elaine frowned.

Holly continued. "I know it felt like we were organising it all, but the book itself knew where it needed to be and it used us as a vector for its own ends."

Elaine glanced at the bookseller expecting to see a mocking expression but he was taking in Holly's words and nodding sagely.

"But how do you know this?" Elaine looked from Holly to the shopkeeper and back again. Holly looked to the bookseller for a cue and he nodded for her to continue, she took a deep breath. "There is a tremendous energy in this place, it hasn't always been a bookshop, and the history of past events is printed deep into the fabric of the building." She paused to see how Elaine was reacting before continuing. "You know how there is often an atmosphere in a place that is hard to explain but most people could agree about?" Elaine nodded. "Well, some of us can go further than just 'feeling an atmosphere' we can 'read' the echo of past events."

Holly looked to the bookseller to continue, he nodded. "There was a great evil done here in the past, hundreds of years ago and retribution was sought. Now finally, there will be resolution once and for all. The book has selected its own target, the men you sent were not the intended goal but they were instrumental in channelling events."

Elaine pursed her lips. "I can't say that I understand what you mean but I have an inkling; I know there are things in the universe that we can't yet fathom and I certainly trust Holly's intuition."

The bookseller counted out ten fifty-pound notes and handed the rest of the money over to Elaine. She held her hand up in protest. "I don't want the money, the book all but destroyed me, I'm just glad to be free again."

"You have to take it, I'm afraid, I have taken out a healthy commission for handling, but the rest is yours. If I were to keep it, I fear it would bring misfortune to me."

Holly agreed. "It's all part of the same thing, Elaine, the money has to be used to bring good from evil. It will help restore the balance you see."

Elaine stared at the cash almost with repulsion. "But why does it have to be me?"

Holly touched Elaine on the shoulder. "For some reason, you got caught up in the cycle; no harm was meant to come to you, I'm sure but sometimes, great power is hard to control. Forces can be unleashed that become channelled in the wrong way."

Elaine held her hand to her mouth. "Professor Cambwell, was he caught up in all of this too? Was he a victim?"

The bookseller stared at the floor and scratched his head before replying. "He was an innocent victim but he knew the whole story and willingly let himself be extinguished."

Elaine drew a breath in sharply. "That's horrible!" She looked to Holly to share her revulsion but Holly's expression was one of calm acceptance.

"I think there was a reason that he let himself be drawn into the whole thing but I can't be sure." Holly sounded as if she was going to continue but her words tailed off.

Elaine frowned. "A reason?"

Holly seemed unwilling to continue. "It's something I felt in the park at the site of Professor Cambwell's passing. I can't really put it into words but I sensed that he was telling me something."

Elaine swallowed hard. "Professor Cambwell?"

Holly looked at her sideways. "Yes."

Elaine showed no reaction, so Holly continued. "He wanted to 'go' for some reason but he wanted to do something worthwhile in the process."

Faltering, Holly looked around her, the bookseller stepped in to help her. "It's like some people donate organs after death, he wanted to glean the best out of a bad situation."

Elaine was even more mystified now. "How come you know so much about it?"

The question was almost aggressive but the shopkeeper was cool in his reply. "Professor Cambwell was a regular in the shop. I sourced many ancient texts for him and he gave me advice about some of my acquisitions. He shared a lot about his personal life to me in the end but I wouldn't divulge any of that to the casual enquirer." His dark eyes were like lasers as he glared at Elaine from under his big bushy brows.

Holly stepped in. "Of course not, you have a duty of confidentiality, it wouldn't be right for us to press you." She paused before continuing. "He had a good reason for allowing himself to be drawn in by the book's destructive power though, didn't he?" The shopkeeper gave a short nod in Holly's direction.

Elaine had the feeling that she had angered the shopkeeper in some way but she couldn't fathom how; she saw he still had the roll of banknotes in his hand, she held her hand out to him. "Are you sure you can't allow yourself to take more commission? You deserve to, you have done a great job with the selling."

He placed the roll of notes in her hand with a shake of the head. "No, ten per cent is the correct amount, any more would be profiteering."

Elaine put the roll in a secure part of her rucksack. "I wouldn't see it like that but I can see you are a man of high principle."

The bookseller lowered his eyes, when he looked up again his expression was softer. "The book will return here, you may like to come back to see the resolution, for my part, I would be interested to see what you decide to do with the money. That is entirely your business of course."

Elaine was pleased that the shopkeeper seemed mollified. "Of course! I'm going to give it to charity but I'll certainly let you know which one."

The shopkeeper's mouth turned down at the edges and he turned to Holly who held her hand up to him and whispered. "It's ok."

Elaine wondered what she had done now but she didn't pursue the thought with a question.

After reassuring the shopkeeper that they would return, she followed Holly out of the shop. Turning to thank him once again from the doorway, she saw that he was already deeply engrossed in the book he was reading, his lion like mane concealed his expression.

Once they were on their way back out of town, Elaine turned to Holly. "What was all that about the money, what's wrong with me giving it to charity?"

Holly glanced at Elaine but kept her eyes on the path ahead as she marched along. "Absolutely nothing, there are lots of very worthy causes which would be very grateful for the money."

Elaine waited before replying. "But?"

Holly wrapped her arms around her bag and hugged it to her chest. "Well, it just seems a bit easy, doesn't it?" She looked at her friend who seemed to be waiting for her to expand her explanation. "You know, it's a good thing to do but isn't it a way for an individual to get the feel-good factor without much effort on their part?"

Elaine frowned. "I've never looked at it like that but to be honest, maybe you're right. I just wanted rid of the money as fast as possible. On the other hand, how would me putting more effort into the giving do any more good than an organised charity?"

They had arrived at the park; the sun was warm on their backs, so Holly went over to a bench and sat down for a moment. "Normally, I would say that it wouldn't make any difference." She put her bag beside herself on the bench as Elaine took a seat. "These circumstances are different, there's a power at work and a balance to be redressed, it's difficult to explain, I don't understand it fully myself."

Elaine paid close attention to what Holly was trying to say. "Is it something like 'no pain, no gain'?"

Holly sat up straight and nodded. "Sort of, you know those exercise machines that you can strap on and can 'exercise' your muscles whilst you're sitting down and watching TV?"

Elaine nodded. "Although they probably have the same effect on individual muscles as going to the gym, it somehow doesn't seem right, does it?"

Holly smiled. "Exactly! Instinctively you feel that it can't be doing as much good and I'm sure that's right. There are probably more subtle factors to consider such as life style attitudes."

Elaine cut in. "Yes, things that it would be hard to quantify but could be very significant."

Holly continued. "I feel it's the same for the money, if it can be targeted really well, then the good that can come out of it will be all the greater."

Elaine looked up at the buds on the branches above. "We'll have to give it a lot of thought." The sun diffused through the waving branches producing a flickering light all around the bench.

"I feel as if I could stay here forever." Elaine leant back and let the winter sun shine full on her face.

"Me too." Holly agreed. "I feel a deep sense of peace sitting here, unfortunately, I have a shift to start this afternoon, so I must get back."

Reluctantly, they stood up and continued their walk back to Cotswold Street in companionable but thoughtful silence.

When Elaine got back home, there was a phone message from Sylvia asking her to return the call when she had a moment; before she could do so, James rang and asked if they could meet up in The Carter's later on. When Elaine spoke to Sylvia, it seemed that both James and Sylvia had some interesting news to share.

Iris was sitting curled up on the bottom stair purring, she had been a happy little cat ever since the book had left the house, now she looked up at Elaine with half-moon eyes. "That money would buy you an awful lot of cat food wouldn't it, puss?" Elaine bent down to stroke the black furry head; Iris responded by thrusting her face into Elaine's cupped palm. As she idly tickled the cat's ears, Holly's words resounded in her head, she closed her eyes against the bright winter sunlight shining through the hall window. This was where she had been found after her tumble down the stairs; maybe she should donate the money to the hospital, they had been very good to her after the accident. Somehow, that didn't seem quite the right thing to do. Something made Elaine recall bits of the dream she had had after the fall, in her mind's eye she could see the man, he was dressed in a long brown robe and sat at a huge bench in a vast space. The man was looking straight at her, his dark eyes full of patience, it was as if he was waiting for her to fulfil a promise. Feeling something small but firm pressing on her leg, Elaine opened her eyes to see Iris climbing up and seeking attention. Elaine laughed. "I think you want feeding, don't you?"

The mood broken, Elaine went into the kitchen to feed the little fur ball.

Chapter Twenty-Seven

Laura was puzzled by her new friend's interest in Dr Sharmer; she suspected that Sylvia had heard of him before although she didn't say so. Later on, Laura had given Sylvia the address of the clinic and a detailed description of how to get there. Sylvia left but she assured Laura that she would fill her in when she had more information.

There wasn't long to wait, later in the week, Laura had a phone call from Sylvia telling her that she wanted to catch up with her and asking if she could bring James too. Laura had hesitated, it was strange, although she felt absolutely fine about Sylvia seeing her chaotic home, she balked at a stranger. In the instant Sylvia had mentioned bringing James, Laura had visualised a scenario where she was being judged by a scornful city gent casting his eye over her humble belongings. Sylvia must have heard the hesitation in Laura's voice because she added that Laura might like to come to her flat instead. This presented a new problem in that Laura didn't want to leave Lilly on her own just yet after her operation. As if reading Laura's mind, Sylvia had added that she should bring Lilly with her too.

Lilly was bright with excitement on the drive to Sylvia's flat. It turned out that she lived not far from the hospital in a fairly new development. Sylvia had given instructions of how to get there and as usual, Lilly had the job of navigating. As they came off the ring road and headed towards the hospital, they had to turn left into a road they had barely noticed before. The road dropped down towards the river, the area had the feel of a village about it, the houses and flats had been designed to look as if the community had grown organically rather than been planned in blocks and rows. Each house was slightly different, and was set at an angle to the next one, the effect on the skyline was pleasing to the eye.

Lilly pointed out a large building that might once have been a warehouse although the clean stonework and perfect alignment of windows suggested that it was a new build. "That's it, Sylvia's flat is in there, the car park must be on the far side."

They continued around the gentle curve of the road and came to a side turning with a structure Sylvia had described; it was a stone post about four feet tall with a discrete keypad and speaker recessed into it. Beyond the post was a ramp leading to large set of garage doors. Laura swung into the turning as instructed and keyed in the number of Sylvia's flat.

Immediately, Sylvia's voice crackled, "Come in," from the speaker and the garage doors swung open.

They descended into an underground car park; Lilly's voice was shrill with delight. "There! That's the visitors' car parking opposite the lift."

Laura reversed into the parking bay and they were just climbing out of the car when the lift doors opened to reveal a beaming Sylvia. Lilly practically galloped over to her.

Sylvia held her hands up. "Hey! Watch that leg, missy!" She shot a worried glance at Laura. Laura replied with a wry smile. "She makes a terrible invalid, there's no keeping her still now and she's off the painkillers too."

Lilly grinned. "My leg hardly hurts now." She stepped into the lift at Sylvia's indication and Laura followed.

The lift ascended three floors and opened out into a corridor with six doors in matching hardwood. The door opposite the lift was ajar, Sylvia went over to it and pushed it open to reveal a small hallway which led straight into a bright open plan room. A stripy multi-coloured sofa and matching chairs took up about a third of the area. Lilly was agog at the magnificent view of the city from the full-length windows which dominated the opposite side of the room.

A man had been seated on the sofa, he rose as they came in and offered his hand. "Hi, I'm James, a colleague of Sylvia's."

Laura took his hand tentatively, the warmth of his smile reassuring her.

Sylvia went over to a vast bookshelf and took a book out; she took it to Lilly who was still gazing at the view. "I thought you might like this." She held out the book. "We get free samples in work." She explained. "It's a true story." There was a picture of a ballerina on the cover.

Lilly regarded it with awe and read aloud the subtitle as if reciting a poem. *Orphaned by war, saved by ballet.* She looked up at Sylvia with sparkling eyes. "Thank you so much!" The sincerity in her voice was plain for all to hear.

Sylvia made a brushing movement. "It's just a little thing."

Laura mouthed a silent "Thank you" in Sylvia's direction.

They sat down. Lilly was the first to flop down in the place next to James who had been sitting on the sofa; she immediately delved into the book, totally absorbed.

Sylvia offered refreshments but Laura declined, she was a little overawed by her surroundings.

Lilly had to be prompted to respond to Sylvia's offer, she was so wrapped up in the book but when she realised, she was being addressed, she politely declined.

Formalities out of the way, James sat forward in his seat and spoke directly to Laura in low tones. "I've been doing some research on Dr Sharmer. It turns out that one of my colleagues in *The Chronicle* is already preparing a piece on him. It appears, he's not all he seems." Laura listened with interest.

James continued. "He has no medical qualifications as we suspected already, but it seems that his doctorate is bogus too. Added to that, he isn't on the Society of Homeopaths Register, he appears to have no qualifications in the field whatsoever."

Laura frowned. "Do you mean he's a con man?"

James nodded. "As good as, what he's doing isn't illegal as far as we can tell although displaying false documents may be; we're still investigating."

Sylvia joined in. "Whatever the legal situation, he's certainly morally in the wrong. He's been accused of fraud before. But wasn't charged, for some reason, the claimant backed down and retracted the accusation."

James continued. "I want to find this claimant to see if they will tell my why. I suspect there may have been coercion involved but I'm not sure."

Laura glanced at Lilly; she was still totally wrapped up in her book. "He seems to know some ruthless people, those men he sent around were pretty threatening."

James looked towards Sylvia then back to Laura. "I have a contact who is in the police force, he knows of those two and he and his colleagues are keeping a close eye on them. Their dealings are often close to the wrong side of the law and they know that if they step over the line, then they will be dealt with. I've told my contact about your experience and his colleagues have communicated the fact that they would be very wise to stay away from you from now on." Laura looked to Sylvia who remained impassive but it seemed to Laura that Sylvia knew all about this already. "Do you think they will take notice of the warning?" Laura turned back to James.

James laughed. "I imagine they will, Laura, I don't think you will be seeing anything more of them."

Sylvia smiled. "There won't be any more demands for money from Dr Sharmer, the so-called agreement you signed is probably not legally binding but even if it was, he would have to take you to court to dispute it and it certainly wouldn't pay for him to do that. The loan company you borrowed the money from is not on the financial services register and you have already repaid the original loan. The governmental illegal money lending team has been informed, so you can put any further fears of claims for payment out of your mind completely."

Laura looked relieved. "Did you report the company?"

Sylvia shook her head. "o, it was your brother-in-law, Rob, actually, he's been helping James with the investigation, he'd already found quite a lot out when we asked him about it."

Lilly looked up from her book and grinned. "Good old, Uncle Rob."

The others looked at each other with rueful smiles when they realised that Lilly had been listening all the while.

Chapter Twenty-Eight

Elaine was puzzled, she had a strong feeling that she was being guided about what she should do with the unwanted cash from the book but she couldn't quite pin down in which direction that guidance was going; she thought about times when people tried to manipulate her into making choices that are not her own and how she always took such attempts as guidance only, a concept that she knew from experience alluded many people. As she walked across to 'The Carter's', she had to push down a slight feeling of annoyance at Holly who had implied that to give the money to charity would be the easy way out. As soon as Elaine walked through the pub entrance, she saw Holly behind the bar with such a bright welcoming smile. Immediately, all annoyance was forgotten.

James, Barry and Sylvia were sitting around a table near the bar. As soon as he saw Elaine, Barry sprung up and intercepted her as she walked towards the bar. "What can I get you? This is my round."

Elaine knew better than to argue and accepted a pint of Gold, she sat down next to the others.

Sylvia shuffled over to make more room. "We've got lots to tell you, James has been very busy."

James gave a modest smile as he sipped his pint.

Garry leant forward. "Holly filled us in on what happened to the book. It looks like our 'friends' got a taste of their own medicine."

Elaine nodded. "The guy with the moustache tricked them so that he could get in there first."

Sylvia could hardly contain herself. "We know a lot more about that man now! James has found out that he's a quack doctor and that he's been accused of fraud on more than one occasion."

James cut in. "It wasn't just me; Barry did a lot of the background investigation."

They all turned towards Barry. "Those two meatheads are not the main villains, Alan Sharmer…" Garry looked at Elaine. "…the man with the moustache, orchestrates their actions to a great extent. He pays them to do his dirty work and he acts the part of a respectable gent, he's ruthless in his exploitation of the weak and the vulnerable though."

James took up the thread. "He started off selling face creams which seems innocent enough except for the fact that his packaging arrangements are less than hygienic and he has a huge mark up. He makes outrageous claims for what is basically a cheap lanolin product."

Sylvia joined in. "In recent years, he's been making forays into alternative medicine and has set himself up a clinic even though he has no homeopathy credentials whatsoever. Most of his clients are hypochondriacs who think he can help them with their imagined illnesses but we know of at least one example where he has been 'treating' Sylvia drew imaginary quote marks in the air 'a serious illness', and the patient was a child in this case."

James nodded. "Not only was he proceeding with a worthless treatment, he was extorting money from the worried parent who could ill afford his demands."

Elaine gasped. "But that's so immoral!"

Sylvia continued. "The victim is a relative of someone we know."

Elaine frowned. "Really?"

"It's Trish's sister and her niece." Elaine didn't reply.

James turned to Sylvia. "It seems strange that Laura came all the way out here to the clinic when there must be other genuine places in town."

Sylvia agreed with him. "I think it was the power of the internet. The website comes up as a first hit and whoever sorted the webpage out has done a very good job."

Elaine frowned. "So, this clinic is near here then?"

James nodded. "Yes, it's at the back of Aldi's near the main road."

Just then Tim emerged from the micro-brewery behind the pub, he took a mug of coffee over to Holly. "You sit down with the others and I'll take over here for a bit."

Holly drew up a chair and slotted herself in between James and Barry; she put her coffee on the table after taking a gulp. "Those two oafs were in here earlier; they weren't too happy with their friend by the sound of things."

James, Barry and Sylvia all fixed their attention on Holly. "I don't think he'll be in here for a while at least, they were very angry with him." James gave her a quizzical look.

Holly continued. "He got to the book first by sending them on a wild goose chase to delay them. They worked out what had happened and they think he's tricked them out of a bargain. They had hoped to make a hefty profit on selling the book."

Barry smiled. "Well, I hope they catch up with him and give him a taste of his own medicine."

"Those sort of people always get away with things, he'll be able to give them some plausible explanation." James said taking another sip of his pint.

Holly twirled her coffee mug around and around on the table. "I have a feeling that he will get what's coming to him this time." She looked at Elaine who appeared to be lost in thought.

Elaine, aware that the attention had turned to herself, looked up. "Holly, I have an idea about what to do with the money."

Holly explained to the others. "The money Elaine got for the book; she wants to give it away."

Elaine nodded. "I've just found out that one of my colleague's relatives has been on the receiving end of that little trio's vile actions."

Sylvia looked towards Holly. "She's a single mother with a sick child and they have been extorting money out of her for a bogus treatment."

Barry interrupted. "It was Alan Sharmer mainly, the others merely did what he told them to."

"I think they enjoyed their part in it though." James added with disgust.

"The bottom line is that she is seriously out of pocket and she is working all the hours to try and get out of the debt they got her into." Sylvia shook her head.

"She should get the money!" Elaine's voice has a steely quality.

Sylvia looked doubtful. "I've tried to help her out but she doesn't like to accept charity."

"There's always a way." Barry rubbed his prickly chin. "We could approach it in a way that it doesn't look like charity. We should be able to convince her that the money is rightfully hers."

Sylvia still looked doubtful. "I wouldn't want to lie to her."

Holly stared into her coffee. "It's not going to be a problem."

Sylvia stared. "What do you mean?"

"Laura will accept the money in the spirit in which it is given."

Sylvia flicked a glance at the others who were looking equally puzzled apart from Elaine.

"You don't know her, do you?"

"We've never met but I know that she is the right person to be given the money and that it will work out satisfactorily."

Sylvia gave a small smile. "Yes, it's good to be optimistic, isn't it?" She glanced at the others in embarrassment but only James seemed to register it.

Elaine came to the rescue. "It's ok, Sylv, I know that it sounds absurd but we're dealing with things beyond our understanding here. Events have taken a certain course and it's as if there is an external entity guiding them."

Sylvia didn't look convinced. "That sounds spooky. Are you sure it's not coincidences which make it look as if there's a guiding hand? The human mind likes to look for patterns and reasons for things where sometimes in reality they don't exist."

Barry put down his beer. "It could be that, on the other hand, if good is going to come out of it, then it doesn't really matter, does it?"

Sylvia could see that Barry was starting to prickle, so she dropped the subject. "No of course not, I'm sure you're right, Holly."

"You are the right person to make it happen, Sylvia, after all, you were the one to befriend Laura, and many people would not have got involved in the first place." Holly's voice was soft.

James glanced towards the door. "I'm sure that Trish would be a good person to help with this."

Elaine bit her lip. "She's a very proud person, we'd have to approach it in the right way, she wouldn't want to take charity even on behalf of her sister."

James agreed. "She is, but her husband is a very personable chap and I'm sure, he would be able to think of some way to make it acceptable to all concerned."

Holly shifted in her seat. "Sylvia is the one." She fixed her gaze on Sylvia, her deep brown eyes full of sagacity.

Sylvia looked uncomfortable. "I'm starting to feel like a sacrificial lamb here."

Holly's demeanour didn't change. "Gold and silver wrought together; I can see it now."

Sylvia made a face at James but Barry and Elaine watched Holly intently as if wanting to catch her every word.

Holly had a faraway expression. "Sylvia, your forebears belong to a line of practitioners of ancient arts. The gift is still within you, you have abilities which you have used little up to now."

"You're starting to scare me a bit, Holly." Sylvia looked to the others for help but even James was listening now.

Holly turned her gaze towards Elaine. "Elaine, there was a tragedy here many years ago. A local wise man's family was slaughtered, his wife and two young children. You have no direct lineage to the family but an accident of genetics means you bear a very strong resemblance to the wife, whose name was also Elaine."

Elaine nodded. "I knew there was something. I've felt it for a while now but I couldn't put my finger on it."

Sylvia was agog. "I'm not sure I like all this; can we talk about something different please."

Holly turned her head towards Sylvia in an almost mechanical way. "Too long have you let your gift lie unused, you need to awaken it now to help your kinsman."

"What kinsman?" Sylvia still looked towards the others for support but they were unresponsive.

"Laura and Trish come from the same shamanic line as you but a different branch. The art has become attenuated and abstracted in this line but they can still be the recipients of votive offering. This will bring about a redemptive exchange and end the cycle of hate and anger." Holly's scrutiny was still focused on Sylvia. "You need to let go of your prejudices and search inside yourself, you will find resources which will surprise you."

Sylvia reached across to Holly and took hold of her hand. "What do you want me to do?"

"Listen to your own thoughts and you will know." Holly laid her forehead on the back of Sylvia's hand.

Sylvia seemed embarrassed. "Are you ok, Holly?" There was no response. "Holly?" There was panic in Sylvia's voice, she looked to the others.

Elaine half stood up and put her arm around Holly and Barry put his hand on Holly's shoulder and looked over to the bar. Tim was already coming around to the table.

Barry's voice was matter of fact. "It's ok, I think she's had a petit mal."

Tim stroked the back of Holly's head. "Ok, love?"

Holly sat up and smiled, her demeanour back to normal. "Yes, Tim, I'm fine." She saw Sylvia's stricken face. "I'm ok, Sylvia, I just drifted off for a bit. Did I miss anything?"

Sylvia looked at Tim perplexed. Tim ignored her and returned to the bar. Barry indicated with his eyes to Sylvia to let the matter drop.

Frustrated, Sylvia tried to make her voice sound normal. "We were just talking about how we were going to get Trish to help us with the task of getting the money to Laura."

Holly stared at Sylvia for a moment, a quiet concern in her expression. "Oh, yes, we thought you might be the best person to persuade her, didn't we?" Holly's voice had the penetrating edge of a laser.

Sylvia was compliant. "Yes, we did, I'll see what I can do."

Holly rose from her chair. "I'm afraid I'm going to have to leave you guys, I promised Tim I'd vacuum pack some hops."

After she had gone, Barry explained. "Holly has mild epilepsy but she doesn't like to talk about it."

Elaine joined in. "Her episodes are very rare but she has had some negative reactions in the past, so she likes to keep it to herself."

Sylvia nodded. "Understood." She looked across at Tim who was lifting a tray of glasses out of the glasswasher. "Tim seems very matter of fact about it."

Barry half turned towards the direction of the bar. "It's no big deal to them, it rarely affects Holly's day-to-day life." His voice sounded prickly again.

Elaine jumped in to change the subject. "So, let's get back to our plan of action, I can have a word with Trish on Monday if you like to broach the subject of a donation for Laura."

Sylvia's eyes lit up. "Would you? I don't think I'd know where to start."

Before Elaine could answer, Barry piped up. "Look who's just coming in!" He glared at the doorway.

The two thugs who had broken Mrs William's gate walked up to the bar. Tim put down the tea towel he had been using to polish the glasses and drew himself up to his full height, he said nothing but his eyes were like polished steel.

The stouter of the two spoke first. "Listen, we want to apologise for letting the old bird's birds out last week." His friend tittered but he continued. "Sorry, that was out of order. We want to help with any repairs as a way of making amends."

Tim's voice was as cold as his steely stare. "The damage was repaired the next day, you're too late."

The man coughed. "I'm sorry about that." He turned to his scrawny friend as if to prompt.

The friend stared blankly at first and then realising, he was expected to speak took off his hat and rotated it between his hands. "I've got a bit of a temper; it gets the better of me sometimes but the old girl didn't deserve that."

Tim was taken aback, he didn't seem to know what to make of the apology, was it genuine or were they up to something.

Barry went over to the bar; his eyes were hard and his body language unyielding. "You really upset Mrs Williams; you know her husband was a war veteran?"

The scrawny one fiddled with his 'help for heroes' band. "I know, I'd kill anyone who did that to my Mam. You've every right to have a go at me. Can I get you a pint?"

Elaine expected things to erupt after that but strangely Barry accepted the pint and before long, he and the two men were having quite an amiable conversation. To Elaine's horror, the stouter man sidled over to their table, he had clearly recognised Sylvia.

"Hello, Doll, bought any good books lately?" Sylvia looked at him in bewilderment.

Elaine chipped in. "You must have heard our conversation about the rare book a while back."

"Yeh, we thought we'd get in on that but we were too late." The man pulled up a bar stool and sat next to Sylvia. "Do y' mind if I join ya?"

James half stood up. "We were having a private conversation actually."

The man, who didn't seem particularly offended stood up again. "Sorry, was just being friendly, I'll leave ya in peace."

"No, it's ok." Sylvia patted the bar stool. "I want to hear more about your plans for the book." The man sat down again and was pleased. "Can I buy yers all a drink?" He got his wallet out.

They accepted the round and another bar stool was drawn up, the scrawny friend joined them and introductions were made. Sylvia did most of the talking, quizzing Colin and Lloyd about how they thought it was ok to try to cheat her and Elaine out of their bargain. Surprisingly, Lloyd made a very good case to justify their actions. He even suggested that they had suspected it might have been some sort of scam on Elaine and Sylvia's part anyway but that they were game for a gamble. He also pointed out that it sounded like they were being underhand themselves in not telling the bookseller that the item was of such value.

Elaine laughed at the last point. "Are you telling me that you would have?"

Colin, the stout one laughed too. "No, but ya wouldn't expect a couple of scumbags like us to. You two are proper ladies, I would have expected better."

Elaine scrutinised Colin's face for signs of irony but saw that he was sincere. "You don't have a very high opinion of yourselves, do you?"

Colin looked towards Lloyd who was staring at his boots and scratching his arm. "Yeh, well sometimes it's hard to get away from your past."

Barry stared at Lloyd, his gaze penetrating. "I remember you at school, you wouldn't go out shooting rabbits with the Biston boys, you said it was cruel."

Lloyd looked at his boots again and muttered. "Aye, well, I soon got that beat out of me by my dad, didn't I?"

Colin laughed. "Yeh, I'd forgotten what a milksop you were. Didn't take long to harden you up though, did it? You were nickin' cars by the time you were ten."

Lloyd narrowed his eyes. "Who are you calling soft? Anyway, you're the one who got all the O levels, ya swotty git."

Elaine shifted in her seat and Lloyd immediately apologised for his language. After that, the conversation turned to light banter but Colin and Lloyd only stayed for the one pint. Elaine had suspected that they had only bought a round in order to get the same back in triplicate but it turned out that her suspicions were unjustified.

It wasn't until Lloyd and Colin had gone that Holly reappeared, she seemed unsurprised when Elaine told her about the two men. "No one is beyond the redemptive power of goodness."

Elaine was unsure of what Holly meant by that but after the earlier experience, she decided not to push her, so she just nodded in agreement. None of the others queried it either, they must have had the same thoughts as Elaine.

Chapter Twenty-Nine

Laura and Lilly were enjoying a rare lunchtime together. Normally, Laura would be at work or busy doing data entry for extra cash. Since the operation, Laura had been able to arrange her shifts so that Lilly didn't have to spend long afternoons on her own. They would have a leisurely lunch together and then Lilly would read or watch television knowing that her mum was in the next room catching up on the computer work. This lunchtime was interrupted by a loud knocking on the front door. Laura frowned and reluctantly went to answer it. Lilly rushed into the kitchen to fetch the mop when she saw who was at the door. Laura reassured her that there was no way that she was going to take the chain off, she opened the door just a crack and told the two men to go away and that there was nothing she wanted to say to them.

The scrawny one crouched down as if talking to a small child. "It's ok, love, we ain't stayin' long, we just need to give you this." He waved a large brown envelope towards the crack in the door.

Laura eyed it with suspicion. "What is it?"

Lilly shouted from the kitchen. "Mum, come away from the door." Her voice was shrill.

"It's ok, love, they can't get in." Laura turned her attention back to the men outside.

"There was a mistake in the accounts, you paid too much." The stouter man was matter of fact.

Laura was puzzled. "What?"

The skinnier man agreed. "Yes, love, you were overcharged, we've brought the cash back."

A squeak came from the kitchen. "Careful, it may be a bomb!"

Laura looked at the envelope, the man had opened up the flap to reveal the notes inside, she called back to the kitchen. "It's ok, love, I can see in the package." Laura turned back to the men. "A mistake? I don't understand."

The skinny man looked to his friend to explain, the friend nodded and tapped the envelope on his palm, and he studied it intensely for a moment. "The thing is, the loan wasn't registered properly, and by rights, you have the option to take the company to court for wrongful dealing. We are returning the interest you have paid, writing off the loan and paying a lump sum in compensation for any inconvenience it may have caused you."

Laura still stared at the envelope in disbelief. "Why wasn't it sent by letter?"

"It's a trick, Mum!" wailed Lilly.

"I'm sorry, I can't accept it, there has to be some mistake." Laura closed the door on the men but she waited to see if they would go. The two shadows she could see through the glass told her that they were still there.

The letter box opened and Lilly screamed, the brown envelope fell onto the floor and the contents spilled out and covered the doormat. Laura gathered the money up and opened the door again shouting at the retreating men. "Come back! I told you I don't want the money."

The two men looked at each other in disbelief. The skinny one came back to the door. "Listen, love, just take the money there's no trick."

The stouter man joined him. "I'll tell you what, we'll wait in the café over the road, have a think about it and come over when you feel comfortable. We'll buy you a coffee and a milkshake for the kid, we can talk on neutral ground and you can ask us any questions, ok?"

"Take the money with you." Laura thrust the envelope at him and slammed the door. The men disappeared from the doorway. Laura went into the lounge to look out the window, she watched as they retreated into 'Polly's Pantry' across the road. Polly and George Eichstädt who ran the café were good friends and neighbours, they often took parcels in for her. When Lilly was at primary school, she used to go to the café after school and do her homework on a corner table whilst she waited for her mum to come home from work. Polly would give her a hot chocolate and a toasted teacake, there was never any charge. George was a big man with a kind heart, he never had a cross word for anyone and yet at the same time no-one ever wanted to risk getting on the wrong side of him.

Lilly joined her mum at the window, she peered out too. "You aren't going over there are you, Mum?"

Laura didn't answer but got out her phone and selected a number. After a few seconds, she was connected. "Hello, Rob? Sorry to call you at work but I've just had a strange visit from two men from the loan company…"

"No, it's ok, they've gone now, they're over at the café…"

"Yes, don't worry, we're both fine, the strange thing is that they were trying to give *me* money…"

"No, I didn't take it. Do you know anything about the company being unregistered?"

"Wouldn't it be more normal to do it by post?"

"Oh, I see. No, there's no need for you to leave work thanks anyway. I'll give Trish a ring later thanks, Rob."

Lilly had been listening to the conversation. "So, Uncle Rob thinks that it might be for real?"

Laura nodded. "Yes, he says that it sounds as if they are trying to keep things quiet and that they might be worried about us publicising what they have been doing so they're trying to buy us off."

"Are you going to go over there then?" Lilly seemed less fearful now.

Laura stared out of the window for a minute. "The money would be very useful and I suppose I've got nothing to lose."

Lilly followed her gaze. "What if the money is forged? You could get arrested or something."

"I'd have it checked in the bank and if there was any problem, I could tell them exactly where I got it from." Laura was almost thinking aloud.

"Let's do it!" Lilly was positively enthusiastic now.

"Oh no! You are staying here, my lady!" Laura's voice was firm.

"Mum, nothing is going to happen to us when George is there, it's quite safe and it would be better than me being here alone wouldn't it?" Lilly's voice had developed an uncharacteristic whine.

Against her better judgement, Laura was persuaded to take Lilly with her but not before they had checked all the locks and windows. Laura made sure the front door was closed firmly behind them. They walked the short way to the pelican crossing a little way up the road and when it was safe, they crossed over to the café.

George was standing behind the counter, a huge presence obscuring his wife Polly, the only thing which gave a clue that she was there was the gurgling and hissing coming from the barista along with the clouds of steam.

George's smile was radiant when he saw them coming in. "Well, hello, ladies, it is so good to see you."

Polly's head appeared around George's left shoulder her golden curls seemed to be a continuation of the steam cloud. "Hi, Laura. Hi Lilly, hey, you're looking good, girl!"

"It is good to see with my own eyes that you are both well. What can I get for you?" George's guttural speech seemed at odds with his benign smile.

The two men who had brought the money had been sitting by the far window, the stout one came across to the counter with his wallet. "I'll get these."

George regarded him for a second and turned towards Laura. "These gentlemen, they are friends of yours, yes?" There was doubt in his voice.

Laura put her hand on George's great tree trunk like forearm. "It's ok, George, I know them, they're here on business."

George grunted but he took the money, his gaze never leaving the man's face.

Lilly had taken a tall stool by the window; she was engrossed with her phone. Laura sat at the same table as the men, but separated by a large gap. An elderly lady sat at the table behind them, she looked up from her cup of tea and nodded at Laura before taking a bite of her teacake.

Laura smiled at her before returning her attention back to the men.

The stouter of the two spoke first. "I'm Colin and this is my mate, Lloyd." The skinny one nodded.

Colin continued. "Listen, you've got nothing to lose in taking the money back, have you? Like I said, there was a mistake in the registration and that put the company in the wrong. We don't want to lose our good reputation, so we'd rather do it that way and then everybody's happy aren't they?"

Laura thought for a moment. "Are you saying that I could sue the company?"

Lloyd jumped in. "That would be very risky for you, we got good lawyers."

Colin held up his hand to warn Lloyd off. "As Lloyd says, we have a very good legal department, so it would cost you a lot to do that and there is no guarantee you would win the case. It could take years."

Laura didn't know whether to believe him but she knew that these things did take time. Colin took the envelope out and slid it across the table, Laura could see the thick wad of fifty-pound notes. "That's a lot more than I borrowed even with the interest added."

Lloyd eyed the money hungrily. "Like we said, there's extra for any distress caused."

Laura pulled the envelope towards herself. "If I take it. will that be an end to it?"

"You'll never hear from us again." Colin downed his coffee and stood up.

Lloyd's eyes stayed fixed on the envelope for a moment and then he too stood up and followed Colin.

Once the men were gone, Laura took the coffee cups over to the counter.

Polly's cornflower eyes were wide. "What was that all about?" George's expression asked the same question.

Laura explained as best she could and both George and Polly agreed she had done the right thing in taking the money. George examined a sample of the notes and could see nothing wrong with them; he was sure they were totally genuine but agreed with Laura's plan to take them down to the bank just in case.

Lilly stayed with Polly whilst George accompanied Laura to the high street, they chatted on the way.

George looked sideways at Laura as he strode along. "You have been having trouble making the ends meet together?"

Laura grinned at him and then looked down at the pavement. "I normally manage fine but when Lilly got ill, balancing the household finances was the last thing on my mind. If this money is genuine, then it will mean I can stop doing extra shifts at work and we can go back to normal life."

"I have a confession." George drew his lips into a tight line.

Laura looked at him in alarm. "What?"

George smiled and patted her forearm with his spade of a hand. "I lied to you about you looking well. You been looking tired, Laura, we worried about you."

"I've not been getting much sleep." Laura admitted. "I've been working from home as well as my extra shifts, I won't have to do that either I hope."

George was horrified. "That is madness, Laura! Why you not ask us for help?"

Laura couldn't answer him, she hardly knew herself. The strictness of her upbringing had conditioned her into believing that ill fortune was a direct result of wrongdoing on the recipient's part. *You made your bed and you must lie in it*, were her mother's favourite words.

"From now on, you must promise me, you will not struggle alone. We are put on this earth to help each other, are we not?"

Laura was still thinking of her childhood, she was glad that Lilly was growing up with the support of kind neighbours. Laura's own childhood had been one of isolation from the community, her parent's strong religious beliefs precluded making friends in the neighbourhood.

George was unconcerned by her lack of response. "Those men, I think that they are not ones that I feel a great friendship towards. They seem very angry at something or somebody. I hear them talking about getting even with someone, perhaps, a business associate? I think that giving you the money was part of the plan maybe."

Laura began to take notice. "Did they say who this person is?"

"They call him Alan only."

Laura nodded. "I think I know who that is, the doctor in the private clinic I took Lilly to, his first name is Alan except that I now know that he's not a real doctor."

"This makes sense." George scratched his chin. "The skinny one he says he is 'sick to the stomach' with the quackery. They speak very bad things about him."

"What sort of things?" Laura had her bag clutched close to her chest; she released it slightly as they mounted the steps of the bank.

George stepped aside to let an elderly lady go past. "Drugs, the skinny one is in rehab and this Alan fellow try to sell him a supply even though he knows he is getting off them."

Laura didn't reply but this lay heavy on her mind.

As they entered the bank, Laura saw that there was just one teller free, the other was serving an elderly woman; Laura was sure it was the lady she had seen in the café.

George stood close by as Laura took the money out and placed it on the counter together with her paying in book. "I'd like to deposit this, please."

There was no sign of suspicion or surprise from the pleasant woman behind the counter. Laura watched her carefully, expecting some adverse reaction. "I'm a little worried about the source of the cash, would it be possible to have it checked in some way?"

The bank lady showed surprise for the first time at this as she looked across at her colleague who was patiently waiting for the older lady to count out her change. "That's no problem, Mrs Palmer if you just wait a moment, I'll have it checked."

The colleague turned his attention back to the customer immediately.

George and Laura waited a little embarrassed at holding up the queue but before long, the cheery bank teller returned smiling to reassure them that the money was fine.

Once the money was deposited safely, George and Laura left the bank, the older lady was still finishing up her transaction. Laura still felt uneasy about taking the money but George convinced her that it was the only sensible course of action and she had to admit that it was a great relief.

When they arrived back at the café, Lilly was helping Polly clear tables.

Polly looked apologetic. "Sorry, Laura, she was getting bored and wanted to help."

Lilly smiled broadly at her mum. "Polly didn't want to let me but I told her that I'm fine and it's good for me to move about."

Laura gazed at her willow like daughter, she was carrying a pile of plates. As she strode across to the sink, her dancer's grace shone through, there was something strong yet perfectly controlled about her movement. At that moment, Laura knew with an inexplicable certainty that everything was going to be alright.

Chapter Thirty

Elaine hadn't been up into her attic study for weeks. It was Saturday morning and she decided to go up there to read James's article in the local paper. Iris bounded up the stairs after her and overtook her at the doorway, she was on the desk in a single leap.

Elaine had to laugh. "How am I supposed to open the paper with you there, puss?" She slid the furry bundle to one side, there was no break in the load purring but the amber eyes took on a look of indignation for just a moment.

The article started on the front page with the headline *Local practitioner exposed as a fraud.* There was a paragraph underneath naming Alan Sharmer as released on bail after having been taken into custody for supplying banned substances. The article went on to reveal that the fake doctor was suspected of using his clinic as a front for large-scale illegal drug importation.

Elaine turned to the third page where the article went on to point out that not only was he thought to have been supplying class A drugs to youngsters but he was also accused of preying on vulnerable people by charging exorbitant prices for worthless 'remedies'.

As Elaine continued to read, she realised from the tone of the article that it was possible that a custodial sentence may not follow. If there was insufficient evidence and if witnesses were unwilling to stand up in court, then the charges might have to be dropped. Elaine was horrified by this thought; she grabbed her phoned and called Holly.

Elaine didn't have to wait long for an answer. "Hello, Holly? Have you seen the paper?"

"Yes, I thought that too, surely he won't get away with it?"

"Why, what do you mean?"

"Okay, see you in five."

Elaine folded up the paper and went downstairs into the kitchen. After shaking out a few bits of dried cat food into Iris's bowl, she grabbed her coat and went out into the road where she saw Holly coming out of 'The Carter's'.

Holly raised her hand to wave, as they drew closer together, Elaine could see that Holly looked quite grave which was quite out of character.

Elaine touched her friend on the arm. "What did you have to tell me?"

Holly hesitated. "Things are coming to a head; it is time for the fulfilment."

Elaine was used to Holly being enigmatic, so she assumed that this was a continuation of what they had been discussing and nodded.

"We should go to the park." Holly headed off in that direction.

Elaine followed but wanted an explanation. "Why are we going there?"

Holly couldn't or wouldn't elaborate. "We'll find out when we get there."

Holly seemed to relax a little when she saw that Elaine was following her without argument. "I found out why Lloyd has a grievance with Alan Sharmer."

Elaine had to run a few steps to keep up with Holly. "How did you get the information?"

"He told me himself. He has a fourteen-year-old daughter and a twelve-year-old son. The mother wouldn't allow him to see them because of his drug habit, so he's been in rehab. He managed to get access to the kids once a week because he had shown that he was really making an effort to stay clean."

Elaine nodded. "How does that fit in with Alan Sharmer?"

"Well, Sharmer had been trying to get him back on the stuff, I guess he felt he had more power over him that way."

"That's awful!" Elaine was genuinely shocked.

Holly continued. "That's not the worst thing, on one of the access visits, Lloyd found that his daughter had been given a packet to pass on to him, she said that a man who said he was a friend of her father stopped her on the way home from school and presented her with it. It didn't take long for Lloyd to find out who the supplier had been. The same man had also given the girl a packet of tablets shaped like teddy bears and told her she could share them with her friends."

"Lloyd must have been furious!" Elaine stared at Holly.

"He's more than angry, he wants revenge."

"Did the girl eat any of the tablets?"

Holly shook her head. "No, mercifully, she had the sense to show Lloyd."

"Not her mother?"

"I asked that, no, she thought that if her mother knew what had happened that she might stop her from seeing her dad again. Of course, you can imagine what was in the package."

Elaine guessed right. "Heroin? He gave a fourteen-year-old heroin to deliver?"

Holly's face was grim. "Unbelievable, isn't it?" They were just coming into the park.

They waited to let an elderly lady pass as she trundled out of the entrance wheeling her shopping trolley, then they headed towards the bench where Professor Cambwell had been found dead.

There was an aged vagrant sitting on the bench reading a book, except that it wasn't just any book, Elaine was sure it was the one she had previously owned.

"How did he end up with it?" Elaine was puzzled.

Holly looked at her, her dark eyes full of understanding. "Look again!"

Elaine looked back at the man and took a few steps closer; she could still only see an old man with a balding grey head and a shaggy moustache. The man was wearing a suit and a shirt that must once have been white, the jacket of the suit was open and as Elaine drew nearer, she could see that there were food stains all down the front of the shirt. The shoes were dusty and scuffed and the trousers of the suit were shiny and crumpled. There was something familiar about the man, he had the beginnings of a grizzled beard. As Elaine drew closer, the man looked up, as soon as he saw her, he slammed the book shut and held it to his chest. Elaine realised who he reminded her of, it was Alan Sharmer, or an older version of him.

The man stood up, when he noticed Holly a look of fear clouded his face. "Stay away!" He shuffled off towards the entrance to the park.

Elaine called after him. "Sorry, I didn't mean to alarm you." She sought explanation from Holly; Holly's face was grim but she said nothing.

The man broke into a shambling trot. Elaine felt the need to follow, she wouldn't have been able to explain why if asked. Holly went with her without question.

When he got to the entrance of the park, the man doubled back towards the direction of town and onto the narrow pavement at the side of the main road. There was heavy traffic on the road, Elaine balked at following him any further and she stood with Holly watching him retreat into the distance.

"He looks so like Alan Sharmer." Elaine was thinking out loud.

Holly smiled. "That's because, it is Alan Sharmer."

Elaine didn't have time to answer because a lorry sounded its horn with urgency and there was a screeching of brakes followed by a sickening thud.

It was as if time was slowed down, all Elaine could do was stay rooted to the spot. Holly fumbled in her bag for her mobile phone. A lorry was skewed across the road holding the rest of the traffic up. People were sitting in their cars gazing ahead blankly.

Elaine felt for her phone in her pocket. "Here, I've got mine handy." She tried to dial the emergency services but her fingers felt like rubber. "Can you do it, Holly? I'm shaking too much."

Holly took the phone and managed to get through. "Ambulance please…on the corner of Market Street and Oxford Road…I don't know, a pedestrian has been hit and he's on the road."

Elaine left Holly and walked towards the incident. The driver of the lorry was still in the cab, he was motionless as was his passenger. Elaine took off her coat and laid it over the casualty, he wasn't moving. He would have been lying face down except for the fact that his head was twisted round at an unnatural angle against the kerb, his staring eyes were filled with blood.

Holly joined her and by now, some of the drivers had got out of their cars and were gathered around along with some of the shoppers who had heard the commotion. Elaine was aware of people's voices, some calling the emergency services, some asking if they had been called but she felt as if she was in a bubble separated from it all somehow.

Still, the lorry driver remained in his cab.

One of the shopkeepers approached. Elaine recognised the wavy blond shock of hair of the bookseller, he was wearing a long black double breasted woollen overcoat.

"It is over." He spoke directly to Holly but they were his only words. They watched him walk off in the direction of the park.

An ambulance siren wailed in the distance; a second siren accompanied it soon after. Elaine was aware of the blue flashing lights; she was stiff with cold and could only stand with difficulty when the round-faced paramedic asked her to give him some space. Holly put an arm around her and pulled her back.

The paramedic took Elaine's coat off the patient and threw it on the pavement, his colleague joined him and shouted at the bystanders to stand back. Some of the people got back into their cars whilst others shuffled about on the spot. Elaine felt that it would be intrusive to retrieve her coat and she felt ashamed to be bothered about getting it back; she didn't want to just leave it there so she stayed around as the paramedics did their work.

The police were here by now and one of them climbed up to the lorry's cab. Shortly after the driver and his passenger climbed down, they were ushered towards the police car.

Elaine heard the driver tell the police constable that the man had fallen sideways off the pavement into the road, the voice was somehow familiar.

By now, there was a long tailback of traffic, the police had closed the road off completely.

Elaine looked up at the empty lorry, there was a sign written on the dark blue door. The writing was ornate and old fashioned, it read, 'Lloyd Payne Scrap Merchant', there was a phone number beneath, it was a local landline number.

Elaine started to shiver. Holly took off her own coat and put it around her friend, she stepped forward to pick up Elaine's coat but the paramedic warned her to stand back. The second paramedic went to the ambulance and pulled out a stretcher with wheeled legs which dropped down and locked into position, he rolled it over to the patient, it happened to track right over Elaine's coat as he did so. With one deft move, the trolley's legs were collapsed again and the patient was lifted on to it. Elaine wondered why there was no spinal collar used. The first paramedic covered the patient with a sheet and together they lifted the trolley up again into its higher position and wheeled it to the ambulance where it rested on one end as the wheels were folded up again and the trolley slid in out of sight.

Holly and Elaine watched as the ambulance drove off, its blue lights flashing but no siren sounding. Holly stepped over and picked Elaine's coat up, they turned to leave but a policeman stopped them. "Did you witness the accident, Miss?" He spoke to Holly.

Holly explained that they heard the horn and the screeching of tyres but that neither of them had seen it happen. They were asked to give their names and addresses and were allowed to leave.

Something made Elaine want to go to the bookshop rather than go straight home. Holly followed her without questioning.

The shop front had changed, instead of the battered car manuals, there were children's books with bright and colourful illustrations on their covers. As they stepped through the door, the low winter sun was shining through the far arched window giving a ruddy glow to the whole interior, the bookshelves were the same but there was an altogether brighter and airier feel to the place. Along with the scent of wood polish, and slightly masking it, was a crisp citrus aroma subtle enough to not be overpowering. There was music playing in the background only just audible, at a guess Elaine thought it was probably Heart Radio.

The bookseller wasn't there; in his place behind the counter was a young woman. As soon as Elaine entered the shop, the woman looked up and smiled, dark mascara gave her sapphire eyes the appearance of two exotic flowers. "Good morning." Her voice had a flute like quality, she trotted around to the front of the counter to welcome the customers in. "My name is Tilly; can I help you with anything or would you just like to browse?" Her dress was a splash of colour with lime green palm tree motive covered with an iridescent butterfly design.

Elaine was confused, she had never seen this lady before, in fact she had only ever seen the one man serving. "I'd just like to browse around, if that's ok?" In truth, Elaine wasn't sure what had drawn her in.

"That's cool," the young woman piped, her glossy red lips revealing brilliant white teeth.

Elaine gravitated towards the shelf where she had first seen her book; on the way, she noticed that the old books were still there but in between there were lots of new ones too, both paperback and hardback. Some of the books were only just in print in fact, Elaine stopped to look at a ballet book that she recognised as one she had seen Sylvia working on very recently.

The bookseller had obviously changed his marketing angle.

"That's a lovely one, so inspirational, it would make a super present for a teenage girl." The voice floated through from the direction of the counter. "Are you looking for a present, perhaps?" The young woman had joined them and was searching through a nearby shelf.

Holly offered an explanation. "We've just had a bit of a shock actually, so we came in here to calm down a bit. You've got a lovely selection of books by the way."

Tilly's face clouded a little. "Are you ok, what happened?"

"We saw a man knocked down just up the road." Holly kept her voice low.

"I heard the sirens." The girl looked towards the window. "You must be feeling shaken up, would you like a cuppa?"

Holly turned to Elaine who shook her head. "Not for me, but thanks."

"I'm fine too, but it's kind of you." Holly smiled.

Tilly returned to the counter. Elaine continued towards the back of the shop. The sun was streaming through the tall arched window, specs of dust looked like tiny gold and silver ingots floating in space. Elaine stopped dead and put her hand on Holly's arm for support. There on the shelf surrounded by crisp new paperbacks was her book. The sunlight shone directly on it making the gold leaf shine. Elaine held out a tentative hand and stroked the spine. As if lifting a baby from its cradle, she took the book from the shelf. As she opened the book, she noticed that there were slight scuffs on the front and back panel, there were small creases in some of the pages too but not to the extent that could be expected considering that it might have been thrown onto the road.

Holly held her hands out and as Elaine passed the book to her, she closed her eyes. After a few moments, she opened her eyes again and smiled at Elaine. "Peace. The energy is still there but it is quiescent."

Elaine nodded and took the book back, she stared down at it admiring its beauty but she felt no particular draw towards it, she placed the book back on the shelf with a steady hand. Holly turned and walked towards the counter. Elaine followed but stopped before she reached the end of the aisle and turned to gaze at the book again; it sat like a contented dowager amongst the newer titles, the mellow sunlight bathing it in a comforting but mystical glow.

As they reached the counter, Tilly greeted them like long lost friends. "Did you see anything you like?"

Elaine and Holly looked at each other and then back at her.

Holly spoke first. "There's plenty I like the look of, the hard thing is choosing but maybe we'll leave it until next time."

Elaine nodded. "Yes, we're still a bit shaken up but we'll be in again definitely." She paused, wondering whether to ask or not but she felt she had to know. "The chap who normally serves here, is it his day off?"

Tilly looked puzzled. "Man? We don't have a man working here. Mind you, we've only been open for a week."

Elaine was surprised. "Oh, it must have been the previous owner then."

The young shopkeeper still looked puzzled. "The shop has been closed for five years, the previous owner had to retire due to ill health, he's staying in the Sandcroft nursing home. The shop has only just come on the rental market. I believe there has been a caretaker looking after it though, cleaning the floor and polishing the shelves."

Holly stepped forward. "Do you mind if we ask his name?"

"Whose, the caretaker?"

Holly shook her head. "No, sorry I meant the owner."

"No probs, it's Ben Auber, why do you ask?"

Holly glanced at Elaine. "I think we'd like to visit him."

The young woman's face clouded. "You won't go upsetting him, will you? He's a very old man."

Holly laid a hand on Tilly's arm. "Don't worry, we'll be very careful. I think he will want to see us."

This time, Elaine was puzzled. "But he doesn't even know us."

"Trust me, I think, he'll know why we've come." Holly looked towards the bookshelves with a faraway stare.

Chapter Thirty-One

Elaine arranged to take the afternoon off to go with Holly to the nursing home. Recently, Sylvia had persuaded Elaine to join her local gym, so that they could go together after work. Elaine knew that this was Sylvia's attempt to help bring Elaine back to full health after the decline she had experienced. Sylvia had the best of intentions and so Elaine was happy to go along with it. Elaine now actually looked forward to their sessions, so today, she arranged to meet before work so as not to miss out a day. Finishing off with the rowing machine, conversation was minimal but Elaine decided to do an early cool down so she could get away without having to wait for Sylvia in the showers. Sylvia's make up regime meant that Elaine was always ready ten minutes before her friend.

Elaine wiped down the machine and waved at Sylvia. "I'll see you at work." Sylvia nodded and smiled.

As Elaine emerged from the shower, she bumped into a familiar figure. "Tessa! I didn't know you worked here."

Tessa nodded. "Just a few hours a week, my dear, I've seen you coming in, sure 'tis grand that you are better again, I was worried about ya."

Elaine was touched. "That's very kind of you, Tessa. Thanks, I'm definitely on the mend again now."

Tessa took up Elaine's right hand between her own and held it as if she was carrying a bird.

"You remind me so much of a friend I had long ago. You may not know it but you have been a kind of catalyst in calming down an experiment that was getting way out of control." Elaine was startled.

Tessa chuckled. "Sure now, you'll be wondering how an old cleaning lady knows about such things."

Elaine opened and closed her mouth unsure of what to say.

Tessa released Elaine's hand. "Now I'll tell ya sometime if you're interested but not now, my dear, you'll be getting off to work won't ya?"

Elaine nodded. "Yes. I'd better be getting a move on; I'd like to sit down together and talk sometime though."

Tessa picked up her mop and walked away giving Elaine's arm a gentle squeeze as she went.

Elaine pondered Tessa's words all morning but come lunch time there was no time to be lost, she was meeting Holly at the nursing home at two o'clock.

The Sandcroft nursing home was a large Cotswold stone country house surrounded by landscaped gardens.

Holly had rung ahead for an appointment; they were greeted at the entrance by a friendly middle-aged woman of generous proportions. They were ushered into an impressive galleried reception area. A delicious smell of coffee emanated from a café just to the side of the main reception.

Beyond the café was an open area leading to double doors over which there was a sign saying 'Cinema'.

The matronly woman took their coats. "Benjamin is waiting for you in the reading room."

They were shown to a large oak panelled room. An artificial log fire flickered in the huge stone fireplace, it was clearly run on gas, but it was very close to the real thing. Around the fire were several high back leather chairs which turned out to be all empty except one.

"Benjamin, these are the two young ladies who wanted to visit you." The woman's voice raised an octave as she projected the words across the room.

The elderly gent had been snoozing, he lifted his head, gossamer hair hung down to his shoulders, his watery blue eyes focused on Elaine as he made a beckoning gesture.

"Come, come." His voice was thin and reedy. "You are the very incarnation of Elaine." Elaine stepped forward, she felt the old man must be confused, he looked familiar but she couldn't place where she had seen him before. "We have been visiting your shop, it's such a treasure trove of books." She enunciated as clearly as she was able.

Benjamin chuckled, then almost snarled at the receptionist. "Yes, yes, you may go now!" He waved his hand as if to shoo away a fly.

The woman gave Holly a wry look and retired from the room.

"Ah, yes, the shop." He continued, smiling at some private joke. He fixed a beady eye on Holly.

"The book, it is back in place?"

Holly nodded. "It's back in the shop now."

Benjamin's chin fell to his chest. "There will be no more harm wrought by it." He muttered.

"My two precious kittens and their mother." He shook his head in sorrow.

"You keep cats?" Elaine's voice was bright; a forced smile crossed her lips.

Holly put her hand on Elaine's arm and gave her a warning glare.

Benjamin lifted his head high; his mouth became a thin line. "How the eye deceives, you are not blood of my blood."

Holly intervened. "No, but she has been a friend to your kin." She glanced at Elaine and fluttered her fingers in an almost imperceptible gesture.

Elaine took the cue and stood far back.

Holly crouched down in front of the old man and whispered. "Benedict had a sister."

Benjamin's eyes opened wide; a lucence emanated from his face as he leaned forward. "She was drowned as a sorceress."

"She survived and escaped and her descendants live on." Holly's voice was barely audible but the old man smiled.

"They fare well?" His eyes glistened with tears.

Holly took his hand. "The newest member of the clan has been through tough times, but she will blossom now, her mother is by her side and they have good friends."

"I would see them before I pass." The old man fixed his eyes on Holly and he once again seemed frail and vulnerable.

"It will be done." Holly's determined expression left no room for doubt.

Benjamin closed his eyes; his head fell forward and he began to snore with surprising volume.

Elaine laughed. "I think we've tired him out!"

Holly released the old man's hand and stood up; there was something in her expression that Elaine couldn't fathom, a kind of excited determination.

Just as they were going to the door the woman who has shown them in reappeared. "He sleeps a lot, bless him."

Elaine noticed Holly bridling at her patronising tone, in an effort to diffuse an awkward moment, she engaged the woman in conversation. "There seems to be a lot of interesting things going on here, I see you even have a cinema."

The woman did not appear to have noticed Holly's irritation. "Yes, there is some sort of event on every night except Mondays, of course, it's the individual resident's choice whether they attend or not; Benjamin tends to shy away from such things to be honest but that's his right of course. We've got the local brownie pack singing tonight." She chuckled. "There aren't very many of them, they will get lost on the stage but I'm sure they will make a cheerful sound."

Holly seemed to perk up. "You have a theatre as well?"

"Oh, yes! It's well used too and we have some big names from London sometimes." The woman seemed proud.

Holly nodded. "But you have small local groups too?"

"Of course! It helps to keep the connection with the community, we think that's very important." The doorbell rang. "Excuse me, I had better go and answer that." The woman waddled off.

Elaine turned back to Benjamin; he was still sleeping soundly. "I think we should leave him in peace for now, Holly, but we could come again, couldn't we?"

Holly had a look of determination. "I have every intention of doing so, Elaine, let me tell you about my plan on the way home; I've just got to pop to the loo first."

As Elaine waited in the foyer, she saw a familiar figure come through the main door.

"Tessa! Fancy meeting you here are you visiting someone?"

Tessa put her hand on Elaine's forearm. "My old friend, Ben, sure I've been cleaning for him for years but we go back along way even before that."

Elaine was agog. "Ben Auber? I've just been visiting him myself."

Tessa chuckled. "'Tis a small world, did you find him well?"

"He was very tired." Elaine tried to be diplomatic.

Tessa cast her eyes down. "He will pass before long."

Elaine tried to change the subject. "Where did you first meet?" Her voice sounded falsely bright.

The old lady considered Elaine for a moment then nodded to herself. "There are some of us who remember previous lives, Ben and myself have this gift, if gift you call it, sure sometimes it can be a great responsibility. In this life though, it was through his physics lectures." She laughed. "Now, you'll be thinking what business has an old cleaning lady got going to a lecture on physics? Sure, I wasn't always old my dear and in my younger days, I had a real appetite for such things."

Elaine shook her head. "No not at all! I just didn't know that Ben was a physicist!"

Tessa threw her hands in the air. "Well, there now, I've taught ya something today! He's a professor at the university, internationally renowned, so he is."

Elaine blushed. "I'm a bit on the arty side I'm afraid; I really should widen my horizons."

"Don't be hard on yourself, Queen." Tessa caught hold of Elaine's hand. "You drive yourself too hard as it is. You've been through a difficult time I know but you're coming back out into the sunlight again now."

Elaine wasn't sure if the kindly old lady was talking about her recent illness or something further back but it didn't matter, the words of comfort were warming to her soul.

Elaine wanted to ask Tessa so many things but Holly came back before she had a chance.

Holly immediately addressed Elaine's friend, the respect in her voice was apparent. "Hello, it's an honour to meet you." Holly held out her hand.

Elaine was puzzled. "Do you two know each other then?"

There was no answer at first as the other two regarded each other with a palpable reverence.

Holly snapped out of her musing. "No, we've never met." Her voice was bright and earnest.

Elaine frowned but Tessa bustled off to visit her old friend and Holly looked at her watch exclaiming that they should get underway to avoid the worst of the traffic.

The nursing home was always busy with people coming and going. There were daily film showings in the tiny cinema which seated only about thirty people. At least, once a week, there was something going on in the little theatre in addition to the regular church and other religious services that were held there. Ben attended none of these. Uncharacteristically, however, about a month after Elaine and Holly's visit, he did insist on attending a small ballet review.

Chapter Thirty-Two

After a hard winter, the spring was especially welcome. Elaine waited in the tea room looking down at the gardens seven floors below, the Sakura was in glorious bloom and its delicate pink flowers were radiant in the vernal sunshine.

Sylvia came breezing in to make a coffee and Elaine sat down, leaving a space for her on the soft corner-chairs. "How are your new neighbours?"

Sylvia rummaged in the fridge looking for milk. "They're settling in really well." She looked around to see if anyone was listening. "Trish and Rob have been amazing, they helped them with the move and advised on all the legal red tape." She spoke in a whisper. "I misjudged Trish, I half expected her to be resentful, after all she and her mother were related to the old gent too and they were left nothing."

Elaine nodded. "The fact that Lilly inherited the estate in trust probably made it seem fairer but I agree, Trish surprised me too."

Sylvia flopped down on the seat next to Elaine. "It was strange how things went; I know that Holly sort of engineered the meeting by getting Lilly's dance group to perform at the Sandcroft nursing home but it was as if some external force was at work the way things slotted into place." Elaine sipped her coffee, an image of the last time she had seen the book came into her mind, resplendent in the sunlight amongst the modern paperbacks. It was strange that it didn't look out of place, it had seemed peaceful and poised like a doyen amongst a cast of less known actors. Over the previous months, she had come to fear the book but now she thought of it only with fondness.

Sylvia interrupted her thoughts. "I always wondered who owned that flat, I know that Tessa cleaned there but I never thought to ask her. Laura and Lilly absolutely love it there and it will be the end of money troubles for Laura since there won't be any rent to worry about from now on."

Elaine nodded. "There's the income from the rent of the shop too which will be a great help. Is Laura going to give up working at the supermarket?"

Sylvia shook her head. "No, but she said she was going to cut her hours down. The bookshop doesn't generate a great deal of income apparently as it's rented out quite cheaply."

"I wonder why?" Elaine frowned in puzzlement.

"The would-be tenants were subject to a rigorous selection process it seems; the estate agents were given very explicit instructions about the sort of leaseholders required and they had to be vetted by someone working on behalf of the owner."

Elaine thought for a moment. "The new tenants were kept in the dark about who had been there before weren't they? They seemed unaware that the man had been in there before them."

Sylvia licked a biscuit crumb from the corner of her mouth. "Laura was told by the estate agent that the shop had lain empty since Benjamin had gone into the nursing home which was three years ago. I'm not sure what to make of that."

"There were never any other people in the shop when we were there." Elaine spoke slowly, formulating her thoughts as she did so.

Sylvia raised her eyebrows. "Hardly surprising, it's not a big chain, all those little shops are practically deserted most of the time."

Elaine had to agree, there was nothing unusual about a deserted bookshop these days.

The click-clicking of Trish's heels made them both hurry to wash their coffee cups. As Trish came into the tearoom, she gave a sad frown. "I was hoping to catch you both before you went back to work. Have you got a moment to spare?"

Sylvia seemed taken aback and didn't reply but Elaine jumped in. "Of course, Trish, there's nothing wrong, is there?"

Trish sat down and patted the chair beside her. "No, quite the opposite, I just wanted to thank you both for the kindness you showed my sister. Especially you, Sylvia, you were a friend when she badly needed one." Trish folded her hands in her lap and looked down at them. "As you know, I'm a very private person, both Laura and I were brought up in a closed community, we were taught not to trust the outside world. We both would probably still be cut off from society had my sister not fallen pregnant and been excluded from the sect."

Elaine had been listening carefully. "I had no idea."

Trish continued, "No, I keep private matters to myself generally. I myself still attend meetings and am in contact with our parents, but even now I can't even utter my sister's name in front of them."

"That must be hard for you." Sylvia's eyes were full of sympathy.

"Ten times harder for Laura and Lilly." Trish put her hand on Sylvia's arm. "That's why it meant so much to Laura to get to know her great uncle even though it was just for a short time."

Sylvia shook her head. "That was Holly's doing, really."

Trish's mouth turned down at the edges, she looked down at her hands and picked at the knuckles. "I'm sorry, but prejudices run through me that I can't get rid of."

Elaine looked at Sylvia who seemed as baffled as she felt herself.

Trish looked up; she could see an explanation was needed.

"Holly comes from a people whose beliefs stray too close to sorcery for my comfort. I was brought up to believe that astrology and the like are of the devil. I know you will think that is very narrow minded but it's a view I can't shake."

Elaine tried not to let her disapproval show in her face. "We all have baggage from childhood, such things can go deep."

Trish looked grateful for the understanding. "It goes very deep with our family. Way back on my mother's side, they were persecuted for the way they lived. We have a very old family bible which has a written record on the flyleaf. This record shows four generations of the family on my mother's side along with an account of Matilda Auber's escape from the town of her birth to the small village which was two days journey away at the time. My great great great great uncle Benedict Auber was what would now be called a man of science but the local folk were deeply suspicious of him. His sister, my great great great grandmother Matilda Auber was nearly hung as a witch."

Sylvia sat on the edge of her chair. "What happened to her?"

"A priest saved her and they left the town and set up home together. He couldn't continue with the church of course but he continued as a man of God by setting up his own church, he gained a good following and the sect survives today."

"That's the one you belong to?" Elaine kept her voice low.

Trish nodded. "Yes, although these days, I'm not so strong in the faith. I have come to see how narrow our outlook is. I see now why the sect has such strongly held principles, they came about as a reaction to the negative events which occurred because the family were associated with the dark arts."

Elaine shook her head. "Benedict and Matilda were probably just people with enquiring minds who could see the way the environment worked better than most."

Sylvia nodded. "It sounds as if they were both deeply spiritual in their own way but it's not surprising that Matilda shied away from any connection with mysticism after her bad experience."

Trish agreed. "Benedict became a recluse after his sister disappeared but that didn't save him from persecution, he was hounded and his wife and children were killed in what we now think was a tragic accident."

"Accident?" A slight frown passed over Elaine's face.

"Yes." Trish continued. "They were found suffocated down a deep dry well just outside the town boundary. They had been held hostage by a couple of local men who had been trying to get information from Benedict."

"So, it wasn't really an accident, was it?" Elaine heard the anger in her own voice and tried in vain to subdue it.

Trish looked both startled and pleased. "I agree! I've always felt that too. It was nothing short of murder in my mind but the culprits were never brought to justice. It broke Benedict's heart, he never recovered from the loss and it was believed that he died in a fire less than a year later, although his body was never found."

Elaine and Sylvia looked at each other for a moment then Elaine turned back to Trish.

"Sometimes, justice takes time to be worked out but I have a strong feeling that Benedict found peace in the end."

Trish picked at her thumb. "I hope, he did."

A silence hung in the air until one by one, they all returned to their workstations. There was a perceptible change in the atmosphere in the office after this brief exchange. Trish stopped finding fault with everything and the others included Trish more in their office banter.

Some weeks later, Elaine felt a compulsion to return to the bookshop, she mentioned this to Holly who agreed to accompany her.

As soon as they walked through the door, Tilly gave them a rapturous welcome. "Hi, you two! I've been thinking about you, how's things?" She didn't pause for an answer. "Have you got over the nasty shock you had?"

Elaine smiled. "Mostly, although I must admit I couldn't bring myself to come along the footpath next to the road."

Tilly lowered her eyes, her downcast lashes looked like the inner petals of a passion flower. "I can imagine."

"We told you we would be back though and we found we couldn't keep away." Elaine felt that she had known Tilly for a long time.

Tilly's eyes sparkled like dew kissed wild anemones. "It's good to see you again, are you here to browse?"

Holly nodded. "We'd like to wander round looking at your vast selection and just drink in the atmosphere for a while."

Tilly's smile grew even brighter. "Of course, let me know if there is anything I can help you with."

Elaine and Holly headed towards the 'magic realism' section; the crisp new paperbacks were resplendent on the deeply polished antique shelves. The shop door tinkled as another customer passed through.

Holly bent her head towards Elaine. "It looks as if business is picking up, that's good to see."

They heard Tilly greeting the man with her customary cheery welcome. "Hi, can I help you?" The man ignored her and went straight towards the dark recesses at the back of the shop.

Tilly seemed completely unaffected.

Elaine rolled her eyes. "Rude?" She said to Holly in a comical voice.

Tilly caught on to Elaine's reaction and giggled, she made towards them with the duster she was wielding and proceeded to buff the shelves nearby. "It takes all types, doesn't it?" There was no hint of rancour in her voice.

Holly smiled. "You have to learn patience when dealing with the public at times, don't you?"

Elaine glanced towards the man. "I don't think I could have the tolerance which you both seem to have."

Holly and Tilly looked at each other with rueful smiles.

The man appeared to sense that he was being talked about, he spun around and looked in their direction. "Are all these books available to buy?"

Tilly took a few steps towards him and confirmed that they were.

The man returned to the dusty shelf and continued browsing, Tilly continued her random polishing whilst chatting to the other two.

After a while, the customer selected a book, it shone out amongst the old and dilapidated volumes either side, Elaine wasn't paying very much attention to this until she saw someone step out from the recesses of the shop; it was the bookseller they had dealt with previously, his long tawny mane looked like spun gold in the few rays of light coming from the tall window behind him, he strode up to the customer.

"I don't think that book is right for you, I know of something more suitable but similar on the other side of the shop."

Elaine was confused, she hadn't realised that the man she had bought her book from was still involved with the shop.

The customer frowned. "I am quite happy with this book, thanks, I think I will take it to the counter." The customer turned towards the counter but before he could move, the bookseller stopped him and took the book away. "I'm sorry, but this section is actually closed to customers and these books are not for sale." His voice was firm, he took the customer by the arm and escorted him out of the area directing him to the refurbished side of the shop before returning to the shadows.

The customer stormed up to Tilly. "You said all the books are for sale! A man just frog marched me out of the back area and told me the book I wanted is not available!" He pointed towards the place he had been browsing.

Elaine, Holly and Tilly stood open mouthed when they saw that the shelves at the back of the shop were all secured by black plastic sheeting.

Tilly was first to speak. "As you can see nobody has been in that area for some time; that is an area that we are developing to be included as part of the floor, we have not been open very long." Her tone was hesitant.

The customer was clearly furious. "I don't know what kind of joke this is but you had better keep your custom well because you'll have none of mine!" He spun around and stomped out of the shop slamming the door behind him.

The bookseller peered out from behind the plastic sheeting, he exchanged a smile with Holly and Tilly. Elaine realised that the other two were party to an understanding which she didn't possess. She watched as he returned behind the sheeting; Elaine could see him through a small gap. He lovingly brushed off the rest of the dust from the book, it looked as if it had been printed yesterday. Elaine could hear the bookseller muttering. "At last, all is right with my world, my duty is done!" The book seemed to be vibrating in his grasp as he returned it to the shelf. "Now we wait idle until needed again." Elaine saw him turn away and then turn back for one last look at the book before she could see him no more.

As Elaine turned back, she could see that something had amused Tilly.

Tilly chuckled. "Don't worry about Tom, he can be a bit fierce but he means no harm."